Dedication

For Matt, who never bats an eye when I interrupt life to take notes. Thank you for your endless support and willingness to share me with fictitious friends. Your enthusiasm makes writing an adventure.

Table of Contents

Chapter One Expectations 1

Chapter Two Encounter... 9

Chapter Three The Beginning...................................19

Chapter Four Discovery 29

Chapter Five Insight 39

Chapter Six A Carnival of Truth 45

Chapter Seven A Life Less Ordinary..............................55

Chapter Eight Forbidden Fairytale........................... 63

Chapter Nine Changes 71

Chapter Ten Complicated 83

Chapter Eleven Whose Funeral? 95

Chapter Twelve What We Found There 107

Chapter Thirteen Responsibility 113

Chapter Fourteen Taken 125

Chapter Fifteen The Truth 133

Chapter Sixteen Confrontation.............................. 147

Chapter Seventeen Desperation 155

Chapter Eighteen Traitor...................................... 161

Chapter Nineteen Unexpected Company 167

Chapter Twenty The Valley...................................... 177

Chapter Twenty-One Transition............................183

Chapter Twenty-Two Reflections 193

Chapter Twenty-Three Family Ties......................... 203

Chapter Twenty-Four Acceptance.............................. 219

Chapter Twenty-Five Ancient History 235

Chapter Twenty-Six Confessions 245

Chapter Twenty-Seven October Rain........................ 253

Chapter Twenty-Eight Resolution 263

Acknowledgements.. 275

About the Author... 277

Also from Soul Fire Press ...... **Error! Bookmark not defined.**

Chapter One
Expectations

"Harry, can you hear me?" I yelled. My mind raced as I weaved a path through the crowd. Holding the phone to my ear, I struggled to make out what he said over the poor signal and blaring noise — then the call died. Lights flashed as the music rang out, pulsating through the ground. I pushed against the partygoers occupying every inch around the pool, trying to make my escape. Rounding the corner of the villa, I smacked into a wall of muscle and bounced back.

"Hey, Ashton! Happy... birthday," Kyle's sentence fell away, his gray eyes pinched in concern. "Where are you going? Is something wrong?"

I shook my head and squeezed around him, ignoring the well wishes and congratulations till the thick horde fell behind.

A valet shot up from his chair and greeted me when I burst through the side gate. He fidgeted with the zipper of his vest while I rummaged frantically through my handbag. I shoved my keys at him and watched him disappear through an alley of luxury vehicles lining the driveway.

I redialed Harry's number, but it went straight to voicemail. Where could he be? Why wasn't he answering? My steel-colored BMW Z4 convertible rolled into view. The dark-haired guy toppled out of my seat and squeezed his slight frame against the inside of the door, trying to avoid me as I slid behind the wheel.

A heavy hand slammed against the doorframe. I jumped and looked up to find the cold smoky eyes of my boyfriend staring back at me.

"What do you think you're doing?" Kevin demanded, his knuckles white beneath his olive skin.

"I have to go!" My voice broke.

"Go where? You can't just leave. Do you have any idea who's here?"

I ignored him, turning the key in the ignition. Music from my favorite band carried across the courtyard as I slid sunglasses on to cover my tear-filled eyes.

"This is your party." His voice grew threatening. "I spent a fortune on it!"

Yeah, happy 18th to me. "Get out of the way, Kevin."

His hand snapped around my wrist, and I gasped. Pain shot through my forearm and the blood pooled in my finger tips.

"Ashton," Kevin growled, his eyes narrowed into slits, "you're not leaving. Get out of the car. Now."

"Hey!" Kyle, Kevin's younger brother, hurried to the car, concern etched in his face. His eyes darkened when they locked onto the hand clenched around my wrist. A silent hostility thickened the air.

"What's going on?" Kyle's voice turned icy. Kevin met his glare.

Kyle shook his head in warning, and their gaze shifted to me. A breath later, Kevin's hand fell away. My tires squealed against the hot pavement as I peeled away, leaving my party, and possibly my sanity, behind.

My arm ached as I zipped toward Pacific Coast Highway. Kevin had some nerve. Angry or not, he'd never hurt me at the risk of someone else seeing him. My purse buzzed, and I reached down to grab the phone.

"Speak of the devil," I mumbled when Kevin's picture popped up. I pressed decline and called information instead.

Information. What city, please? Para continuar en español, marque ocho.

"Los Angeles."

What listing?

"Los Angeles International Airport."

Press one for flight schedules, a recording began, *press two for ticket information ...* I tapped the icon and waited to be connected with customer service. Smooth saxophone music droned on in the background, creating an unsettling contrast between my agitated mood and the intended relaxing tone of the melody.

Traffic slowed to a crawl. My fingers drummed against the steering wheel as I inched forward to sit in idle. It was Friday and rush hour — not a convenient combination when you're in a hurry.

"Ticket agent, how can I help you?" A nasal voice came on the line.

"I need a flight into New York," I ordered.

"One moment..."

Please, take your time, I thought and rolled my eyes.

"I'm sorry. It looks like the weather has grounded all flights in and out of the New York airports indefinitely. If you want, I can search for flights in neighboring..."

My father's attorney Harry Waterford's picture flashed across my screen, and I hung up on the agent midsentence. "Harry, where have you been? Why wouldn't you answer your phone? I've been calling for over an hour! Look, I'm stuck in traffic, and the stupid airports are shut down over there, but I think I can—"

"Ashton..." he interrupted me, his voice strained.

"Harry?" A cold fear washed over me.

"Ash." The silence stretched on before he took a shaky breath. "Your dad, he ... he had a heart attack. He didn't make it. I'm so sorry."

My hands shook around the steering wheel, tears blurring the highway. Harry's words echoed through the crunch of the gravel as the car came to an abrupt stop in the emergency lane.

"W-w-what?"

"I'm sorry," he repeated. "The doctors did everything they could, but his heart suffered too much damage."

I stared at the blue and white insignia in the center of the steering wheel, the colors blurring through hot tears. This had to be a mistake. Harry had to be wrong.

"I realize this is the worst time possible, and I hate to ask, but I need you to meet me in Kentucky. It's where he ... where we need to finalize everything."

"Kentucky?" My voice sounded distant, small.

"This isn't the best time for explanations," Harry urged gently. "Meet me in Cumberland on Thursday. It's in the southeastern part of the state. I'll email you the directions and more information."

I couldn't answer.

"Do you understand, Ashton?" His tone deepened with a sense of urgency.

"Yeah. Kentucky. Southeast. Six days." I stared mindlessly into the setting sun. A gust of wind carried across the ocean, taking my breath away.

"Ashton, say something, please. Should I call Kevin? Perhaps he should escort you."

"No, it's fine," I said quickly. "I'll see you soon. Bye."

My body went numb — all except the ache around my heart — as I fought to keep the tears at bay. I drew a deep breath and forced my emotions to shut down, years of practice making it possible.

"Excuse me?" A voice spoke beside my car, causing me to flinch. I looked up. Pale-blue eyes of a police officer greeted me with concern.

"Are you all right, Miss...?"

"Blake," I murmured.

The officer nodded, his shoulders relaxing. "Are you sure? Is there anything I can do for you? Someone I should call?" His eyes fell on the white-knuckle grip I had on my cell.

"No. Thank you," I whispered as my empty gaze shifted across his decorated uniform. "I have to go."

Somewhere in the reasonable part of my mind, I registered the fact that he didn't ask for identification or question me in any way. That seemed odd in comparison with the multiple law enforcement interactions I'd experienced in the past.

"Look, I don't know what's happened to upset you, but it's going to be all right. Do you hear me? Everything will work out," he assured.

I thanked him and offered a pitiful excuse for a smile. He nodded and turned back to his car, lifting his cell phone to his ear as he walked away.

I switched on the GPS and entered Cumberland, Kentucky into the destination box. Tracing along the interstate, I noted the route ran through Granbury, Texas. Charlie, my father, had a home there. I marked the city on the map and drew a deep breath as I thought about what to do. Six days was more than enough time to get to Kentucky. If I left now, I could avoid Kevin and kill a couple of days at Charlie's lake house. That wouldn't be too life altering.

A cool breeze brushed across my exposed shoulder. I shivered, watching dark clouds roll in. Rain pattered the soft roof as I pulled onto the highway.

Shifting in my seat, I tugged at the waistline of the black satin digging into my side. The mid-thigh cocktail dress hugged a little too tight. Even though it looked great, I couldn't help make the correlation that it was like everything else in my life ... it restricted me. My naked toes breathed a sigh of relief as I worked my feet out of the evil stiletto heels. Why they labeled them Italian when torturous was more appropriate, was lost on me.

After an hour and a half on auto-pilot, a billboard ahead flashed with pictures of a San Bernardino mall. I pulled into the closest spot, quietly groaning as I stuffed my toes back into the heels, then hurried inside. Thirty minutes and two credit cards later, I headed back to the car with a three-piece luggage set and enough clothing to last me a week.

The phone buzzed again as I merged on to the interstate. The image of my smiling best friend lit up the screen. "Hey, Kyle."

"Ashton, thank God you answered," Kyle spoke quickly, his tone little more than a whisper. "Are you okay? What's the emergency?"

"My dad had a ... a heart attack." I swallowed against the knot in my throat. "He didn't make it."

"Oh, Ash, I'm so sorry. I don't know what to say." Kyle sighed. "I know you guys weren't especially close, but still, he's your dad."

My stomach tightened. "Yeah. I know he wasn't much, but he was all I had."

"You always have us." His voice deepened. "Is there anything I can do?"

"Yeah. Do me a favor and don't tell Kevin. I'll deal with him when I get home."

"You sure?" Kyle's voice rose in surprise. "You know he's going to feel like a jerk for acting the way he did."

"If I could only be so lucky," I muttered. "Look, I'm sorry I didn't get to see you much before I left. I know it's been a while since we got to hang out."

"Please, don't apologize. Just focus on you right now. Do you know about the funeral?" Kyle asked after a moment of silence. "I can meet you if you want. Kev doesn't have to know."

I hesitated. "The details are still being worked out. I'll give you a call in a few days."

"Ash?" His tone grew soft yet serious. "Please watch out for yourself. And know if you need me, I'm here."

"I will. I'll talk to you later, okay?"

"As you say, Monet," Kyle whispered on a sigh and disconnected.

I tossed the phone into the backseat and concentrated on the double yellow lines of the highway. My thoughts drifted back to memories of my childhood...

"Happy birthday, dear Ashton," Harry and my nanny, Ms. Lynn, sang with a smile. "Happy birthday to you!" Their applause carried through the open air, echoing across the endless lake at our home in Louisiana.

The sound of loons swelled in the background as the cheers faded away. My best friend Allie smiled from across the picnic table. I leaned forward, prepared to blow out the candles dotting the pink cake. I had one thing in mind, one gift that I wanted more than anything. I squinted in thought, my unspoken wish more of a silent prayer, then blew out the flames.

Harry wrapped an arm around my shoulders. "Thirteen, huh? You look older. Do you feel older?" His eyes bored into mine, as if my answer were somehow vitally important.

"I'm just joking, kid." He grinned at my guarded expression.

My heart grew heavy as I eyed the vacant seat across from mine.

Ms. Lynn patted my back "Your dad has a lot of business going on right now. I'm sure he'll pop up in a bit."

I sighed, disheartened as Allie wove her arm through mine.

"So—" Her blonde curls bounced as she plopped down "—what was it you wanted for your birthday?"

I searched over gift after gift, each one wrapped in the same, shimmering paper, knowing that what I wished for had chosen the office over me.

Harry offered the first present. "Well, kid, have at it."

A half hour and many thank you's later, one package remained unopened: a simple envelope with my name scrawled across the front. Lifting the flap, a knowing smile tugged at my mouth as I caught sight of a photo.

"She's beautiful." I admired the chestnut mare in the picture.

Just then, a whinnying sounded behind me. I turned to see a stable hand leading the graceful horse toward us.

"Happy birthday," the three called together. Harry pulled me into a tight hug as my eyes fell back to my father's empty chair. "Go ahead. She's been waiting for you." He took the reins and offered to help me up.

The familiar scent of a hayfield after the rain filled my memories as it always did with the thought of Harry. My heart ached in my chest as exhaustion weighed heavy on my eyelids.

A dimly lit vacant sign just off the interstate flickered to life, distracting me from my reverie. I exited and pulled into the lot. From the outside, the two-story building appeared more like an oversized duplex than a hotel, constructed of taupe vinyl-siding and stacked sandstone. Arms full of shopping bags, I lumbered toward the front desk, trying to stay conscious.

"Good morning," the desk clerk greeted, her curious eyes sweeping over my zombie-like state. "How many nights?"

"Just tonight … er, morning. Whatever." I stifled a yawn.

She held her hand out for my credit card and driver's license. Her eyes widened as they locked onto my extended forearm. I glanced down to see the imprint of a palm and four fingers in the form of a bluish-purple bruise beneath my skin. I grimaced — not the first time Kevin left his mark — and pulled the arm behind my back.

"Check out is at eleven. Your room is down the hall; take a right at the ice machine." She eyed the clock before glancing at me. "Do you need a wake-up call?"

"Sure," I mumbled, remembering I'd left my phone in the car. "Eight o'clock, please."

The hall dead-ended at my room. I trudged inside and tossed my stuff onto one of the full-sized beds. Slipping out of the dress and heels, I slid under the blankets, welcoming the emotional release sleep might offer.

Chapter Two
Encounter

An ambient glow filtered through the drapes from the streetlamps outside, casting the room with just enough light to make sleep impossible. My leg twitched as I watched each hour tick by on the wall clock, the second hand goading me as it made its pass. A heavy downpour beat against the glass as the wind howled and danced with something metallic outside my window. I sighed and threw my arm over my eyes, but it was no help.

Several sleepless hours later, my wake-up call rang in. I stumbled out of bed and threw open the useless curtains, shaking my head as I caught sight of a flooded parking lot.

Climbing into the shower, I turned the heat up and let the spray beat against my back, massaging away the stress. The water soothed my nerves and invigorated me more than a restful night's sleep ever could.

Eventually, the hot water faded into cold, and I climbed out. I towel dried my hair and pulled it into a messy knot. Loose brunette strands curled out along my temples and the nape of my neck — an unmanageable feature I inherited from my father, though the waviness and color were the only genetic similarities I shared with the man. Harry always said I looked like my mother. I took him at his word since I'd never known her.

I gazed into the mirror over the sink, taken aback by the change of my oddly blue eyes. The color seemed more vivid, even through the tiredness. My fingertips moved across the unexplained blush on my cheeks. Must be the stress, I reasoned as I pulled the tags from my new slacks and tank top to dress. Slipping into some flip-flops, I wheeled to the front to check out.

A mass of a man stood behind the counter. To my unease, the closer I moved, the more he grew. Easily a twelve inches above my five and half feet, he towered over me. He ran a hand through his disheveled hair as a predatory smile parted the five o'clock shadow darkening his skin. I noticed the name "Oren" was scrawled on his nametag as I shifted my focus from his face. He reminded me too much of Kevin.

"Good morning." Oren's voice, deep yet smooth, sent chills across my skin.

"If you like driving through a monsoon," I said, shifting my bag on my shoulder as I waited for my receipt.

"Well, you sure don't seem to care for it, huh?" A glint of humor sparkled in his uniquely gray eyes as they raked over my silhouette. The way he spoke and looked at me felt like a lion stalking its prey. "No rain on our date then. I can keep you dry with no problems."

"I don't think so," I replied, growing uneasy with his seemingly serious banter.

"So that's it then? You're just leaving?"

"Yup, I have to get going. Things to do." I snatched my bags, trying to make an exit.

"Right. Well, in that case ... I'll see you around." His voice carried a sudden lack of interest but there was an unsettling edge of expectancy in his tone.

Doubtful, I thought and wheeled away.

"Keep dry!" Oren's voice echoed across the tile as I reached the front.

I turned my face to find he'd vanished. Scanning the lobby, I shivered and hurried outside.

A bellboy held the door open for me. I paused beneath the awning and pulled out a ten-dollar bill and my keys, hoping he'd get the message. His eyes moved from the money, to the rain, and back to the money before he nodded. I pointed out my car, and he hurried into the downpour. At least I wasn't in over my head, yet.

It's not that I didn't enjoy the rain or any water for that matter. In fact, I'd always found it refreshing and almost energizing. But spending the better part of the day in dripping clothes wasn't exactly appealing.

As I drove, thoughts of the past two days filtered through my mind. Things would never be the same for me again. True, Charlie and I had never been close — that distance had only grown over the past few years — but he had taken care of me, provided me with every imaginable luxury. We rarely spent time together, but I was used to that; it was something I had grown to accept as a fact of life. Even still, as far as I knew, my family line had ended. I was officially an orphan.

Blood hammered through my veins as I attempted to fend off what I could only assume was the pressure from the surmounting stress. Come on, Ashton. This is no big thing. Get it together. My knuckles ached around the steering wheel. I sucked in a deep breath through my nose and blew the tension away.

Blinding headlights raced up out of nowhere, reflecting off the glass of my rear-view mirror and into my eyes. I smacked the mirror away and slowed down, hoping the driver would pass. After several seconds, I peered behind me to see the silver SUV inches from my bumper.

"Go around, jack-wagon!" I threw my hands up.

As if he heard my rant, the car drifted into the opposite side of the two-lane and inched up beside me. I glared through my window, sending a silent message with the hope the driver could see. A figure shadowed by tinted glass moved behind the wheel. The vehicle lingered beside me as I looked back to the road and let off the gas even more.

Oncoming headlights forced the driver of the SUV to hurry around me. A dark shape blurred past, going the opposite direction. I watched in wonder at whoever would drive at that speed — especially in the rain.

As I looked ahead, bright red filled my vision. The SUV locked up and slid sideways, blocking both lanes. I stomped against the brake. My tires screamed as they bit into the wet pavement. The back-end of the BMW shuddered from one side of the lane to the other before coming back around.

A wall of brown and green encircled the car. The scent of burnt rubber and smoke filled the air. My heart hammered in my ears as I battled momentum, trying desperately to end the spinning. What felt like minutes later, the wet squealing gave way to squishy crunching as my tires found the shoulder of the highway and settled into a ditch.

I took a shaky breath and tried to still my hands shaking in place. Rain pounded against the muddied glass as I looked out my window. The driver of the silver SUV stood, his arm slung across the top of his open door as he stared my way. The distance and bucketing rainfall obscured his face, but his aggressive posture spoke volumes.

I moved my foot from the brake to the gas. A wave of mud and gravel slammed into the belly of my car as the tires fought for purchase. Terror gripped my chest. The car wasn't moving and the man was. My breaths came too fast as I reached behind my seat, searching for the cell phone I'd tossed back yesterday. Risking a glance, I frantically pawed around the tiny area but came up empty.

In full panic mode, I looked ahead to see the brawny figure halfway to my car and moving with purpose. Just as I'd given up hope, he froze mid-stride, his hands balling into fists at his sides. My stress began to ease when he took a step back ... and then another. With one final hesitation, he turned, climbed in his SUV, and screamed out of sight.

I exhaled in a shaky breath and dropped my head against my hands. A sharp pain shot through the skin above my eye. Fixing the rear-view mirror, I wiped at the bloodied gash over my left brow.

A rapid knock against the window caused me to jump, ratcheting up my adrenaline once more. An unfamiliar figure stood outside my door, trying to peer through the slightly bloodied glass.

A guy wearing a black skullcap motorcycle helmet gestured for me to lower the window. Sensing he probably wasn't part of the insane posse who ran me off the road, I rolled it down.

"Do you need some help?" the stranger asked, shielding his face against the rain. His focused locked on the cut above my brow.

I peered up and gasped. His eyes were the most distinctive color, like the Caribbean ocean — a faint orange circled his pupil, turning the palest shade of blue in the center, before fading into a deeper blue-green toward the outer ring. They were framed with a fringe of long dark lashes that had to be the envy of every woman. His blue irises created a striking contrast with his sun-kissed skin, kicking my heart rate up.

"Miss?" His voice brought me back to my senses.

"Hmm? Oh, yeah, please," I mumbled, trying to concentrate. "I'm pretty stuck though. I don't see anything short of a tow truck getting me out of here."

If only I could find my phone.

"I'll give it a shot." He stared at my predicament with a little smile. "Just try not to run over me."

I gave him a disbelieving head shake and put the car in drive, watching for his signal from my mirror.

"All right," he yelled, "get ready to—"

And I floored it.

"Stop! Stop!" he sputtered, spitting and gagging as he waved his arms.

I grimaced as he brushed senselessly at a thick layer of sludgy road grime and sand down his front.

"Sorry!" I called back, my face growing warm. He waved me off and repositioned himself behind my bumper.

"Okay, ease forward a bit now," he directed.

I very carefully applied a little pressure to the gas pedal. To my surprise, the car lurched forward without effort. The grating sound of metal on metal screeched through the air at the same time something jarred beneath me. I threw the BMW into park and jumped out.

My shoulders slumped as I peered at the twisted metal lodged beneath my bumper. A crumpled motorcycle fender and black handlebars peeked out. I dropped my head into my hands and moaned. What else could possibly happen today?

"Is that my bike?" the stranger asked from behind me. I startled and slipped in the mud, going down to one knee.

"Easy there, Grace." He laughed and pulled me to my feet.

"That was an accident," I groaned. Heat scorched to my hairline. "I was watching you and not looking ahead. I can't even begin to tell you how sorry I am."

"It's fine. At least I wasn't on it, right?" He winked and wrenched a large bag off the back of the seat.

"But I killed your bike. I'm happy to pay for it or whatever you need..." My voice trailed away as I considered giving him a lift.

You should probably return the favor, I thought. Yeah, but what if he's crazy? What if I end up dead in this ditch, waiting to be covered by the evening news so someone can identify my body? The other part of my brain argued. If he'd wanted you dead, you'd be dead. He didn't have to help you, remember? It's not like you can leave him stranded in the rain just waiting to be mugged. What if the crazies who ran you off the road came back?

Obligation beat sensibility.

"Can I give you a ride somewhere? My cell is MIA, or I'd call the police right now," I said.

He hesitated, his eyes scanning the emptiness. "Yes, thank you."

"Oh, please. It's the very least I can do." I climbed in the car and grabbed a crumpled quilt from the floor, spreading it across his seat.

Mr. Biker tugged the drab green pack through and shoved it at his feet. He closed the door, and the air stirred with a woodsy aroma. The delicious scent of cedar heated by the sun lingered with the fresh rain. A strange warmth settled in my chest.

I ignored the sensation, as well as the scraping sound of metal, as I backed up and pulled onto the highway again. My new traveling partner never looked back as we drove away.

Water dripped from the brim of Mr. Biker's helmet as he unfastened it and sat it on his knee. He appeared to be around my age — maybe a few years older. He tucked a mop of longish auburn hair beneath a Gatsby style hat. A gray thermal clung to his chest, the washed out fabric settling nicely into the contours of well-defined muscle. A sense of familiarity wrapped around me.

"Have we met?" My head fell to the side as I studied his face.

He laughed. "I think I would remember meeting you."

His musky scent worked its way into my head as I considered the truth behind his statement. It'd be impossible to forget eyes like that.

"There's a truck stop just ahead. I'm sure they have a phone we can use." I said, struggling to think over the fragrance flooding the tight space. "We can also grab a bite to eat, if you'd like. My treat of course."

"That's very kind, thank you."

"I maimed your motorcycle. Lunch doesn't even scratch the surface." I shook my head. He grinned, and I lost myself in his dimples.

"I'm Ashton, by the way," I spoke after a moment.

"Nice to meet you. I'm Gabe." His hand lifted as if to shake mine, but he pulled it back and wiped it against his leg. "What are you doing out in this nasty weather?"

"I'm headed back east."

"Yeah? Me too. Aren't you a bit young to be traveling cross-country alone?" he asked.

My eyebrows fell. I hated that everyone made that assumption. "No younger than you." I scoffed, and Gabe bit back a smile. "I'm actually eighteen..." I stopped short of announcing today was my birthday. This wasn't turning out to be a birthday I wanted to remember.

"What happened to your forehead?" He pointed to the caked blood there.

"I ... I hydroplaned and slid into the ditch," I fudged. "I must've hit then."

"It seems to have stopped bleeding at least. That's a good sign." He smiled, but it felt off.

I felt Gabe watching me as we pulled into the truck stop, like if he concentrated hard enough, all of my secrets would be revealed. I tried to ignore it and grabbed the door handle.

Gabe reached for an umbrella on the floor and hurried around to open my door. He ducked down to measure closer to my height, his hand resting lightly just above my jeans. The heat from his palm blazed against my damp shirt, sending an electric charge through the small of my back. Gabe's warm breath tickled against my bare shoulder, and I shivered.

"Hopefully it won't be too cool in here," he said, opening the door.

I shrugged my shoulders and looked down so he wouldn't see the rush of color flooding my cheeks. I wasn't about to tell him that my reaction had nothing to do with my own temperature.

Gabe followed me to a small booth in the back of the dining area. An empty spot in the corner held an overflowing vase of orchids. Gabe took a seat, but I excused myself and hurried to the restroom, my eyes floating by the time I reached it ... in just enough time to stand in line. I considered charging the men's room, but decided against going the route of having myself dismissed from the establishment.

Gabe's voice caught my attention as I walked back to our table. He gestured discreetly as he spoke with a waitress. From his expression, they seemed to be discussing more than the menu. I paused in the archway, straining to read their lips.

"Excuse me," a gravelly voice spoke at my back. I turned to see a burly man in a plaid shirt trying to get around.

"Pardon me." I moved to let him pass.

When I looked back, the waitress had vanished. Gabe stood and smiled as I approached. The vase of flowers now sat two tables away. A waitress in a pale-blue and white uniform came around the corner. The same woman he'd spoken with moments ago. She appeared to be a couple of years older than me with a shining smile and fair strawberry-blonde hair that hung like satin below her shoulders. An unexpected pang of jealousy swept over me. My hand slipped into my pocket, and I discreetly swiped a layer of gloss across my lips.

"Hi, welcome to the Truck Haven diner. I'm Lily," she drawled with an unexpected southern accent. Her lavender eyes lit the room with warmth. "What can I get you two to drink?" She pulled a pen from behind her ear and replaced it with her hair.

"Ashton?" Gabe offered, keeping his eyes away from the pretty girl.

My heart leapt a little hearing my name from his lips. I sighed and cleared my throat. "Do you have sweet tea?"

"Certainly." She nodded.

"Lily, I'd like the same." Gabe winked at me from across the table.

"Sure, I'll be right back with those if you want to take a moment to think about what you want." Lily lifted an eyebrow at me. She turned and walked back the way she came.

"Would you excuse me, Gracie? I'm going to clean up a bit," Gabe said, smiling when I narrowed my eyes at his nickname.

He stood and shouldered his bag. The strap tugged at his shirt, exposing a hint of skin at his hip. "Would you mind ordering something for me?"

"Umm ... sure, yeah," I answered and pulled my eyes upward. "What do you want?"

Gabe laughed softly. "I'll leave that up to you."

My thoughts assumed a wistful tone as I admired him walk away. He carried the air of someone who had lived life — both the good and the bad — but came away the better for it. And Gabe liked sweet tea. Kevin only ever drank some strange herbal tea that he'd never share and always hid.

"Here we are, sweetie." Lily stopped at the table. I turned to see her setting our glasses down as she glanced around the diner. "Now where did your friend disappear to? Did you need more time?"

"Hmm? No, thank you." I fumbled with the menu trying to regain my focus. I paused, catching that it was upside down, and warmth stole to my cheeks.

"So, what can I get you two?" she asked, her pencil tapping against her notebook.

My teeth locked around my bottom lip as I looked over my choices. I hadn't thought to ask Gabe if there was anything he didn't like.

"May I make a suggestion?" Lily offered as the time drew on.

"That's probably a good idea," I said. "Thanks."

"Well, we're known around here for our mushroom burgers," she stated.

"Ehh," I wavered. That didn't seem like a win-win option. Not everyone liked mushrooms. I loved them, but I also liked to eat my fries with mayonnaise and mix peanut butter and syrup together for dessert. I'd always been a little quirky when it came to food.

"I guarantee you'll both be glad you ordered it." Lily pointed at me with her pencil.

"All right Lily, you convinced me. But if he doesn't like it, I'm blaming you," I half teased.

"Well, when he falls in love, you won't have anything to worry about." She laughed as she walked back to the kitchen.

Chapter Three
The Beginning

I fidgeted with the sugar cubes as I waited. My gaze fell on the vase of flowers, and Kevin flitted back into my mind. Orchids surrounded his villa. They weren't the bright, cheerful color most people chose, but a dark-plum, almost black, giving his place a slightly dangerous feel — kind of like Kevin. I rubbed the imprint of his hand on my forearm then tucked the bruise beneath the table.

I sighed and looked up to see Gabe sauntering around the corner. The ragged cap was gone, and his dark hair waved down the back of his neck. He wore it loosely pushed away from his forehead with just the hint of rebellious curl. A pale-blue button up replaced the frayed thermal, the sleeves rolled to his elbows. A sense that I knew him from somewhere hit me again, nagging at me like a fly buzzing around my ear. Feeling lightheaded, I realized I'd stopped breathing and sucked in a lungful of oxygen.

"Sorry to have kept you waiting." Gabe slid into his seat.

"No worries. I've just been..." My sentence trailed away. I didn't really want to bring up my hot-tempered boyfriend with the guy I was strangely attracted to.

"You've been what, building an empire?" he asked and pointed to my condiment formation. "You have a nice little town going there."

An embarrassed chuckle slipped out as I shoveled the cubes back into the dish, careful to keep my bruised arm hidden on my lap.

Lily reappeared and sat her tray down to divvy out the food.

Gabe moaned from across the table and sniffed at his burger. "I love mushrooms."

I slid a sideways glance at Lily.

"Enjoy your meal." She winked.

"Did you get in touch with someone about your bike?" I took a gulp of tea.

Gabe nodded. "I spoke with the police. They're sending someone to clean up the mess, and said they'd get back with me. My cell was crushed, so I told them I'd check back in a couple of days."

Add new phone to your list of costs, I thought.

"What will you do until then?" I frowned. "Can you get home or wherever it is you're headed?"

"Not exactly," he wavered. "I'll likely wait here. There are bunk houses in the back there. I can rent one for a day or two."

"Well, like I said, I'm headed east," I explained. "I know I have a history of mudslinging and destruction, but you're welcome to ride with me as long as you want."

"If you're comfortable, I'd really appreciate that. Riding the bike in the rain was getting tired anyway." His dimples sank in.

I wasn't sure the reasoning behind the offer but it felt right having Gabe around, and that wasn't a feeling I was used to. I welcomed it without a second thought for what it could mean.

After we finished eating, Gabe excused himself to use the restroom. My eyes tarried on his figure as he walked away, the nagging familiarity still chewing away at my brain.

"He seems very special," Lily spoke, startling me. "Sorry, sweetie."

"You're fine. I guess I was daydreaming." I finished the last of my tea.

"Can't say as I blame you." Lily smiled as she sat the check on the table. "You guys be safe and have a great day."

I lifted the tab as she walked away, and I frowned. It was almost blank. Lily hadn't charged me for anything, she'd just written one sentence along the bottom. It read: The best things in life aren't free ... they're priceless.

Gabe returned to find me mulling over the huge gesture scrawled onto an insignificant square of receipt. I discreetly tucked what should've been the price of our meal plus a hundred under the tab on the clipboard.

Gabe watched me for a second, like he'd somehow seen my kind gesture, and then motioned for me to lead the way out. I grinned as he opened the umbrella, and we stepped out into the downpour.

"Where exactly are you heading?" he asked as we hit the road.

A tidal wave of anxiety hit me. I ground my teeth together and tried to cover the flurry of despair and panic that simmered just below my composure.

"Umm, a funeral," I managed to choke out in a betraying tone.

"Funeral?" Gabe's voice sounded strained. He drew a deep breath. "Family?"

"Just a friend," I answered, though I questioned whether or not it was misleading to call Charlie a friend. We weren't even that close.

"A friend?" His expression darkened with remorse.

I couldn't answer him.

"I apologize. I didn't know." Gabe shook his head and stared through the window, his mouth set in a hard line.

I bit down on my lip and focused on the highway.

"Are you from Arizona?" he asked, changing the subject.

"No, I live in Pasadena more often than not," I said, relieved to talk about anything else. "I spent my first thirteen years in Louisiana. With the exception of the summers in New York, I've been in California since my freshman year of high school, studying at a private arts academy."

"Why spend summers in New York?"

I hesitated. "Family. I go back home when I'm not in school."

"You don't like the east coast?" Gabe laced his fingers together and listened as if my life were somehow interesting.

"No, it's fine. I just prefer sun and warmth. And Idyllwild, my art school, was a great place." I shrugged. "It really helped me get ahead of the game."

"That's a lot of traveling. You must be serious about school. Will you go to college in California?"

"Well, I'm taking some time off for now." It was a hollow and pitiful explanation, but I hoped he'd either assume I meant time off for summer break or drop the matter altogether. Fact of the matter, college demanded more effort than I cared to exert given the choice.

"So, you're working then? What do you do?" Gabe turned his head, eyeing my discomfort. He almost seemed to enjoy it. I paused, trying to regain the lead of the conversation.

"I've been working in the social setting, you know? Trying to meet the right people and broaden my opportunities." A.K.A. lame lingo for bumming it. It sounded ludicrous, even to me. "What do you do? Are you in school?"

Gabe's hands curled into fists at his knees. "I'm in acquisitions."

"You must've graduated early then," I surmised. "What are you, like twenty-one?"

"You're good," Gabe said, wearing an awkward smile. "I was on the fast track through school, and then lucked out on this job."

"What kind of things do you acquire?" I asked.

Gabe hesitated, his leg bouncing against the door. "It varies from time to time. Can you believe this rain?" he asked and made a show of staring out the window.

We filled several more hours with superficial chatter. I was cautious not to bring up topics that could lead to my family, and avoided the ones he flirted around. We talked about music — he found my distaste for country to be funny given that I grew up in the South.

"Classical?" He lifted a brow.

"I'm a fan of Bach and Debussy. Vivaldi is my favorite." I grinned, hoping he didn't think I was a nerd.

"I'll bet you like poetry then, too?" His blue eyes danced as he smiled.

"Yeah. How did you know?" I quirked an eyebrow.

"'Sometimes a troop of damsels glad, an abbot on an ambling pad,'" Gabe quoted.

"Sometimes a curly shepherd-lad or long-hair'd page in crimson clad, Goes by to tower'd Camelot; And sometimes thro' the mirror blue. The knights come riding two and two. She hath no loyal knight and true...'"

"'…the lady of Shalott,'" we concluded together.

I turned and faced him, my eyes narrowed.

"Why are you looking at me that way?" he questioned.

"You like poetry?" I asked, my focus falling on the helmet resting at his knee.

"Very much so. That just happens to be my favorite. I love how Tennyson's words flow so effortlessly. He invokes true emotion with his work."

"Tennyson is my favorite poet." I glanced at him from the corner of my eye.

"You know what they say about great minds." His dimples sank in. "Do you like the classics?"

"I do," I said. "And Greek and Roman mythology. If I hadn't gone into art, I would've chosen something literary related."

Gabe watched me with curious eyes. A hint of amusement toyed around his mouth.

It was unbelievable that in all the years I'd spent traveling around world, the person I seemed to share a kinship with was a biker with a penchant for literary treasures who I ran across outside of Flagstaff, Arizona. It was almost comical. My lips turned up at the thought of what Kyle would say if he knew I'd picked Gabe up on the side of the road. My smile turned derisive when I imagined Kevin's reaction.

What started out as a gloomy morning transformed into a stunning evening. The rain died away by the time we reached Amarillo. The horizon flaunted a striking display of color with running streamers of pink and purple throughout a canopy of blue. Wispy clouds filtered through the air, adding depth to the endless sky.

The shadow of a towering white hotel enveloped the car as we rolled into the parking lot. I climbed from behind the steering wheel, and Gabe gestured for me to go ahead inside while he gathered our luggage. Checking in, things went much smoother than in Arizona. I laughed to myself, recognizing the reason. I didn't feel uptight and on edge; it was actually quite the opposite. It almost seemed wrong to feel so okay. Not only did it cause me a fair amount of guilt in the current circumstances, it confused me to no end.

Gabe made his way into the lobby with our things as I grabbed the keycards.

"I didn't mean for you to pay for the room," he grumbled.

"I'd be here regardless," I said. "I don't expect anything from you."

Gabe sidled up beside me, and we rode the elevator to the top floor. Lifting the keycard from my pocket, I opened the door to the suite.

"Here, let me get those. You aren't a pack mule, you know." I smiled.

"You didn't have to do this." He frowned as he gazed around the lavish suite. "In fact, I wish you hadn't. The least I can do is help you with your things. Where do you want them?"

"Oh, I'll take care of..." I began. Gabe ignored me and carried everything into my cattle baron inspired bedroom, situating my suitcases beside the dresser.

"Thanks again." I reached forward to nudge him in the arm with my elbow.

"You're welcome again." Gabe mimicked the motion. His gaze held, and I lost myself in the blue-green sea of his eyes. There was a warmth there I'd never seen in anyone else. An invisible connection hummed between us like a current. My heartbeat picked up, bringing a twinge of guilt for the enjoyment I felt in the moment.

"I'm just going to find some blankets and take the couch." His voice grew husky as he backed toward the door.

I rolled my eyes and scoffed. Did he actually believe that I planned to ditch him on the too-short loveseat? I walked back to the sitting room and opened the door against the wall housing the entertainment center. A spacious second bedroom appeared.

"Wow. You have expensive taste. This is too much." He shook his head then pushed the hair from his eyes.

"No, it's fine. Like I said, I'd be here regardless and still in the suite. I do have good taste ... in some stuff," I murmured.

"Well, thanks again." He smiled.

"Sure. G'night."

"Sleep well, Grace." Gabe grinned and began toward his room.

I started to bed then turned on my heel. "Oh, I left my other bag in the car. I have to get my MP3 player. My Zune helps me get to sleep."

"I'll get for you," Gabe offered.

"No, it's fine. I'll be right back." I smiled and hurried for the front door before he offered again.

Gabe's warm cedar and rain scent lingered in the elevator, wiping my mind of coherent thought. I was downstairs and halfway across the parking lot before I realized my keys were still inside.

"Really bright, Ashton," I fussed. "Geez. One gorgeous guy shouldn't make your brain stop working."

"They say I have that affect on women," a deep voice purred behind me as a rough hand swept around my throat.

Impulse pulled my eyes toward him.

"Don't even try it," he ordered and yanked my chin forward. My back slammed into his chest with enough force to knock the wind out me. The heat from his body bled through my clothing like a furnace. Sweat prickled and trailed down my skin as my heart battered against my ribcage. I tried to think over the panic — to remember how to escape an attacker — but the overflow of adrenaline did nothing more than make me lightheaded.

I choked and clawed at the fingers around my neck.

"Stop fighting," he growled and pinned my arms down with his free hand.

Tears flooded my eyes as he lifted me up until only the balls of my feet touched the ground. Air wheezed through my tight windpipe. My eyes felt like they were about to explode from the pressure on my carotid.

"Behave and we'll have some fun." He laughed once. "Now, walk backwards and don't turn around."

My footsteps faltered. A hollow ringing filled my ears, and dots floated in front of my eyes.

"Move," he demanded. The hotel swam in and out of focus as he dragged me in the opposite direction.

"Hey!" Gabe's voice echoed from across the parking lot.

My assailant growled under his breath. I strained through the black spots to see a figure moving toward us. Two blue reflections twinkled in the distance. It looked like an animal blinking in headlights.

The blazing fingers tightened around my throat. Tears spilled down my face as I braced myself for what followed next. Without warning, the hand loosened and fell away. Wiping my eyes, I stumbled in blind panic toward the figure from the shadows. Somewhere behind me, heavy footsteps retreated into the dark.

"Ashton?" Gabe gasped. I fell into him, trembling as his arms wound around me and lifted me up. "Are you hurt?"

His arms tightened as my strength give way.

"No," I panted, trying to fill the lungs that burned with need for air.

"Come on," he muttered blackly. "Let's get you upstairs."

Gabe's eyes scanned the parking lot as we hurried back inside.

"Here, sit down and I'll get you something to drink." He led me to the sofa in our room.

"No! Please, don't leave me." I clung to his arm.

The cushion gave way as Gabe eased beside me. I curled into his side, breathing in his comforting scent, and tried not to cry. He wrapped his arms around me, a tentative hand sliding along my back.

"Shh," he soothed, his voice strained. "It's all right. You're safe."

"Sorry." I sniffled, feeling weak and vulnerable. "I don't know why I'm shaking."

"Someone attacked you." He backed away but kept one hand around mine. "You're experiencing an excess of adrenaline. Your body will calm down in a minute."

I nodded and drew a tremulous breath.

"Did he say what he wanted?" Gabe's voice became low, tight.

"He didn't say much at all." My breathing hitched. "I can only imagine what he wanted."

Gabe held his breath for a moment, his knuckles whitening as he clenched his hand into a fist. "And you have no idea why he came for you?"

I shook my head. "I must have been in the wrong place at the wrong time. Why? Do you think it was something more?"

"No. You're probably right. I'm just relieved I followed you down." Gabe raised my chin and grimaced as he saw my neck.

"What is it?" I asked.

He lifted a silver tray off the side table and held it at eyelevel so I could see the reflection. My fingers moved to the skin below my jaw. Another handprint.

The room radiated with fury. Gabe's expression darkened as he caught the hand at my throat and held my arm out. His gaze lingered on the fading mark there, his turquoise eyes burning with resentment. Like so many times before, I tried to hide the result of a quick-tempered boyfriend.

"These aren't men," he murmured with disgust. His gaze softened as tears prickled in the corner of my eyes.

"Could you … would you mind sleeping in my room tonight?" I whispered.

"Sure." He gave me a tight smile. "I'll make up a spot on the floor." Gabe stood and went to his room. He carried some pillows and a blanket into my room and made a pallet on the carpet beside the bed.

"Come on." Gabe helped me to my feet and into my room. I collapsed on the bed, and he tucked me in, brushing a strand of hair from my forehead.

"What were you doing out there?" I slurred, exhaustion finally catching up with me.

"You left your keys on the counter," he whispered.

"Lucky me, I guess." My voice faded. "Thank you for saving me…"

I drifted off but not before I thought I heard, "I'll not fail you again."

Chapter Four
Discovery

Last night's emotions hung heavy in the air. My stomach rolled like the ocean. I chugged a glass of water and grabbed my luggage by the night stand. Gabe's muscular silhouette held my attention as he leaned against the door to the patio. He turned and smiled when I wandered into the living room. Serenity enveloped me. Had I not been at ease it would've bothered me that he had such control over the rhythm of my heart.

"Good morning." Gabe weighed my expression. "How are you feeling?"

"Never better." I smiled. "You?"

"Glad you're okay." He returned my smile, but it didn't meet his eyes. "Are you ready to leave?"

"Yup. Let's hit the road."

My fingers tapped the beat of the song on the radio while we drove east. Gabe's glance caught my attention. Again.

"What is it?" I looked at him then back to the highway.

"I know it's none of my business, and feel free to tell me so, but can I ask a favor of you?" he asked.

"After last night, you can ask anything."

"Would you mind to not go off alone? Only for a while," he said. "I just need to know you're safe."

"Yeah, that's not a problem." I smiled. "Thank you again, by the way. If you hadn't been there…" I shook my head at the same time Gabe did.

He offered a genuine smile — likely relieved that I'd consented without throwing a Miss Independent fit.

"Gabe, my dad has a lake house in central Texas. If you don't have any objections, I'd planned on stopping by. I've never been there, and since it's sort of on the way, I thought it might be a good time." I left out the fact that Charlie had previously forbidden me to go there.

"Central Texas?" Gabe's shoulders tensed. "Sure, that sounds fine."

He drew a deep breath and toyed with a brown leather cord around his neck, looping it around his finger at the smooth skin at his collarbone.

I stared through the windshield, wondering for the thousandth time why Charlie had forbidden it in the first place. This had the potential to be a very difficult experience: my father's restriction of visiting, the fact that it was my mother's home, so to speak. It had emotional disaster written all over it. Anxiety knotted in my stomach, and I worked to smooth the worry lines across my forehead.

Gabe stared idly at the nothing of the sprawling desert. I suppose the brown sparseness was beautiful in its own monotonous kind of way. Still, I preferred a more dimensional landscape. It felt too open in the desert, like I was somehow more exposed to being hit by a falling meteor or an earthbound satellite.

"So, where are you from exactly?" I asked.

His eyebrows creased in thought. "I've lived here and there."

"You don't have a home?" My words sounded sadder than I would've expected.

"A house isn't the only place you can have a home." He gave a half-hearted smile.

That began the wheels turning in my mind again. I didn't exactly understand his meaning, but on the other hand, I suppose I understood perfectly. Even though I had access to a half-dozen houses across the world, I never felt like I had that special place where I felt safe and loved. The place that I could always run to when the world became too much for me. Not now anyway — not now especially. My heart ached realizing I needed that haven — that place where I felt safe and loved. It had been missing all of these years, but I'd refused to see it.

Kevin was willing enough to provide that place, in a sense. Or rather, he had been. Things weren't going so well for the two of us. We'd been fighting more and more lately, almost to the point of me threatening to call it quits. For some reason, and one I would never admit, that notion didn't bother me like it should. Kevin always seemed to be grooming me for some sort of life he wanted me to lead but with no regard for what I wanted — an act I'd only recently noticed.

"So where do you feel your home is?" I asked, suddenly feeling very empty inside. I saw him shrug from the corner of my eye as he sighed.

"I don't have the answer to that," he murmured.

I swallowed air, silently agreeing with him.

"Are we heading to Granbury now?" he asked.

I cleared my throat. "Um, yeah, I—" My sentence cut short when I realized that I couldn't remember speaking the name of the city where we were headed. "How did you, I never—"

"It's starred on your GPS." He winked. "I'm not crazy."

"Right." I laughed, feeling foolish. "Charlie, my dad, has a house on the lake, though I don't know the last time he visited. He built it for my mother as her wedding gift. He didn't have the wealth that he does now, or did, so it was a very romantic gesture on his part. She always loved it. He kept it for her, I imagine."

"Your mother doesn't love it now?" Gabe watched me from the corner of his eye.

"She passed away when I was a baby," I explained matter-of-factly. "No one ever spoke about her more than necessary. To this day, I don't know how she looked or what her interests were." I laughed once without humor. "They wouldn't even tell me her name."

I bit down on my tongue. Why did I tell him that?

Gabe leaned his head against the seat, his eyebrows low. "I'm sorry. I had no idea," he spoke, his tone sad yet surprised. "That must've been hard growing up."

"It's different with my mom," I explained. "I never knew her, so there wasn't as much to lose. I still miss her though. Sounds crazy, huh? Missing someone you've never even met."

"That doesn't sound crazy at all. It's hard not having a mother." Gabe's eyes filled with compassion. "But I do know trying to understand, trying to figure out why, can drive a person mad. Sometimes you just have to accept the hand you've been dealt." His voice trailed with a hint of bitterness.

My teeth cut into my bottom lip.

"You're much stronger than you realize, Ashton." Gabe's tone softened. "Always remember that."

"I'm not so sure that's true," I murmured, remembering the mind-numbing terror that overrode all logic.

"What happened yesterday was in no way a sign of your being weak," he spoke sternly.

Maybe not, I thought. But my life is a sign of weakness. Kevin's face flashed through my mind as I glanced down to see the bruise had all but faded. Never once had I stood up to him.

Gabe's expression confused me as I peered at him. It settled somewhere in the realm of remorse.

"What's wrong?" I asked.

"Nothing," he assured. "I have a lot on my mind. It's been an unusual couple of days. Things still surprise me."

I laughed once. No truer words were ever spoken there.

"I guess that doesn't come close to summing up your last few days though, does it?" He sighed. "Sorry, I shouldn't have said that."

"Please. Don't worry about it. You know, there's been a lot to change for me in the past forty-eight hours. Some of it has been really crappy and confusing, and I wish it hadn't happened. But some of it has been amazing, and I wouldn't change it for anything." I looked down as my cheeks flamed red. "I don't know much about you or your life or what's going on, but someone once told me, 'What matters, matters.'"

Gabe's eyes flashed on mine. "What did that someone mean?"

"You shouldn't feel bad about something that's important to you just because someone else has issues you think are more significant. What you're going through matters as much as what they are."

Gabe's brows furrowed as he turned his quiet assessment back to the highway, his hand slipping to the leather necklace around his neck.

A couple hours later, the Granbury city lights came into view. Signs plastered to poles announced that tomorrow was the fourth of July and there was to be a carnival, live music, and a fireworks display over the lake. I imagined Gabe would enjoy watching the pyrotechnics over the water. Guys seemed to enjoy explosions, even if they were pretty.

The city stood quiet as we crossed a bridge stretching over a wide ribbon of the lake. Muted light shone from the antiquated shops' window displays. Brick storefronts glowed softly from the staggered streetlamps along the sidewalks.

"Hmm, North Houston Street," I muttered to myself, catching sight of a street sign.

Gabe cocked an eyebrow as I eased into an empty space along the road.

"I need the address. Excuse me a sec." I switched on the map light beneath the mirror.

Gabe flinched and moved his hand to his eyes. "It's bright."

"I'll try and give you a heads up next time." I smiled and pulled a thick stack of papers from the glove compartment. Sorting through them, I looked up the address for Charlie's house.

"What is that?" Gabe asked.

"This is a book with information on all of my father's properties. Pass codes, spare keys, phone numbers, everything is in here," I said. "Ah-hah, there it is." I held the book closer to the light and read it aloud. "Let's see, North Houston runs into Weatherford and that takes us where we need to go."

I entered the address, and the voice in the GPS told me to make a left. We followed a narrow one-lane road for several miles, the houses growing few and far between as we drove to the last lot on the peninsula.

An iron gate stood at the mouth of a stone wall. The silhouette of an elegant manor loomed across the courtyard, the roof stretching high into the darkness. A recent rain left its fingerprint in the form of wispy fog settling along the ground.

My tires splashed over the damp driveway. As I entered the security code on the keypad, the black gate groaned as it slid to the side, the chain links ticking in unison. The air seemed to cool as the quiet yet unnerving sound ceased with a clang.

My headlights washed across the square revealing well-groomed blooms and green shrubs. Sensors caught our motion, flooding the front lawn with light. An expansive Tudor home with a turret in the center, stretched toward the sky. Gray stone wrapped around the three-story exterior, the rock interspersed with patches of wood panels. Ivy trailed the corners, enveloping the stone in a mask of green.

A sudden stab of guilt twisted through me for defying my father's wishes. Charlie's gone, I told myself. There's no one left to care anymore. The heart that had been racing began to ache.

I parked the car at the front of the house, and we grabbed our bags. Standing at the front door, I counted five places to the right of the doorbell and began wiggling the rectangular stone.

"Huh, clever," Gabe murmured.

"Tell me about it," I grunted, jarring the rock till it gave way. Inside the well-disguised cubby was a ring with multiple keys attached, each labeled in regards to what it opened.

I unlocked the dead bolt and turned the knob. My hand stilled as Gabe's wrapped around my fingers.

"Ashton..." He drew a breath but didn't continue. Finally, his head fell and he sighed. "Thank you for inviting me here. I realize this is different than staying at a hotel, with it being your family's home and all."

"Sure. I trust you not to make off with the silver while I'm sleeping," I tried to joke, but the familiar current hummed through my skin where his hand lingered, making it hard to concentrate.

Gabe offered a weak smile then dropped his arm.

I took a steadying breath and pushed the door open. The soft fragrance of lilies filled the doorway. I flipped the light switch and peered around the foyer. Two wooden staircases curved in opposite directions, winding up to the second floor. Watercolors dotted the sage colored walls that curled around the stairs. The marble tile was a grayish-green, reminding me of the Pacific after a storm when the water was troubled and frothy. A compass design was inlaid in the center. Large statues and sculptures stood guard over the entryway. While each piece of decorative furniture and art was different, they flowed harmoniously, sharing a likeness that I couldn't quite put my finger on.

"It appears we have some hiking ahead of us." Gabe nudged me back into reality, his eyes focused toward the landing atop the steps. "Then again..." His sentence drifted off as he walked through a passage between the staircases. He veered to the left before stopping. Gabe turned, wearing a satisfied grin, and stretched his hand forward to touch the wall. I looked on, confused, until I heard a familiar ding and the sound of doors sliding open.

"Your father's home is meticulous," Gabe offered as we stepped into an elevator. "I'm assuming there's a staff of sorts?"

"No doubt." I hit the button for the second floor. "Leave it Charlie to have a lawn service for a house he doesn't even visit."

"Will the staff mind you're here then?"

"I don't see how it's any of their business." I shrugged. "I imagine they're off for the holiday anyway."

"Then promise me this, if we're caught in this house together, and there's trouble, you can't blame me." Gabe grinned, his dimples sinking in.

"Scout's honor." I lifted my left hand to my forehead.

"That's not the girl-scout salute," Gabe pointed out, staring at the two fingers I held to my brow.

I tried to readjust my number of fingers. Gabe reached forward, grabbed my right hand, and positioned it to my head in place of the left.

"Wrong hand, Gracie." He winked.

"Oh," I murmured, trying to maintain a healthy pulse. "I was never in the girl-scouts."

"I'm not sure what that says about your promise then," he laughed.

My humor faded as I stared into his eyes. Something like liquid fire burned through my body, melting away my defenses. The invisible connection sang to life, drawing me closer. I searched his face, wanting to know what he was thinking. How did he feel at this exact moment? Why did he wear that expression? What did it mean?

A bell chimed as the doors opened on the second floor.

"Sorry," Gabe murmured, severing the tenuous thread that stretched unseen between us. "I'm in my own world. It's been a long day."

Of course he's just tired. I jerked my luggage out of elevator and down the hall. What would a kind soul like Gabe ever want from an emotional shut-in like you?

I sighed and turned to see Gabe still standing at the elevator, his hands balled at his sides.

"I—" He paused before saying something else. "Where would you like me to sleep?"

I cleared my throat, still thick with emotion. "You can pick any room you want. There seem to be plenty to choose from."

"Sure, thanks, Ashton. Nite." Gabe hoisted his bag and started down the hall to the left. He opened the first door and vanished into the darkness.

Fresh tears welled as he closed the door. Maybe Charlie's death was affecting me more than I realized. Being here only added to my emotional instability. The house made me curious about the life and love my mother and father shared. I had never seen that kind of love in him. It was impossible to imagine him having the capability. But he did.

I looked over the banister to the floor below and realized that this was my mother's house, her personal space. Charlie must have adored her to have it kept in such pristine condition all these years. Feminine touches were stamped in every way, and my heart ached at the thought that I never knew the woman who meant so much to him.

A strange remorse coursed through me. I never knew this wonderful woman — I never even had the opportunity to know her — but I also never had the opportunity to lose her. Charlie did.

For the first time in my life, I pitied my father.

"Ashton?" Gabe appeared from the shadows and paused a few feet away. Our eyes met, and his features grew serious. He took a tentative step toward me.

I drew a breath. "Yeah?"

"I need to tell you ... I think I forgot to lock the front door." Gabe swallowed hard, his expression tight. "Did you get it?"

"Yeah, thanks."

"Good." Gabe swept a curl from my forehead and tucked it behind my ear. He shifted his body just enough to lean in a little more, and the current surged over me.

Stop it, I ordered myself, but it didn't lessen the pull between us.

"We should probably call it a night," I whispered, trying to control the trembling in my voice.

"Yeah, you must be tired," he murmured. The corner of his mouth pulled down as he backed away, leaving a chill where he'd stood.

"Right." Frustrated, I wheeled around and slammed into a table that stood behind me. It balked under the force, jarring a crystal container of wild flowers. As the vase toppled over, Gabe lunged forward in an attempt to catch it.

The loud crash of shattered crystal echoed through the hall. I stared down in horror, my eyes fixed on the deep gash running across the inside of Gabe's right forearm. Blood ran freely from the wound, dripping onto the rug. He gripped his arm with his free hand, trying to stop the flow.

I dropped to his side and yanked the zipper open on my toiletry bag. Pulling out a shirt, I knotted it around the bloodied mess.

"We'd better get to the bathroom and clean you up. Here, elevate it." I lifted his arm.

He rose on a groan but hesitated. I stuck close in case he turned out to be a fainter. Not that I could catch him, but I could come between his head and the floor if nothing else.

"There's a bathroom in my room." He gestured toward his wing of the house. We walked down the hall and paused outside his door. Gabe's knuckles whitened around the shirt as I turned the knob and flipped on the light.

I led him into the bathroom, hitting the switch with my elbow. Gabe grudgingly lowered himself into an armchair. His head plopped back and he stared up toward the ceiling.

"I'm going to look for some bandages. Don't try to get up," I warned.

I wiped my bloodied hands on a hanging towel then rummaged through the cabinets until I found a full-sized first aid kit.

Gabe tilted his head toward me as I knelt in front of him. He drew a slow deliberate breath in through his nose and blew it from his mouth. I moved my hand to the shirt but Gabe caught mine in his.

"I can take care of this. You should go on to bed."

"Gabe, you're bleeding everywhere. You can't do this one handed. It's probably going to need stitches regardless. Just sit tight and let me help you."

Gabe sighed in resignation and fell back against the seat.

I gently unknotted my shirt from his forearm and gasped. The bleeding had all but stopped. A deep cut remained but it was clean and dry less the crusted blood from moments ago. It looked like it had been formed from clay. I turned his hand in mine. How was that possible? The only way blood doesn't flow is if it can't. Something was very wrong with his arm.

Chapter Five
Insight

"It's all right, Ashton." Gabe grabbed my hand, his eyes locked on me.

"Right..." I managed, my focus still glued to his arm.

"Please, don't be upset," Gabe pleaded. "It isn't ... I swear everything is fine."

"I don't understand how?" My mind fumbled around for an answer. Just a moment ago, he needed stitches, and now, the wound healed before my eyes.

"You're confused, and I'm sorry." Gabe looked pained as he tried to explain. "I wish I could say something." He paused. "I just can't right now."

"I don't know what to say to that. I think I need to lie down." My fingers moved to my temples.

Gabe nodded solemnly, not giving me anything else to go on.

The overwhelming events began to weigh on my suffering state of sanity. I tried to smother the anxiety and searched for a reason to excuse myself and run away.

"Well, I guess I understand why you didn't want help. Sorry I pushed you." My voice was a distant whisper. I didn't know what to feel as I stood up in a panic and rushed out.

I lugged my bags into an open room and hurled them through the darkness. The wall protested with a thud. I fell backwards in the center of the canopy bed, wanting to go to sleep and escape this alternate reality, but my foot wouldn't stop twitching. I threw my arm across my eyes and willed myself into unconsciousness. It was no use. All the day's occurrences crept back in, sabotaging any hope I had of rest. I jerked up with a growl and tugged the chain of the lamp on the nightstand.

I picked up my bags and placed them on the leather bench at the foot of my bed. The first suitcase held my clothes. I chose the pink cotton tank top and matching pajama bottoms.

Yanking the new tags off, I caught sight of the brand. Apples to Oranges. A little image of the two fruits sat beneath the title. It seemed ridiculous that the commonplace emblem should bother me, but it did. The words were parts to one of Charlie's frequently used quotes. *You're trying to compare apples to oranges, Ashton. That's neither here nor there.*

I sighed and walked into the bathroom. Every argument we ever had almost always consisted of him using that phrase. The last conversation I shared with my father echoed through my mind as I filled the tub.

"Ash," Charlie pleaded in his thick southern accent, "please come home for the weekend. It's your birthday."

"Dad, we've been over this. The weather is going to be bad in New York in the next few days. I'll come after this whole hurricane thing is past. Besides that, Kevin's throwing me a party Friday."

"All right. Will you come the week after next then? Or even mid-week? Please?" he nearly begged, which was atypical for my father. He didn't ask; he demanded. And more than that, he never begged.

"Yes. Look, I'll talk to Kevin and see what we have going on, and we'll try to get up there as soon as we have time."

"You can come without him. You know that, right?"

"Yes, Dad, I do realize that Kevin's presence is not required for my trip, I just thought you might want to get to know each other a little better, you know?"

"Right," he said dryly.

I sighed and opened my mouth to say goodbye, but Charlie interrupted me.

"Well, what are you doing with yourself this summer?" he pressed, pushing the conversation into the realm of uncomfortable.

"Uh, I don't know yet. Kev mentioned us going to Europe for a few weeks, I think." I tried to sound excited, but I wasn't so

confident about the recent change in my relationship status. Though it was nowhere near official, Kevin had been hinting at him filling a more permanent position.

"So, have you guys … discussed anything?" he hinted, his voice gruff with poorly masked irritation.

"Yeah, we've not really talked about stuff," I said, my thoughts going a thousand different directions. "That kind of thing is a long way off."

"Sure. Well, I guess just let me know if y'all end up going to Europe. I'll set you up with what you need." Charlie's sudden acceptance caught me off guard. He was usually trying to convince me to wait on men in general, though Kevin seemed to hold a special place on my father's blacklist.

"Yeah, I'll keep you up with everything." I looked at the clock. "Well, Kev's waiting for me, so I guess I'll talk to you later."

A long silence passed.

"Dad? Are you there?"

"Yes… but before you go, just promise you'll come soon, with or without Kevin. I'd like a chance to talk to you, really talk."

"No problem, Dad. We'll come soon. I promise."

Charlie sighed, frustration seeping through. "All right then. Take care of yourself out there."

"Sure. Talk to you later."

"Goodbye, Ashton."

The impossibility of not ever having the opportunity to be with my father again hit me with sudden force. I couldn't call him. I couldn't see him. My time was over. Granted, I didn't take advantage of those opportunities before, but I knew they were at my disposal. It kept me selfish. It meant I could hold the cards; I could call the shots. And I'd used it to manipulate situations to fit my will.

Why wasn't I closer? Why didn't I go see him when he invited me last week? It was too late to fix now. My family was gone, and I was alone.

Grief swam in my chest and my knuckles ached around my pajama shirt. Just leave it alone. I unclenched my fists and opened the bag with my Zune and favorite book inside. I sat the MP3 player and dock on the bathroom vanity, and tuned it to quiet harp music with Gymnopedie No. 1 playing first.

Slipping into the tub, I wanted to forget everything and everyone. My ragged collection of Tennyson's poetical works waited on the floor. I flipped through to The Lady of Shalott — the poem Gabe had quoted from earlier — but I couldn't get into it. Gabe's rich voice echoed in my mind.

Laying the book aside, I sank below the surface, and stared at the scalloped ceiling from beneath the water. I thought about the lady in the poem and how she might have felt living as a non-human in a world that didn't accept her. A vision of Arthurian Camelot filled my imagination. The fairy-lady in her confinement, watching the world pass by through no more than a reflection — always existing on the outside. Till suddenly, what she never knew her heart longed for most appears, only to have no hope of attaining it. Not only hopeless but cursed.

An impossible situation.

My nose broke the surface, and I blinked as droplets filtered through my lashes and into my eyes.

It seemed that my Zune was set on shuffle because the previously relaxing tune had morphed into a melancholy account of the same grief that clouded around me. Unable to hold it in any longer, my sorrow echoed off the marble walls. Finally, the water turned cold, leaving me to only hot tears.

I struggled out of the tub, toweled off, and forced myself into pajamas. Empty and bewildered, I collapsed on the bed and fell into a restless sleep.

∽ ∽ ∽

Darkness opened to a dense unfamiliar forest. Slivers of light filtered through the canopy above, breaking through the green that sheltered me as thickly as a rooftop. Sweat trickled down the back of my neck, though I shivered with cold. My hands chafed against my bare arms as I searched an empty wood.

The sharp snap of breaking sticks drew my attention to an opening in the vegetation. A familiar silhouette made his way through the gap.

"Gabe?" The thick air sat heavy in my chest, sapping my voice of power. Gabe strode toward a body of water barely discernable through the trees. Moisture trailed across my skin and my shirt clung to my back. My muscles burned as I pushed my legs harder, trying to close the space between us. He turned his face every now and then, wearing the same torn expression but never stopped moving toward the water.

"Ashton?" The distorted whisper of my name echoed from behind me.

"Charlie?" I pivoted. A gust of wind carried a wave of dead leaves across the empty path.

As I turned back, the scenery shifted. I was alone inside the cemetery where my father was to be buried. Dusk settled in quickly, smothering the sun behind the mountains. Rolling fog snaked around faceless headstones, casting shadows that swayed with the breeze. I shivered and struggled forward, my fists pulled tight to my chest as I tiptoed around the graves.

The shadow of a massive oak stretched across the land, the clouds casting the ground in a sick shade of green. A chill swept my hair into my eyes, carrying the scent of rotting earth and decay. The profile of a coffin sat in the shade beneath the trees. Darkness stretched from the outline of the forest as if it reached for me, drawing me closer. My feet moved of their own accord as the crunch of dead leaves sounded under their path.

A gust of wind howled through the passage, turning my stomach as the scent of death filled my lungs. Suddenly, the lid swung open with a groan. Dread seized me, my uncontrolled gaze drifting across the figure inside. Gray long sleeved shirt, hands folded across the torso ... I froze as the face came into view. It wasn't my father that lay pale and lifeless. It was Gabe. A hot metallic taste coated my tongue as my teeth sank into it to keep from crying out. Finally, my knees buckled, and I crumpled to the ground in despair.

Chapter Six
A Carnival of Truth

I jerked up in bed panting and soaked in sweat. Images of Gabe lying ashen in a coffin burned in my memory. I shuddered at the thought of my Gabe being gone ... then I remembered he wasn't my Gabe at all.

With a deep breath, I lay back down and closed my eyes. Piano music from my Zune continued softly in the background, lulling me into unconsciousness. I imagined my own fingers moving across the keys — something that had become a habit since beginning to play at the age of five. Before the first melody was over, I was close to slumbering again, or perhaps the place in-between. Whatever the state, I almost smelled Gabe's blissful aroma. Serenity enveloped me as I shivered only once before surrendering to pleasant warmth.

A strip of white light traced the border of the heavy drapes as I sat up and stretched. Oh! My eyes popped wide. The clock read 11:50 am. I'd slept the morning away!

"Crap-dang it!" I tumbled out of bed, my legs tangled in the blanket, and thumped my arm on the nightstand. Rubbing my sore elbow, I hurried to my bag and chose the first thing I came to: artificially-faded plaid shorts and a Kelly green tank top. Hopping on one foot, I jerked my pajamas off and dressed quickly.

"Good morning!" Gabe smiled when I came into the kitchen. "Or should I say afternoon? Is it still technically morning?"

"I am so sorry. I can't believe I slept this late. This never happens." I mentally kicked myself for getting so worked up last night. I felt like an idiot this morning like I knew I would.

"Hey, it's fine." He rubbed my arm and my heart stopped. "Don't worry about it. Your body knows what it needs. You might try listening every now and then."

I laughed nervously and forced my eyes to the table to see an elaborate brunch set out. "What's all this?"

"I figured you'd be hungry." He grinned. "Hope you like omelets."

"I'm amazed there was food in the house to begin with." I pulled a chair out and plopped down.

"About that, I borrowed your car to go to the grocery." His eyebrows pulled together. "I didn't want you to wake and have to go on an empty stomach."

Heat warmed my face as I stared into his ocean-view eyes. He thought of me ... that was sweet.

"You didn't have to do that," I said and looked down. "Thank you."

A smile lit his face, giving him a boyish look. "You're more than welcome, Gracie."

We sat in silence as I shoveled my food in faster than I knew was ladylike, but everything tasted so delicious. I finished my last bite and looked at him. "That was fantastic. By far the best omelet I've ever had."

Gabe smiled. "I'm glad you enjoyed it. It's nice being useful."

He shook his head and carried our dishes over to the sink.

"I'll get these washed and—" he began.

"And I'll dry," I said before he could offer.

Gabe rolled the sleeves of his white button-down to his elbows and started the water. I squeezed a small amount of soap into the basin and waited for it to fill.

"So, are you up for some celebrating today?" I asked after he shut the faucet off. The dish slid through his fingers and fell into the sink, slopping us with soapy water.

"Sorry," he muttered and handed me a dry dishtowel.

"And you call me Grace," I teased.

Gabe smiled and dabbed a towel across his soaked garment; it clung relentlessly to his torso, fitting to the pattern of his sculpted chest and stomach. My eyes lingered on the faint gray pendant sitting at his breastbone. He made a pass across the dripping counter, and I would've offered to help, but I lost myself in the outline of his shirt.

"Celebrating?" he repeated, a wary look on his face.

"Well, yeah, it's the fourth."

Gabe's eyebrows lifted as he turned his head toward me.

"The fourth," I repeated, certain he understood. Nothing. "Of July?"

"Ohh," Gabe breathed. "Yes, right. Independence Day. 1776. That was a big deal." He grinned and reached up to smooth a loose strand of hair from his forehead. A white square of bandage grabbed my attention.

Gabe caught me staring at his dressing.

"I'm sorry about last night," he muttered, offering the last plate.

"You're sorry? It was my fault. I shouldn't have freaked out like that."

"You had every right to react the way you did," he insisted.

"Regardless, you needed help, and I just bailed on you." I stretched on my tiptoes to put a glass mixing bowl in the cabinet.

"I'll get over it. A few years of counseling, some kind of support group or electroshock therapy, but eventually, I'll cope," he teased.

"In that case, send me the bill." I nudged his arm.

Gabe's smile melted as his gaze shot to the shelf over my head. I followed his gaze to see a glass mixing bowl teetering on the edge of the shelf. In a flash, his body pinned me to the counter, his arms over my head. Gabe's knee slid in between mine as he forced the bowl back into place, and my heart sprang into my throat. The scent of cedar swam in my chest, drowning me with the need to be closer.

Gabe looked down at me, his hair curling into his eyes. I bit my lip and reached up to brush it back into place. My focus trailed to his mouth. It was entirely perfect ... and entirely alluring.

The sharp clang of a skillet tipping over caused us both to start.

Gabe backed away, wearing a tight smile.

"You'd think this place is haunted or something." I sucked in a shaky breath.

"Maybe." He laughed once and moved to pick up the fallen cookware.

"I need to take care of a few things." I made for the stairs, my face flushed with desire and embarrassment. "But we can ramble around town after, if you'd like."

"Sure. Do what you need to." Gabe's eyes met mine as he shoved his hands in his shorts pockets. "I'm not going anywhere."

I so wanted to take that as a promise.

"I'll be back in a few." My voice wavered as I climbed the stairs. He nodded and disappeared to the parlor.

With my cell phone MIA, I needed another way to get in touch with Harry. My laptop sat on the mahogany writing desk in front of my bedroom window. I connected and opened my email, ignoring any not from Harry. The most recent he sent held one word in the subject box: Arrangements.

Dread twisted my insides as I clicked on the message and scrolled down to the body. The email was short and to the point. Harry briefed me on the time and place where the funeral was to be held, making quick mention that I hadn't returned his phone calls, and finally asked if I wanted to hold a private ceremony.

I responded in the same stoic manner as Harry had written, apologized for not returning his calls, and told him my phone disappeared. Pressing send, I logged off and tried to shake off the depression that accompanied any thought of Charlie.

Gabe waited for me in the driveway; knowing eyes raked over me in concern. I forced a smile, but he didn't seem to buy it.

"You ready to go?" I chimed, climbing into the car.

His eyes searched mine, but he nodded.

The winding road led us back toward the shops. The quaint town overflowed with people as we rolled into the city limits. Posters and flyers clung to every noticeable surface announcing the events planned for the day. I found an available parking space and pulled in.

Live music and children's laughter filled the atmosphere with excitement and a sense of wellbeing. The smell of funnel cake and corn dogs tickled my nose as my eyes flitted from the Ferris wheel to the brightly colored game tents.

"Ooh, a carnival!" I stared through the windshield at the festivities. "You want to go have some fun?" I grinned playfully.

Gabe shook his head as we climbed out, but his eager smile belied his casual attitude. I knew he wanted to play as much as I did.

"Oh, come on. Let's go win a bunch of junk we don't need." I tugged on his hand.

His eyes warmed, but still, he shook his head no.

"You worried I might show you up?" I teased.

He raised his eyebrows in surprise. "All right, Gracie, show me what you've got."

Gabe made his way toward the makeshift game booths. We paused in front of a pierced teenager manning a game with a few softballs and an angled basket. Gabe pulled out a crumpled wad of cash and paid the attendant.

"Ladies first." He gestured toward the pyramid of three balls.

"Thank you." I smiled. "Watch and learn." I lifted the first one and lobbed it toward the wicker container. It met the rim with a clank and shot to the side, grazing the punctured youth in the knee. He stifled a groan and took a step back.

"Sorry! Sorry!" My ears burned red.

Gabe let out a snort of laughter.

"Something funny?" I asked.

"Nope." He battled a smile.

"Let's see you pull it off." I tossed him the second ball.

Gabe stepped up beside me and flicked his hand forward. The ball floated from his fingertips and settled along the inside wall of the basket.

"Show off," I muttered. He winked on a grin, and his dimples sank in.

"It's all in the wrist." He moved behind me. "Here, I'll show you. Grab that last ball."

I squeezed it in my palm, blood rising in my cheeks as his body settled into mine.

"You have to hold it softly, like an egg," he whispered, his breath tickling my ear. Gabe's palm slid over the back of my hand, encouraging my grip to loosen. His body moved flat against mine, and heat flooded the places they touched. The rhythm of his heart beat against my back, drumming in my head as if it were my own. I forced a slow steady breath through my nose, hoping he didn't notice my reaction.

"Relax." His free hand glided down my other arm. I closed my eyes, trying not to hyperventilate.

"Now, hold the ball facing down and flick your wrist to create backspin."

His chest flexed as he demonstrated the motion, sending me into arrhythmias. I opened my eyes in time to see the ball glide through the air and catch the inside lip. It rolled in next to the first.

"Perfect," he commended. "Nice throw."

"I did it!" I turned and wrapped my arms around his neck, realizing the moment my chest met his, what I was doing.

"Yes, you did," Gabe's voice lowered, his hands tightening around my waist for a brief moment. "You're a natural."

The shadow of carnival rides stretched over the grounds throughout the afternoon. Gabe's eyes lingered on me as we played games and shopped the different venders. By the time we circled the grounds, our arms overflowed with knickknacks.

"Do we have enough junk we don't need now?" Gabe smiled at me.

"I think we have enough for ten people." I laughed. "You never lose."

Gabe held his finger up and jogged across the parking lot to a group of young kids climbing into a bus. The writing on the side said Children's Home. I looked on with a smile as he talked with a worker, gesturing to the toys. The worker nodded enthusiastically.

Gabe knelt down to their height and divvied out our winnings among the smiling faces. Squeals rang across the parking lot as each child jockeyed for position. Gabe, lost in the mix, laughed and ruffled the hair of the smallest boy as he handed him a fuzzy green alligator. His smile warmed as a little girl in pigtails wrapped her arms around his neck.

The children piled onto the bus and lined up at the windows, waving as it pulled away. Gabe turned and made his way back, a satisfied twinkle in his eyes.

"That was very sweet of you, but I think you missed one," I said, pointing to the tip of a baggy showing from his back pocket.

"Hmm. I suppose I did. Here, why don't you take it?" He lifted a green square box out and offered it to me.

I lifted an eyebrow and removed the lid. Inside, laid a ring with a woven silver band and a blue-green stone in the center. The color matched his eyes perfectly.

"Where did you get this?" I picked up the ring and studied the round stone. "This is incredible."

Gabe took it and slid it over my index finger. "I hoped you would like it."

"I love it," I said. "Thank you so much, but if anything, I owe you. I did kill your bike if you'll remember."

Gabe smiled. "There are worse things in life than spending a few fun-filled days on a road trip with pleasant company."

My face warmed, and I looked away. "You want to head back and settle in before the fireworks?"

"That sounds like a good idea," he said, his gaze settled on me, watchful. I wanted to believe it was because he enjoyed the view but his frequent glances toward the crowd forced my opinion in another direction. I got the feeling he wasn't over the incident in the hotel parking lot. Neither was I for that matter, but something about Gabe made me feel safe, even if I shouldn't.

Gabe appeared to be lost in thought as we drove back. When we got to the house, he walked upstairs. I slipped my shoes off and headed for the sitting room. An elegant grand piano situated in the corner caught my attention. I brushed my hand across the glossy black and white keys, enjoying the coolness of each one. It always amazed me that no matter the temperature of a place, the keys always felt chilled, like the piano was more relaxed than everything else around it.

I hadn't so much as touched an instrument since I was fourteen. It felt foreign but familiar at the same time. My fingers danced across the ivory, finding the peaceful melody I'd learned as a child. Grief swirled around me, but I ignored it, welcoming the warmth of the tune.

Suddenly, the air stirred as Gabe came in the room, and my hands stilled. "Sorry, I got carried away."

"I haven't heard that song in years." Gabe paused in the entranceway, his head bowed.

"You know it?" My eyebrows rose.

"It's ... a lullaby. Where did you learn to play?"

"It was the first song I ever learned. Charlie would have me play it over and over again." A sad smile pulled my mouth up.

"You play beautifully." Gabe's eyes darkened with a regret I didn't understand. He cleared his throat and moved toward the front door. "I thought I'd take a walk. If you need me, I'll be outside."

His gaze hesitated on the piano for a moment before he left.

I offered the keys one last touch then stood and wandered to the backdoor overlooking the lake. A long dock jutted out into the water, the latter half covered by a green tin roof. A sport boat floated in the furthest slip, beckoning a visit. My fingertips traced the ridge along the skin of my cheekbone — a faint scar from my first attempt at wakeboarding.

I pocketed the boat keys hanging by the door and crossed the yard. A breeze danced from the shore, filling my lungs with the scent of lake water and excitement. I closed my eyes and drew a deep breath. The sound of children's laughter echoed from the trees. Suddenly, I found myself on the banks of the lake in my Louisiana home.

"Girls, come inside!" Ms. Lynn called.

I ducked below the surface, smiling at Allie as we waited below the waterline.

The shadow of Ms. Lynn waved into view at the edge of the grass. She crossed her arms, foot tapping, and shook her head.

"Ashton." Her voice carried through the liquid barrier like a hollow drum. "Ashton?"

"Ashton?" The voice became clearer. I slowly opened my eyes.

Gabe stood a stone's throw away, his head tilted in question. "Are you all right?"

I sent him a tight smile. "Uh, yeah. I guess I was daydreaming."

"What are you doing out here?" he asked.

"I thought I'd check out the Moomba," I said. He lifted a brow. "The boat." I nodded toward the slip.

"Ah." His eyes shifted toward the water. "Were you going for a ride?"

"I was thinking about it. Want to come?" I smiled and followed the wooden planks to the edge.

"That depends. There's nothing left for you to run over but me." He grinned when I scowled.

I paused halfway to the boat. My eyebrows fell as I dug around in my pockets.

"Something wrong?" he asked, a mischievous grin on his face.

"I swear I brought the—"

Gabe made a slick move with his hand and dangled a set of keys in front of my face as if he'd pulled them from my ear.

"Looking for these?" He winked.

"How did you do that?" I moved forward, playfully lunging for the keys. My toe caught an uneven plank, and the dock came sailing toward me. Warm hands wrapped around my waist, pulling me close, the motion bowing our bodies across the railing. My heart leapt into my throat. Gabe's face, inches from mine, sent his mouthwatering scent across my skin.

"Thanks," I breathed.

"Are you okay?" he asked, his tone distant.

That's a loaded question, I considered but nodded.

"Good. Did you want to..." His sentence fell away as he peered around.

"What are you looking for?"

"The keys." He sighed in frustration. "They fell."

I didn't understand his aggravation till I saw that the ball-chained ring they were on had snapped in two. The floating part of the key chain lay on the dock; the keys on the other hand, had slipped through the cracks.

"Hey, no worries. I can order new ones. It's not a big deal." I shrugged. "Besides, I'll take consciousness over a boat ride any day."

"Hmm..." He slid a contemplative eye toward the water.

"Hmm, what?" I questioned with a frown. He couldn't possibly believe that the keys were retrievable, but he probably did.

"I'm curious, how deep do you think the water is?"

"Deep enough," I insisted. "You can't just—"

Without hesitation, Gabe dove headfirst into the lake and disappeared beneath the surface.

"Gabe?" The water rippled from the center then dissipated like sound waves. "This isn't funny."

The wind brushed across my face, my eyes scanning the surface. Silence stretched on, and the water smoothed to glass.

"Gabe!" Still nothing. In a flurry, I dove in.

Chapter Seven
A Life Less Ordinary

O pening my eyes, I didn't expect to see anything, but somehow water shone as clear as if I were wearing goggles. I fought the urge to gasp as things came into focus. Wisps of lake grass swayed along the bottom, a variety of fish weaving in and out of the vegetation. Bubbles gurgled up from the silt, zigzagging their way to the surface.

I shook my head and spun around, searching for Gabe. A human-sized silhouette floated just in the shadows beneath the dock, suspended as if it were hanging like a lure. I squinted into the darkness and set out swimming. Algae licked up the columns and filtered through the water, obscuring my view. Frustrated, I kicked to the surface.

No sooner than my head met the air, did I hear an amused chuckle coming from behind me. I whirled around to catch sight of Gabe hiding by the boat.

"What the—?"

"You know, a guy could drown waiting for you," he teased.

"How could ... you ... don't ever..." I sputtered. Visions of a lifeless Gabe in the coffin lingered too close. I splashed him angrily and swam toward the bank.

"Ashton, don't be angry. I didn't mean to upset you. I was joking," he implored, the humor still not gone from his voice.

Mixed emotion hummed through me as I huffed across the lawn. How could I not be upset?

"I apologize. I didn't think. Gracie, wait. Please." Gabe's slick hand wrapped around mine, encouraging me to turn. His turquoise eyes burned into mine. "Forgive me?"

"Fine," I conceded with a sigh. He grinned. "That doesn't make it funny though." I shoved him away a little.

"I know," he answered, his tone apologetic. "I'm truly very sorry. I didn't think about your reaction in the water ... I won't ever do that again." With that, he raised his left hand to his brow, two fingers extended. "Scout's honor."

"Ha ha." I rolled my eyes but half-smiled.

Gabe stuck his hand in his pocket and pulled out a pair of keys. "Look."

My eyebrows rose as I opened my palm to catch them.

"How did you..." I didn't even finish my question. I knew the answer — sort of. Gabe seemed capable of almost anything. He looked like he wanted an explanation for my silence, but I figured if he wanted to be mysterious, so could I.

Gabe absentmindedly toyed with the leather cord around his neck.

"What is that thing?" I stepped closer, trying to get a better look. "You tinker with it when you're anxious."

His smile turned to surprise before he hurried to brush it off.

"Force of habit." He laughed once. "It's nothing really. A family heirloom."

"May I see it?" I risked another step. His chest tensed, pulling my eyes away from the necklace for a moment.

"Sure." He looped his thumb under the cord and lifted the charm from beneath his shirt.

I stared at an intricately carved willow tree with long wispy branches. The silver glistened in the sunlight as I traced over the trunk to the roots. The bottom curved out, forming a small V-shape. Something seemed familiar about the design, but I couldn't quite put my finger on it.

"See, no more than a boring tree," he said. "Now, how about that boat ride?"

We stayed on the lake most of the day. As dusk made its approach, we docked and found a soft patch of grass to settle down on. Just as the last ray of sunlight ducked below the horizon, a brilliant red lit up the night sky in the shape of a heart. A flash of blue streaked east as a blaze of green soared the opposite way. Distant ooh's and ahh's sounded from various boats scattered across the lake. Gabe and I sat shoulder to shoulder on the grass, his warmth bleeding into mine as we stared transfixed at the darkness that served as a canvas.

I snuck a glance at Gabe who continued to watch the show. A brilliant white shot across the horizon, illuminating the entire sky. I gasped as the light filled his eyes. A strange blue flickering shone back like an animal in the night.

Gabe heard my gasp and quickly turned his head down, his breathing picking up.

"Your eyes," I said in a whisper. "Wh-what is that?"

"Nothing," he wheezed. "It's the light from the fireworks on my... retina." Gabe sighed. "It's an odd genetic anomaly."

"But they glowed!" I continued to stare, dumbfounded.

"No."

"No?" My voice shot up. "I saw them."

"No, they didn't glow." He glanced at me, his mouth quirked up. "They just caught the light at an angle and it ... refracted back. Thick corneas or something along those lines." He laughed nervously. "It's nothing to trouble yourself about."

"Sure." I narrowed my eyes.

There had to be more to it than that.

Gradually, the lights died away and the crescent moon peaked through the haze.

"Well, I'm beat." Gabe yawned as we made our way toward the house. "I think I'm going to head upstairs."

"Oh." I looked up, hoping to prolong our time. "Did you need anything before bed? Are you hungry? I can get you something."

Gabe's turquoise eyes traced over my face, an enticing smile on his lips. He drew a long breath, lost in an emotion I thought closely resembled my own, and then he shook his head.

"Are you sure? I don't mind." I looked up at him through my eyelashes and gave him a playful smile.

Gabe moved closer, his hand on the doorframe. He shifted on his feet, leaning in. The heat from his body pinned me in place, leaving me wanting to close the distance. I lost myself in the sea of his eyes and let out a sigh.

"I should go now." Gabe's voice grew husky, and he backed away. His hand swept again to the charm around his neck, almost as if it were some talisman.

"All right. 'Night, then," I said.

"Goodnight. Sleep well." He held the door open for me, and we walked through the foyer. Gabe vanished into the shadows on the second floor, the echo of another yawn lingering in the stairwell. Having slept all morning, sleep couldn't be further from my mind.

I tiptoed upstairs and followed the hall to the last room in my wing of the house. Turning the glass knob, I opened the door. The scent of stale air tinged with patchouli oil brought a twinge of anxiety. Something about this room felt familiar.

I switched on a lamp. Pale light illuminated the dust-covered trinkets scattered across a table near the doorway. The walls reflected the same shade as the sky on a cloudless day. Gilded-framed watercolors scattered the walls, splashing the background of blue. Though difficult to make out what they portrayed, I stood in front of them one at a time, blowing away the thick layer of dust. Each depicted various bodies of water surrounded by vibrant wildflowers. One large painting showed a towering willow overhanging a lake. The long branches hung low, skimming the surface of the deep. Beneath the tree sat a beautiful couple. A man with dark hair reclined against the trunk while he held a woman with golden tresses waving down her back. My eyes tarried on the painting, wishing I could see them better — I couldn't make out the faces through the dust, and I didn't want to smudge the painting by rubbing it.

Antique-white furniture stood lonely, abandoned along the mullioned walls, a long forgotten rocking chair hiding in the corner. As I walked toward the dresser, a draft carried across my bare feet. I glanced toward the windows. The heavy curtains drooped motionless. Another kiss of cool air tickled my toes. I bent down to see a bare spot on the wooden floor where the wind moved.

The draft came from behind the dresser.

With a grunt, I worked the furniture away from the wall, gasping as the arch of a door came into view.

Sweat dewed on my brow as I inched toward the tarnished handle and tugged. Worn and narrow steps ascended into the darkness. A silent breeze traveled through the empty passageway, sending a chill racing down my spine.

"Ashton?" Gabe's voice broke the silence. I jumped, feeling like I'd been caught spying or reading someone else's journal.

"You scared me," I said through a shaky laugh.

"I thought you might find your way in here." Gabe sighed. His eyes narrowed as they locked on the passageway behind me. "You are clever, aren't you?"

"You knew about this? How? That's not even possible." I frowned, a thousand questions swirling through my mind.

Gabe laughed without humor. "The realm of impossibilities is a tricky place."

"I don't know what you mean. This doesn't make any sense."

He shook his head, a sadness filling his eyes. "You're right. Few things are sensible. I should call you Alice for all the rabbit holes you fall down. But this is one thing you should understand."

Gabe flipped the switch on the stairs and reached down to take my hand, leading me through the doorway. The stairs creaked and groaned as we left a trail of footprints through the dust. Gabe pulled on a chain hanging from the ceiling at the landing and row after row of lights flickered to life.

An expansive room spanned the top floor. The roof sloped toward the edges with exposed beams. Shelf after shelf stood, lined floor to ceiling with dusty books of all shapes and sizes. The scent of old leather, musty paper, and linseed oil set my heart aching as a sense of déjà vu washed over me.

Moonlight filtered through the semi-circle window, acting as a spotlight to an easel, table, and various painting tools. Tubes of paints, pallets, and pencils lay strewn across the stained surface, and a small green sofa sat against the wall opposite the window.

"Can you believe this?" I mumbled to no one in particular.

I ran my finger along the leather-bound books squeezed onto the shelves. Much like my own library, there was no rhyme or reason to their order. Several memorable titles caught my eye as

I drifted from one to the next. Gabe walked behind me, his fingers still wound through mine. I peered around the attic, admiring the paintings scattered throughout. Some filled the blank spaces between the shelves, while other were stacked flat or tucked in a corner. Each had one of two things depicted: a family or a different view of the same body of water. Consistent brush strokes and style pointed to each being crafted by the same artist. The tugging in my heart led me to believe it was my mother.

"I can't believe my mom had all of this. Where did she find the time to paint these pictures or read these books? It would take me a lifetime."

"For some, one lifetime offers more opportunities than others. I imagine you're capable of most anything."

I didn't need to turn to hear the smile in Gabe's voice.

"We aren't all super-human. In fact, most of us are quite ordinary." I sighed.

Gabe pulled me around to face him. "Most of them, Gracie. You are anything but ordinary." He brushed his fingertip down my nose, and my heart stuttered in my chest.

I turned my eyes down and struggled to work my way around the room. A small box, the same shape as a miniature trunk, caught my attention. I tilted my head, trying to make out the designs on the side.

Gabe's arm stiffened, pulling me to a stop as I tried to move closer for a better view.

"What's wrong?" I asked.

"Ashton," he started then paused. "I don't want you to..." His voice faltered as he searched for the words. I waited for him to continue but he didn't speak.

"Gabe, please. What's going on?"

His hands rose to either side of my face, his thumbs stroking my cheekbones. Gabe stared deeply into my eyes, searching. My heart ached as his expression fell.

"I can't do this anymore." He sighed and shook his head. "This is wrong. I didn't mean for this to happen. It wasn't supposed to."

"Can you please just tell me what's happening?" I begged.

"I need you to try your best to hear me out. Allow me explain everything before you speak. Can you do that for me? Please?" He studied my face, his torn.

I nodded.

Gabe tugged me over to the faded green sofa and pulled me down beside him. "How to begin?" He glanced around the attic. "Here, open it." Gabe picked up the dirty trunk from the table and offered it to me.

I lifted the box and focused my attention on the detail as I turned it around in my hands. I tried to raise the lid but it stuck. A familiar looking tree locked the top and bottom halves together.

"That looks like yours," I said. Without thinking, I pulled the collar of his shirt to the side and gasped. His necklace wasn't there.

Gabe extended his hand, the tree charm flat against his palm. "You deserve to know," he whispered.

I rolled the metal between my fingers, seeing what I missed before. A key. The curved end fit perfectly into the opening in the front. I took a breath and carefully raised the lid. A memorable tune chimed from the wheel inside. The same melody sang to me as a child — the same one I had unthinkingly played on the piano.

My eyes found Gabe. He motioned for me to search the box further.

I lowered my hand into the hollow space. A delicate silver locket lay inside. The front was engraved in a language I couldn't read but recognized. I lifted the locket and unfastened the catch. Affixed within the oval halves were two photos. A flowering meadow with a pool of water was tucked in the left side. On the right was a photo of my father with a woman that could only be my mother because she looked very much like me, only much more beautiful.

My breath caught in my throat.

The couple smiled as the man stood behind the woman, both their hands around her swollen abdomen. Tears blurred my vision.

"How ... how did..."

"I know this?" he finished. "I'm going to tell you, but remember your promise." Gabe squared his shoulders. "I'm not who you think I am, not exactly anyway."

Chapter Eight
Forbidden Fairytale

"What does that mean?" My eyebrows fell.

Gabe continued, gauging my reaction with every word. "I'm not exactly normal." He laced his fingers together and stared at the floor.

"What are you trying to say?"

"This is harder than I imagined." He frowned. "Your mother wasn't average either. I knew her long ago. She was a very dear friend of mine — my best friend."

I felt the speculation on my face. "How is that possible? You're not much older than I am."

The corner of his mouth pulled down as he shook his head.

"Were you ... together?" I grimaced.

"No, no!" he said quickly. "We were only friends. Nothing more. She was more like a sister to me."

"So, you actually knew her?" My heart swelled with unfamiliar hope.

Gabe nodded. "Your mother was royalty in a sense. She was the daughter of the most powerful family in our world — and mostly happy to be so. She loved her people and wanted to be a generous and loving leader, but to lead by example. The one exception to her happiness was she didn't want to live her life loveless and empty."

Royalty? Shock coursed through me.

"Your mother spoke with her parents often, asking them to allow her to find a mate so she could fall in love the real way, marry, and have a family. They refused her time and again, stating that outsiders could never be part of our world."

My eyes narrowed. "What kinds of people forbid love and families?"

Gabe's tone softened. "Our ruling families have certain ways of doing things. If those guidelines aren't followed..." He shook his head. "The repercussions don't outweigh the benefits. A few of us are allowed to venture among the world. We gain both experience and connections to share with others. Some choose to live permanently with the people they meet, but that comes with ... consequences."

"Well that's stupid," I spouted, not caring if I sounded like a child. "Why didn't she have a choice?" A sense of resentment boiled inside. How did she feel about everything?

His voice turned solemn. "You have to understand, the royal family never has that option. Your mother had responsibilities to her parents and her people. Her purpose would be served there. End of story."

I sighed, at a loss for how to feel.

"What are you thinking?" Gabe's eyes met mine. "You aren't saying much."

"What can I say to that?" I shrugged.

Gabe shook his head with a disbelieving laugh. "I'm confessing to you that I'm not normal, that your mother wasn't anyone that you could have ever imagined, and you're taking it all in as if I were explaining the migratory pattern of locusts. This isn't how I expected you to react."

Yeah, me either. "I knew that you were too special to be anyone average. That part doesn't exactly surprise me. And my whole life has been a question mark. Until a few days ago, I really never cared. It was always about me." My gaze fell as shame warmed my face.

He brushed a finger down my flushed cheek.

"Then you showed up and turned my life upside down. In a good way," I said when he frowned. "You caused me to think about my meaning and purpose, the affect that I have on those around me. In taking stock of my life, I realized just how screwed up I'd become. But meeting you, getting to know you, I wanted to be me again. I wanted to know you, and I wanted you to know me, but I didn't know me. How could I explain me to you?" I bit down on my lip trying to control the depth of my honesty.

"Ashton, I'm not admirable. You can't believe that about me. There is so much I would change. I only came here to..." He sighed and looked away for a moment. "I came here to tell you the truth."

"About how you know my mother?" I peered up at him, hopeful.

He gave a half-hearted smile. "Yes. I followed her one day when she left to visit relatives. I watched from afar as she came across a man in the forest. Something happened between them. A spark, a connection. I very nearly killed him myself then and there, just to keep her safe, knowing what it would mean, but Edlyn—"

"Edlyn? Her name was Edlyn?" I interrupted, hearing the word for the first time in my life. Joy swelled inside me like I would've never expected. "It's beautiful."

Gabe nodded, his expression tight. "It means 'noble waterfall."

"Wow..." I straightened on the sofa, relishing in the small intimacy of knowing her name. "What happened between her and Charlie?"

"I saw something in her eyes that I had never seen. I knew then that she'd found the one she was searching for. In that instant they were in love. Edlyn sent word to her relatives she wasn't coming for now, and sent word back to her family that she had arrived safely and would remain there. She and your father ran away together."

Gabe gestured around the area as he continued. "After some time, I traced them here. I have a sort of knack for finding people — some people." He frowned. "I needed to know she was safe. Your mother and father were married and she was happier than anyone I had ever known. I went home content that she had made the right choice for herself."

"Wow. What do I say to that?" I thought aloud, rubbing my fingertips across my temples.

Gabe met my gaze. "Ashton, this is a very selfish thing I'm doing. Don't think I'm offering you anything. People cannot know about us. It's not allowed. Those of us who choose to live among humans are at a continual threat of being dealt with."

"Dealt with?" I repeated quickly.

"Your mother violated our laws. Even being royalty wouldn't exempt her from the aftermath." He paused, his face torn in anger and remorse. "I couldn't protect her, and now I'm exposing you to the same. How could I be so selfish?" he moaned, his face hidden in his hands.

"Don't say that. You are not selfish. Why would you think that?" I put my hands on his face and lifted his teary eyes to meet mine. The smell of a warm cedar and fresh rain filled the air.

"I've followed her, Ashton," he said as if I'd missed the point. "I'm as guilty as she."

"I don't understand." I frowned. "How did you follow her? You mean back then? She's gone now, how could you be guilty of anything?"

The familiar exasperated look crossed his face, but with a hint of a smile this time. "Is it not obvious? Every moment that we've shared together, do you not see how crazy I am about you?"

I shook my head, drowning in question.

"And against my better judgment, I've subjected you to this danger," Gabe said on a sigh. "What's wrong with me?"

"You ... you're crazy about me?" Of everything he'd told me that was a stretch. Gabe was perhaps literally one of a kind. Not even at my best could I ever do anything to be desirable to him. This was the first thing he'd said that sounded like a lie.

"Ashton," he whispered. He lifted my chin. The back of his finger brushed away the tear running down my cheek. The blue-green I'd come to love burned with fervor. Passion and hesitance weighed heavily on his face.

Gabe's focus trailed to my mouth; his thumb swept feather-light over my bottom lip. Warmth sparked from the place he touched and spread throughout my body. His eyes flickered to mine once more, caution registering there, before he slowly leaned in and met my mouth with his.

Gabe's lips lingered on mine, soft and testing. His scent enveloped me like smoke. Our current sparked to life and heat blazed beneath my skin. I pressed into him, wrapping my arms around his neck. Gabe's lips parted with a moan as he knotted his fingers in my hair, securing my mouth to his. My heart beat unevenly in my chest as his hands fell, roaming the length of my back, and settled at my hips.

I sighed against him, and he groaned then slowly pulled away.

"Wow," we both spoke at the same time then laughed breathlessly at the other. Gabe reached up to stroke my face with the back of his hand, his eyes burning with adoration.

I inched closer and gently pushed him against the back of the sofa. Snuggling up beneath his arm, I laid my face against his chest and listened to the rhythmic pace of his heart. He wrapped his arms around my body, pulling me tighter.

"Ashton," he whispered, laying his cheek atop my hair. "You mean the world to me. I know it changes things, with what I've told you."

He began to pull away, but I held him in place.

"I want you, Gabe," I confessed, the words bubbling up with sincerity. "Whoever you are, or have been, or will ever be." My lips trailed his, but he backed away.

"Wait," he breathed. "There's more to explain."

"There's more?" I tried not to grimace.

"You need to know what this entails, what you're committing to." His hands balled up. "It's the only way that I could live with what I've done."

Gabe reached into the box and lifted out a ring — it appeared to be a man's wedding band and was crafted from a golden-tinted crystal. The material faintly sparkled in the soft light. Etched along the outside, the band was inscribed with the same words that the locket carried.

"Charlie loved Edlyn more than life." Gabe smiled, rolling the ring between his fingers. "It was impossible not to love her. She was so vibrant and joyful, especially after they met."

"You knew Charlie?" My voice rose.

"We met once. He was a fool for your mother." His smile slowly faded.

"What happened?" I asked carefully, not sure I wanted an answer.

"Edlyn never knew that I'd followed her the day she left. More than a year had passed since I checked on her, so I had no reason to suspect her family of watching me," he murmured. "I wouldn't have even made my presence known, but when I saw she was pregnant, I couldn't help myself. I knew she would be pleased to see me once she understood that I wanted to celebrate her life, not betray her.

"We spent the day together. She gave me the locket you held. The phrase inscribed on it and the ring that you found says, 'With all the love I possess.' She gave it to me as a token of our friendship and her new life here. I couldn't understand it at the time, but I could appreciate it, envy it even. After seeing her and Charlie look at each other the way they did, it only sparked my own desire for love," he laughed softly and ran his fingers across my arm. Warmth radiated from his touch, leaving a tingling trail across my skin.

"I went away that day with the promise of returning around the time of your birth. So I took the locket and left her," he breathed, his voice thick with emotion.

We sat in silence as Gabe tried to maintain his composure.

"Before she met Charlie, Edlyn had been betrothed to another — a male who fell under a particular lineage," Gabe explained, an edge to his voice. "It keeps everything tied in as far as bloodlines, but it's extremely complicated and was only magnified by the agreement." His voice turned cold on the last word.

Gabe caught the questions in my eyes. "With our kind, there are requirements of us and differences among us. Those found in the mountain ranges — like the mate meant for your mother — are generally more temperamental and harder to get along with. They're not ... well, they're different.

"The man sent his brother to follow me here. He saw me with your mother as we sat by the beach at the water's edge that day.

More importantly, he saw that she was pregnant with you. Oren apparently reported his findings to Darach."

My blood felt like ice in my veins, and my breath caught in a startled gasp.

Oren...

Chapter Nine
Changes

"Oren?" I rasped.

Gabe nodded, his face twisted in disgust.

My stomach churned. I leaned forward, arms around my waist, and shut my eyes.

"What's going on?" Gabe asked.

"Is Oren about six-five with black hair, gray eyes, and kind of creepy?" I breathed and looked up. Dread washed over me as anger marred Gabe's face.

"You saw him?" he spoke through clenched teeth.

The room began to tilt despite my being upright. Just days ago, I had been within inches of the man responsible for my mother's undoing. Why? What did he want?

"Ashton." Gabe shook me trying to get my attention. "Where did you see him?"

"The day I met you. He was manning the front desk at the hotel in Arizona where I stayed. He was wearing a nametag?" That didn't make sense. Why would he parade his identity?

"It's a threat. He's warning me, flaunting that he's found you," Gabe answered, his face red with fury.

"Why me? What did I do?"

"Nothing. You didn't do anything." Gabe leaned his forehead against mine and shut his eyes. His embrace turned possessive. "You just don't know the rest of the story."

"What happened?"

"Cowan, Edlyn's father, had me locked up. After I returned from my visit, he saw the locket in my hand. You have to understand, Cowan has a unique talent. He knows beyond question when someone is being truthful. He'd know if I lied, but still I refused to tell him where to find Edlyn, so he put me away. After discovering Edlyn was pregnant with you, he feared Darach would come. Cowan released me and ordered me to come here in secret and bring you and your mother to him. He didn't want to follow the rules, but if he could get the two of you back, he could send you both away. No one would ever know.

"I left right away, running as fast as I could. It had been two weeks since I had been in the water, and I was weak." The questions on my face were apparent but we both knew there wasn't time for deep explanation. "I reached the lake before the house, so I was able to swim some of the way and regain a bit of strength. I wasn't fast enough though. When I arrived at the house, she was nowhere to be found. I searched the entire property for her, hoping she'd perhaps taken to the water if she had somehow sensed Oren coming for her. I waited for several minutes and then swam out to look, but she never surfaced.

"I decided to wait inside the house. I don't know why, but I kept hoping maybe she was gone for the day and would come home. I didn't want to risk her coming back and finding him instead of me. But when I saw the flowers on the table, I knew."

"Flowers?"

"It's like their calling card. Demented really. I hate them for it." Gabe shook his head. I wondered if he meant he hated the flowers or Oren and Darach, though it was probably both. I thought back to his reaction to the flowers on our table at the truck stop.

Gabe sat silently for a moment before his tone changed and he continued with a wistful smile. "I heard a baby crying. I ran upstairs to the empty nursery and listened. The dresser had been pushed against the passageway and the bassinet wasn't in the room anymore. I pulled the dresser away from the door and ran up. The bassinet sat here, in front of this sofa, and there was the most beautiful baby lying inside," he whispered, sounding awed and heartbroken together.

"You found me," I stated, recognition sinking in.

"You remember?" Gabe's tone rose.

"Not like a real memory, but the color of your eyes, your scent ... they're familiar but hazy."

Gabe smiled briefly. "I lifted you up. You were so tiny, only a couple of months old. She saw Oren in enough time to hide you. She knew he'd want you, too."

He sat silent for a beat. "I still don't know how she managed to hide you so well or how long you kept quiet, but she saved you. I can't even do that. Now I've done worse."

"You did everything you could." I met his eyes. "That wasn't your fault, and it isn't your responsibility to handle now."

Gabe sat quietly, his expression torn.

I stood and walked over to the window, looking out over the moonlit water.

"They're after me now, aren't they?" My breath fogged against the glass.

Gabe's arms wound around my waist from behind as he rested his head against mine. "Yes," he murmured.

"What do they want with me? I didn't do anything. Why would he even care? I don't mean anything to anyone now."

"That's not true," Gabe said.

"But, I mean Charlie's gone, my mother is gone." I turned in his arms. "Why would he be bothered with how you feel? Is it because I'm human, because I know too much?"

"No, Ashton. He isn't coming to kill you, and it isn't because of your knowledge," Gabe muttered. "I said humans couldn't be aware of us. Technically, you don't fall under that category."

I thought about that for a minute before pulling away to study his face. He gazed back with an immense sadness. Realization took hold.

"My mother," I breathed. She wasn't human — neither was I.

Gabe's jaw clenched tight. He gave a slight nod.

I stared off, bewildered. What was happening? Just a few days ago, everything was normal — normal as far as I was concerned anyway. And now I was standing here with the guy of my dreams, neither of us is human, and some crazy man is after me — and very close to accomplishing his goal at that.

Did Oren wanting me specifically have something to do with it? If I didn't know too much, and he wasn't going to kill me, what was left?

"You're the last," he murmured.

"The last for what?" I whispered.

Gabe didn't answer. He rested his forehead against mine, motionless as a mountain.

"Look, whatever it is, we can fix it. Okay?" I tried to reassure. "We'll just work around it."

"I couldn't save her, but I will save you." Gabe's eyes snapped to mine. "I'll keep you safe. We need to get out of here. Oren knows this place."

"Do you think he'd come here looking for me?"

"I don't know, but I'm not going to chance it. I have no idea why he didn't take you when he had the opportunity, but I'm not giving him another one. He's sure to think that I'm with you now, or will be soon." He encouraged me toward the stairs.

"Hang on." I freed my hand to grab the trunk with the locket and ring. "I don't want to leave them."

"I suppose we should gather our things," Gabe said. "Pack your clothes. We'll leave tonight."

I nodded and let out a shaky sigh.

"Everything will be fine, love. I promise. I'm just being cautious." Gabe kissed my forehead then stepped out of the room. "I'm going to pack. We'll leave in a half hour."

I gave him a weak smile and watched him down the hall. As I crossed the threshold to leave, something pulled me back inside.

My eyes flitted from the antique covered tables to the overflowing shelves of the room. Pulling out the desk drawers, I coughed and sneezed but didn't come up with anything special. I followed suit around the space, lifting knickknacks and looking inside boxes, but the gnawing inside me wouldn't stop.

I walked the perimeter of the room, looking over the same pictures as before. I paused at the image of the couple under the willow tree, realizing the hidden faces were that of my parents.

"What are you hiding?" I asked the painting. "What am I trying to find?"

Not surprisingly, the picture didn't answer.

I stared at the canvas, frustration growing as I stayed in place. What was I missing?

Out of time, I decided to give up. I grabbed the painting of my parents and lifted it off the hook. A sharp thud sounded by my feet, and I looked down to see a weathered book lying on the floor.

I bent down and picked it up. It seemed to be an old leather journal. The front held the emblem of a coat of arms situated in the center of a unique lock. Points jutted from the middle like a star, each angle with a different curve or tooth in the indentation. I felt along the jagged edges of the parchment paper, wishing the flap would open, but it was no use. The lock didn't budge.

"What good is this without a key?" I looked at the painting again.

"Ashton?" Gabe called from the hall.

"Coming!" I answered and grabbed the painting.

Gabe lifted an eyebrow when I closed the door behind me, canvas in hand.

"I didn't want to leave it behind," I said, keeping the book behind my back. It wasn't that I didn't trust Gabe as much as instinct told me to keep the journal to myself for now.

"We need to decide where to go from here," Gabe directed as we hurried down the hall.

"What do you mean? We have to meet Harry for the funeral," I said, hiding the journal in my toiletry bag.

Gabe paused. "We can't be any place that Oren could find you."

"But Gabe, my … Charlie!" My voice caught in my throat.

"We can't. I'm sorry but it's too dangerous. If Oren knows about Charlie, and he has to, he'll know to expect you. He'll be waiting and not alone this time."

My vision blurred with tears. "I can't not tell him goodbye. I know he's not there now, but I didn't come when he asked me before. I can't do that. This is my last chance to make things right. I'll never see him again." Salt water spilled down my cheeks.

Gabe pulled me forward, tucking my head beneath his chin. "Shh, it's okay. You're right. I won't take that away from you. Forgive me for even thinking of it." He sighed. "We can figure something out. We'll just drive to New York and—"

"Wait. We aren't going to New York. We're going to Kentucky."

"Kentucky? Why would we go there?" Gabe asked, confused and uneasy.

"Harry told me to meet him there. That's where the funeral is going to be held. Is that bad?"

"Harry?" Gabe repeated.

"Yeah. Harry is Charlie's best friend."

"Harry." Gabe paced around the room grabbing my things and stuffing them into bags.

"Gabe, what is it? Is Kentucky a bad place to go? Is there something going on with Harry?"

"Parts of Kentucky are mountainous. Remember I told you about Darach and Oren? The forest and mountains aren't safe. Which part of the state would we be going?" he asked.

"The southeastern part, in Cumberland."

Gabe's knuckles whitened around the handle of my suitcase. "Why did Harry want to meet there?"

"He never said specifically. Just that he would explain later, but he sounded weird." I tried to replay our conversation in my mind, but it was somewhat blurry from the chaos.

"Ashton, please try and remember." Gabe peered down at me, his eyes hard with concern. "What exactly did he say? How did he sound weird?"

"He kept insisting that I meet him," I answered. "It was his tone that was strange. He was sad but more than that, he sounded worried, insistent, like he thought I might not come."

"What is Harry's last name?" Gabe swallowed hard.

"Waterford. Why?"

"Of course." His posture relaxed.

"What? Do you know him?"

"In a sense. Everything is going to be fine for now. We have some help. Harry is like me," Gabe implied. "I'm guessing that he's taking us to a place that Oren wouldn't consider looking for you. He would never think of Kentucky."

"Oh. Huh," I murmured, not really understanding. "That's good then."

"Yes, very. Though I'm curious about your father and Harry's involvement," he deliberated, not really talking to me anymore. "Obviously Charlie knew our little secret, and Harry has been involved with him all of these years afterward. That's highly unusual. It leaves a lot of questions to be answered."

"How do you know that Harry is like you if you don't know him?"

"His surname," Gabe explained. "We do that when we choose to live among humans. We pick last names that refer to our native homes and landscapes. It makes it easier to identify each other. His name refers to a wet place."

Considering that, I realized that in all this time I had never asked Gabe about his last name.

"Willoughby," Gabe answered my unspoken question, a smile on his face.

Willow. Of course.

We finished gathering my things and loaded the car. Gabe locked the door and put the keys back in their hiding spot. I sighed, feeling a strange emptiness, like I was leaving a part of me behind.

Writing it off on stress, I clicked my seatbelt on as we rounded the drive toward the highway.

"What are you thinking?" Gabe brushed my hair over my shoulder. "You're tense."

"I have so many questions." I sighed. "Is it okay to ask questions?"

"Yes, of course." Gabe offered an encouraging nod. "You must have countless things that you want to know. What would you like to ask first?"

"If we aren't human, what are we?"

"It's somewhat difficult to describe. We have human descriptions, most of which are unflattering and rather offensive at times." He rolled his eyes. "Humans truly have no grasp of what we really are, which is a good thing. It means we've done well hiding ourselves and blending in."

"Gabe, please." I eyed him.

"Well, I suppose the human definitions will work the best for now." He glanced at me, his perfectly arched brow lifted on one side. "You have to remember that any concepts you may have of our kind are most likely entirely inaccurate, so please put away any preconceived notions."

"Fair enough," I said.

"What do you know of mythological beings?" He shifted in his seat to face me. I couldn't help but smile at his business-like tone.

"A fair amount, I suppose. You know the books I've read and the authors I like. Mythology is right up my alley."

"Precisely." He laughed once. "That is my whole motivation behind the terms speech. You might have a difficult time grasping this, especially with the fairytale world you seem to enjoy so much."

"Oh, come on, it can't be that bad. What are we, pixies?" I teased. He leveled a cynical glance my way. Taking his hand, "I mean whatever you are, I am, right?"

"Sure. You were warned however, and you'll do well to remember that when this discussion is over." His eyes crinkled into a smile.

"Fine. I'm good and warned," I teased. "Let's hear it."

"Where to begin? I explained to you about being locked up for those two weeks and needing water. So far, I really haven't been able to tell if you had an inclination for it."

Inclination? Of course I liked water; we talked about that. We obviously weren't mermaids. Well, I didn't think we were — though the whole flipper notion could be way off. Mermaids could have legs. No, that was ridiculous. Maybe.

"Are you going to tell me or make me guess?" My question was meant to be lighthearted but the curiosity burned through.

"Fine," he sighed. "Eleionomae. Does that sound familiar?"

"Elay-oh-no-may?" I repeated.

"Yes," he said slowly.

My forehead creased as I stared out the windshield trying to remember where I'd heard the term.

"Would you like a hint?" Gabe grinned.

I scowled a little but nodded.

"One word," he said. "Hylas."

"Hylas? Hmmm, let's see. He was an Argonaut and the supposed son of the Greek demigod Heracles, right?"

"Very good," Gabe praised cautiously. "Do you recall what happened to him?"

"Of course. He disappeared because he was seduced and fell in lust with a—" My sentence was cut short as understanding sank in. Laughter filled the car.

"What's so funny?" he questioned, his tone disbelieving.

"Oh ... come ... on ... Gabe." I struggled to stay on the road, my eyes wet with tears. "How could that even be possible? It's absurd!"

"I told you." Gabe's face turned disapproving. "I said that you were going to have to throw out any preconceived notions."

"But a ... a nymph? That's impossible! Nymphs are all female and lusty and..."

"You see, this is why we don't tell people. And you think I'm crazy."

I tried to stifle my laughter.

"Are you quite finished?" Gabe asked, crossing his arms, playfully put out. "I thought you wanted to know about all of this?"

"Ahh, I think so. I'm sorry. I just can't get that Waterhouse painting out of my mind. You're not Hylas, are you?" I crooked an eyebrow.

Gabe rolled his eyes. "One poor fool and suddenly we're a disorder." His head shook. "And more appropriately, we would be Naiads if we're maintaining labels. While it's true that a vast majority of nymphs are women, they certainly aren't all female, as you can see."

I couldn't suppress the smile, but the snort I kept to myself. "So what are the Eleionomae again? The term sounds familiar, but I don't remember what it means."

"Well, it mostly refers to our particular dwelling. We inhabit marshlands. The Potameides reside around rivers. Pegaeae live near springs and the Limnatide lakes. Those are basically the water dwelling nymphs you need to know."

"Wow. I didn't realize there were so many."

"We aren't that different in most ways. It mainly comes down to our preferred living areas, or homewaters, I suppose you could call it. Each clan has a certain knack in our individual places. It's a matter of being in an area where you can regenerate most efficiently. We're much more similar to one another than we are with the Dryads."

"So, the Dryads, they live in the forest or trees or something like that, right? Or is that just another human assumption?" In my mind's eye, I had image of a wispy tree-lady that looked like she had limbs for fingers. Not a picture to be taken seriously.

"No, that one is correct. They do live around forests and there are more ways to classify them than us. There are the Hamadryads which are by far the most populous. They dwell around the oaks. The list goes on, but it's not important right now."

"I guess I have a lot to learn," I mused.

"That isn't the half of it. Our world is so much more complex than this one." Gabe waved his hand. "I think that's why so many of our kind tend to stick around the humans. It's easier at times, until you fall in love with one." His fingers traced across my palm and up my arm.

After a moment, I remembered to breathe. "I'm only half human, you're forgetting. Speaking of which, what am I?"

Gabe laughed at my choice of words. "Well your mother was Eleionomae like me, but she chose that as her family often lost their homes. They began making adjustments in their settlements. You see how things can get complicated?"

"How do you keep it all straight?"

"That is an excellent question," he said with a hint of an idea behind it. "Can you repeat everything I just explained?"

"What?" I looked at him.

"Repeat what I told you." He nodded, his eyes locked on me.

I rattled off, word for word, everything Gabe had just spoken about nymphs. My eyes rounded. "Why do I know this?"

"Amazing. I've never encountered this before."

"Gabe, what is going on?" I was feeling a bit strange — I had been for days. My erratic emotions were so clear and sharp, my intensified desire for water, and the minute differences I saw in my physical body. I'd just attributed my craziness to the stress.

"You're showing some Naiad-like tendencies, as if you're developing new instincts. I've heard of this happening, but have yet to see it firsthand. This doesn't occur with full Naiads. It's fascinating. How do you feel right now?"

"Freaked out is how I feel! Naiad-like tendencies? What's that supposed to mean?" My voice shot up in panic. What was going to happen? Was I going to develop gills or flippers? Would I be overcome by some commanding lust? My grip tightened around the wheel.

"Ashton, love, calm down. You aren't going to sprout a tail. A majority of it is heightened senses," Gabe soothed. "For instance, you asked how I could keep everything straight. That's because we don't forget anything. Ever."

"Oh. That's not so bad, I guess." It would be nice never having to write phone numbers down or have reminders for birthdays. But then heightened senses, new instincts, how would that play out?

"It's somewhat reminiscent of puberty," he chuckled. "You reach a certain point, eighteen to be more precise, and bang, it's set in motion. Like I said before, this isn't at all the norm. In fact, it's extremely rare."

"Puberty? I don't want to go through puberty again." It was bad enough the first time around. I did a lot of crying then, too.

"No, no. It isn't anything like human puberty. Your Naiad body seems to be altering. You shouldn't concern yourself. Nothing bad will happen."

"I'm really thirsty." I closed my mouth, my tongue dry and sticky feeling.

Gabe's eyebrows shot up.

"What?" I demanded. "Gabe, you have got to stop doing that. It's weirding me out!"

"Sorry. I'm at a loss for what to think right now. You seem to be resurrecting the makeup of a Naiad. The thirst, the memory, the desire for being in water. You're showing signs of a true nymph, not a half-breed, for lack of a better term."

"What are you saying? I'm turning into a real Naiad!"

Chapter Ten
Complicated

"**I** have no idea," he said. "I need to talk to someone who knows more about it."

"That's just great then. I'm some super-nymph freak. Maybe I should get a cape." I rolled my eyes.

Gabe laughed louder than I'd ever heard him.

"Nice to know I'm entertaining," I replied a little sharper than I meant, my dry throat feeling like sandpaper.

"I apologize. I know it's confusing. You're so calm and collected about everything." He smiled at my sigh. "All right, calm about mostly everything. This is new for me. I've never had to deal with telling someone they're part of a mythical world. Actually, it's been just the opposite. It's been my duty to hide it. But you're so composed, just taking it all in. I should've expected more of your mother in you."

"What does my mother have to do with that?" I spoke through a raspy voice.

Gabe reached into the floor and pulled out a liter of water. He removed the lid and handed it to me.

"Thanks." I lifted the jug to my mouth and drank ... and drank. Gabe watched intently. I thought his eyebrows would touch his hairline as I drained the container.

I sighed. "Mmmm, that's much better."

"Are you satisfied?" he joked.

"Yes, very." I ignored his tone, happy to be satiated.

"How close did you say you are to eighteen?"

"Shouldn't you know?" I challenged. Gabe gave me a sarcastic smile. "This is my third day."

He scoffed. "The day we met was your birthday?"

I nodded and moved to another topic. "So finish telling me about the different types of nymphs." The word was becoming easier to say without causing me to giggle like a schoolgirl.

"What do you wish to know?"

"What are the differences between Naiads and Dryads? I mean besides where they live."

Gabe sat quietly for a moment; conflicting emotion crossed his expression. "Naiads, obviously suited for water, are more streamlined," he began. "We have smoother skin and fairer complexions and features. For instance our eyes, we all have light colored eyes ranging anywhere from pale green to deep blue and every shade in between. Then of course there's this." He lifted his flashlight from yesterday and held it at an angle near his face. Light rays slanted across his irises, the blue reflection reappearing.

"I knew it!" I gasped and forced my focus on the road. "Genetic thing my butt."

Gabe laughed and clicked the light off. "It's entirely genetic, I can promise you that."

"It's like an animal," I marveled.

"Yes, very much so. We call it eyeshine," he said. My eyebrows rose. "Don't worry, you don't have it."

"Why do you?" I asked.

"The same reason as a deer, dog, or fish — to see in the dark. Of course the fish analogy is a little more fitting. We also have an extra layer across our eyes that allow us to see more clearly underwater. We swim as well as anything and faster too."

"I can sort of imagine that." I grinned. "I was always the fastest swimmer at camp. It felt unfair though. Swimming didn't tire me out like it did everyone else."

"Figures." Gabe smiled to himself.

"So what else?"

"As you've just experienced, we need water, although your experience was quite intense. I can only guess that it's because everything's so new. Typically, Naiads can go up to a month before it becomes dire. Our store depletes quickly after that. Not a good situation to be in, but it rarely occurs here."

"How does it all work? Why can we swim so fast? What are the mechanics of it?" I asked.

"Naiads are like dolphins in a sense. We actually share many similarities. Dolphins have nearly smooth skin, like satin but rubbery. Our skin is very similar that way, only not so rubbery." He tugged at the skin on the back of his hand. "That's why we try to avoid getting wet in sight of anyone too close. It's why I wouldn't let you touch me at the lake or after you picked me up in Arizona."

I thought about Gabe diving for the boat keys. "That's still not funny, by the way."

He grinned and continued. "The big difference is that when our skin is dry, it very much resembles human skin. No one would ever notice a difference except we aren't particularly hairy. This creates a more laminar flow by reducing drag in the water. And like dolphins, we shed our skin cells more frequently. I'm sure you've noticed how we have very smooth skin. Good for wrinkles."

My youthful appearance suddenly made a lot more sense.

"Oh, and we heal at an amazing rate, which you witnessed yourself," he said. I grimaced remembering the incident. "Though our skin isn't very tough. It doesn't take as much to damage it. Speaking of which—" Gabe pulled the sleeve of his injured arm up and peeled the bandage away "—it's all better now. See?"

My mouth fell open at the sight of his unblemished skin. "Why do you still have it bandaged if it's healed?"

"I hadn't planned on telling you about any of this. I figured it would kind of give me away if my formerly stitch-worthy arm was all better out of the blue." He smiled grimly.

I didn't care to think about that night. "How else are we like dolphins?"

"Naiads have excellent eyesight, both in and out of the water. Our hearing is unmatched. We can detect frequencies much higher and lower than a human and at a greater distance — up to about twenty miles away underwater. Like dolphins, we use something similar to echolocation to position things and similar sounds to communicate. It's very convenient across long distances. Our sense of touch is quite sensitive."

His finger trailed down my arm and settled in my palm, tracing lazy circles. I drew a slow breath, my skin warming as I struggled to watch the highway.

"This is incredible," I managed. "How long can you hold your breath?"

"That is one way that we absolutely differ from our mammalian counterparts," he said. "You see dolphins, like humans, breathe air. Full Naiads have the ability to stay submerged indefinitely."

"Indefinitely? As in, you don't need to resurface to breathe?"

"That's right." He grinned. "Even though we don't breathe, you learn to taste the water, and in this you can actually smell what's there. We don't do as well in salt water as fresh, though. The salt water obviously is saltier, denser. It isn't impossible to draw oxygen from it, but it's very uncomfortable. Also, the salt tends to be dehydrating — it sort of works the opposite in that way. There are nymphs, Nereids to be exact, that live around the seas, but we don't have much interaction with them. They're the most different among the water nymphs."

"How do you draw oxygen from the water? Do you have gills?" I asked solemnly. I didn't even want to think about where those would be.

Gabe took one look at my expression and burst out laughing again. "No. No gills!" he promised. "Once again, our skin makes it possible. It works much the same as gills but without the creepy appearance."

"Where do you think I fit into all of this?" I asked.

"That's really hard to say," he considered. "You're the first hybrid I've ever witnessed going through this change. You have to understand that despite the rumors of the insatiably lusty Naiads—" he winked "—it's uncommon that we have that kind of relationship with humans. It happens on occasion because there aren't as many male nymphs as female, but even then, the transformation you're experiencing rarely occurs."

"So not all half-nymphs go through a change?" I merged onto the main highway as I spoke.

Gabe shook his head with a small grin. "You're very much the exception, not the rule."

"Then why do nymphs have relationships with humans at all?" I wondered. "It seems like they'd be sad not to have kids that weren't extraordinary."

"Because to some, average is better than nothing."

I cocked my head in question.

"Children are rare among our kind," Gabe explained, a touch of sadness in his tone. "The Naiads who choose to live as humans, like your mother for a while, typically can't stay with the same partner forever. It's a hard life for those who choose it. Then you throw royalty into the mix, and it gets complicated."

"Complicated how?"

"It goes back to the ruling families and how they have their own way of doing things, when there's no other option, at least." Gabe shifted uncomfortably in his seat. "Generally speaking though, given the option, males are paired with equal females first. It ensures the bloodline is uncontaminated."

"What happens if the bloodline is broken?"

Gabe knew what I was alluding to. My mother had more than stepped out of line with her choice. Who knew what lay ahead of me?

"To my knowledge, it's only happened once before and it nearly started a war," he said, all traces of humor gone.

I frowned, wondering if that was a result of her actions. "When was this?"

"Well before your mother's time," he assured, though his face showed no relief.

"I don't understand one thing," I said. "If the bloodline is supposed to stay clean, why would my mom need to marry outside of it? Into another race especially."

Gabe's shoulders tensed as silence stretched on.

"There was a treaty," he eventually spoke, his voice hard.

"What kind of treaty? Why?"

Gabe stared through the windshield, his eyes narrowed against the sun. "Your grandfather's brother Leith betrayed who knows how many of his own kind. The treaty was created to settle the factions between the Naiads and Dryads."

"And my mother was a part of that treaty?"

"She would've been, yes," Gabe answered reluctantly.

Disheartened, I concentrated on the passing cars along the interstate. Neither of us spoke much before we reached a small town outside of Memphis. I pulled into a station just off the highway, low on fuel and full on water.

"You should go ahead inside. I'll take care of the car," Gabe offered. He smiled softly as he reached across to brush my hair away from my heavy eyelids.

"Thanks," I said through a yawn. I smiled back then climbed out to hurry inside.

Gabe waited in the driver's seat as I made it back out. I stared in question.

"You look as if you need a break." He nodded toward the open passenger's side.

I didn't oppose as I slid in and reclined the seat.

ⴞ   ⴞ   ⴞ

I awoke enveloped in warmth and surrounded by the scent of cedar and rain. The quilt Gabe used in Arizona covered me. I held it to my nose and breathed in.

Gabe lifted an eyebrow.

"I love your smell." A dopey grin pulled at my lips. "Thanks for letting me sleep. I feel much better. I don't know why I'm so tired."

"It's part of the change. It gets better. The more time you can spend in natural water will help." He reached over and pulled my hand from beneath the quilt. "I'm glad you slept well, but I'm happy you're awake."

"I guess you're probably pretty tired, huh? I can drive now if you'd like," I offered.

He gave a sigh and tucked his palm around my face. "Really, that's not what I meant."

I leaned into his hand. It was strange, but also normal, how comfortable it was with Gabe. It felt like we'd always been together. Like the invisible current tied us together in a way that was more than just attraction or chemistry.

"So, where are we?" I idly brushed my lips back and forth across his wrist, pausing to inhale the scent of his skin.

"We're just outside of Nashville." He drew an unsteady breath.

"You really didn't have to drive all this way. Aren't you tired?"

"Not at the moment." Gabe eyed my movements intently. "Perhaps we should find a place to spend tonight though."

The GPS directed us to a hotel overlooking the Cumberland River. A valet greeted opened my door and offered his hand. Gabe studied the doorman attempting to usher us inside. Men in Stetsons and bolo ties nodded as they passed, the heels of their leather boots clacking loudly across the marble foyer. My gaze traced over the lobby as we checked in. High archways and transitional chandeliers colored the room in understated elegance, adding dimension and style to the classic architecture.

"Was the governor's mansion full?" Gabe murmured as he tipped the bellboy and dropped my luggage inside the door.

"Funny guy, huh?" I teased. "Why don't you take a nap? You're looking a little glassy-eyed."

"I'll be fine. It isn't anything a little water won't fix. Would you care to join me for a late lunch?" Gabe extended his elbow.

I laughed and wound my hand through his arm.

After lunch at the hotel restaurant, we passed the indoor pool. I sighed in longing, wishing it was open.

"You want to swim?" Gabe lifted a brow.

"It says the pool is closed while they replace the floor." I pointed to the sign. "But if you want to sweet talk the front desk into letting us in, I'm game."

"I can do better than that." He glanced around then gave me a devilish grin and flipped the door handle. Somehow it popped open.

Just then, a deep voice carried down the corridor. Gabe grabbed my hand and tugged me inside before anyone could see. Cold tile met my back as Gabe's body pressed into mine. He held me in the shadows, the voice lingering near the entryway.

My nose brushed against the soft skin at his collarbone. I breathed in and sighed. My fingers, flat against his chiseled torso, began to wander. Just as my heart picked up pace, the voice faded into the background.

"Voila." He winked and moved away.

I let out an unsteady laugh, and turned my heated face from him, thankful for the dimness of the room.

Gabe turned beside me, staring at the pool. "Unfortunately, this is chemically treated water. It won't be as fulfilling, but it will refresh you all the same."

"One small problem," I said and gestured to my clothing.

"You're going to allow something so small as no bathing suit stop you?" He stepped to the edge of the pool and yanked his shirt over his head, exposing smooth skin over tight muscle. My eyes widened as he went for the snap on his shorts.

"Perhaps, I should keep these on." He laughed, his abs tightening, and stole over the ledge into the water.

My gaze followed the water droplets rolling over his shoulders and down the curve of his back. Gabe glanced up and caught me staring. He smiled impishly before motioning with his finger for me to join him.

Remembering to breathe, I worked my shorts away, grateful I'd gone for nice underwear in my shopping trip. Gabe kept his focus on the water, but I felt him watching me from the corner of his eye. Hurrying to remove my top, I slinked into the deep end.

Our party of two swam uninterrupted long enough to feel somewhat reenergized. It wasn't quite as liberating as I'd hoped, given the confines of the pool wall and the biting taste of chlorine, but it was pleasant nonetheless.

Gabe met me at the shallow end as I resurfaced for a breath. He moved closer; the silky feel of his skin brushed against mine. I slid my hand up his arm and past his shoulder, tracing the ridges and valleys of muscle. On the surface, it didn't look dissimilar, but to feel, there was a remarkable difference. His skin was soft and smooth, but there was a slippery quality to it now. I imagined him trying to move swiftly through the water. My fingertip swept across my own arm. The skin there felt different somehow but not to the extent as Gabe's. I wondered if that would change with the other things or if I was different being only half Naiad?

Gabe drew an unsteady breath as my fingers continued their course over his bare chest. He pinned my palm over the hard muscle above his heart. I smiled as the tempo increased. Turquoise eyes burned into me, warming me from head to toe as his arms encased my body like a cocoon. My skin met his and heat slashed though my stomach. Gabe's hands slid along my back and down to my waist.

"My Gracie." His mouth brushed against mine.

I wound my arms around his neck and our lips met. Gabe sighed, the sound amplified by the empty room, as his fingers tightened around my hips. He lifted me to the edge of the pool and moved closer, his kiss growing eager. The taste of cedar and chlorine danced on my tongue. His lips trailed down one side of my neck and back up the other in a torturously slow way.

I slid forward, wrapping my legs around Gabe's waist as his fingers snaked up my arm and wound through my strap. His free hand tangled in my hair as he slid the strap away, grazing my shoulder with his teeth.

The sound of someone clearing their throat caused me to jump.

"The pool area is closed for construction," a voice said. I peered around Gabe to see a man in a hotel uniform, his arms crossed as he lifted a speculative eyebrow.

"Right," Gabe huffed, his forehead falling against my shoulder.

"We would also encourage the use of proper swim attire." The worker's eyes lingered on the lacy strap dangling across the top of my arm. My cheeks flamed as I ducked behind Gabe and tugged it up.

"I'll give you a moment to dress then you two clear out of here." The man shook his head then stepped out of the room.

I padded across the patchy tile and hurried to yank my clothes back on. The fabric clung to my wet skin despite my tugging it away. Gabe dripped to the towel stand and unfastened his shorts. I closed my eyes and turned around as he wrapped a towel around his waist.

We hurried back to our room, picking up wandering glances along the way. I slipped into my pajamas and sat in bed, while Gabe changed. My pulse hammered in my ears as I waited, not knowing how the rest of the evening would play out.

Gabe opened the bathroom door but hesitated, glancing between the sofa and the vacant spot beside me.

"What are you doing?" I questioned.

"There's only one bed," he stated as if I'd missed the obvious.

"Yup." I ran my hand over the crisp king-sized sheets. "You didn't want me to get the double."

"I asked you to not get the presidential suite." His eyes lingered on the sheet at my waist. "Had I known these were single-bed rooms, I would've thought otherwise."

I scoffed with a disbelieving smile.

"That wasn't ... I didn't mean for us to share the bed," he mumbled.

"I realize that," I said bluntly. "I wasn't laughing for humor's sake."

"Why did you laugh?" he asked, his eyes narrowed.

"No reason." I sighed and pulled the blanket to my chin. "You're welcome to share the bed. It's plenty big enough for you to have your own side."

Gabe lowered himself on top of the sheet, pinning me beneath it, and settled along the far edge of the mattress. His tense posture and the rapid rise and fall of his chest told me he wasn't trying to sleep, despite his closed eyes.

I lay on my side, content to watch him breathe. There was more to Gabe than just a pretty face or beautiful body — though they were perfect. My feelings for him ran deeper than attraction. It didn't matter that we'd only known each other a short time or his life was little more than a question mark to me. The connection we shared was unlike anything I'd ever felt, and I knew with every part of me, he was meant to be in my life.

"What are you staring at?" He cracked one eye and looked down at me.

"You." I snuggled into his side, burying my face under his neck. "I love you," I whispered, my heart pounding in my chest.

The seconds ticked by in silence, and fear drummed inside me. You shouldn't have said that, Ashton. That was stupid!

My breathing stopped. I peeked up, terrified why he didn't respond. I didn't worry long as he seized my face in his hands, sustaining my gaze for only a second, before his mouth covered mine. His intensity was nearly alarming, but the pounding in my ears made thinking all but possible. Gabe held me close, his fingers twisting in my hair, and I gasped. His lips trailed from mine, blazing a path of fire as they slid along my jaw to trace the ridge of my neck to my collarbone. I buried my face in his hair, inhaling his intoxicating scent. My head spun — a combination of his overwhelming aroma that seemed to sit aching in my chest, and the lack of oxygen that was slowly catching up through my breathlessness.

"Ashton," he murmured, his voice husky.

"Mmmm?" I moaned breathless.

"Wait." Gabe grabbed my wrist, his eyes hesitant. "I-I need to tell you something…"

My heart fell.

"What is it?" I whispered.

Chapter Eleven
Whose Funeral?

"Sleep well," he murmured as he drew away.

"What?" I huffed, pulling myself into a sitting position. "What do you mean 'sleep well?' Where are you going?"

"Perhaps I should sleep on the sofa tonight," he said breathlessly.

"The sofa? I just told you that I loved you. And then we were ... and now you're just going to—"I sputtered then scoffed, trying to maintain my broken dignity. "Yeah, sure. Sleep on the sofa. That's just great."

I snagged two down pillows from the bed along with the duvet and dragged them into the living room.

"Here you go. Goodnight." I turned and sulked back to bed. Alone.

Gabe hesitated in the doorway. "I enjoyed being with you today, Gracie — perhaps too much." He laughed once. "Goodnight."

The door closed, leaving me alone with my thoughts. Why did I have to go and tell him I loved him? How could I be so stupid? Gabe probably thought I was either insane or so flighty he'd never want to be with someone like me.

I tossed and turned the rest of the night, praying I hadn't shot myself in the foot, until I finally fell asleep.

❧ ❧ ❧

Sunlight poured through the front window. We dressed with exaggerated slowness as we prepared for our trip to Kentucky.

Gabe watched me closely as I moved around the room, gathering our things. His constant contact was reassuring though, as he brushed his fingers across my face or squeezed my hand each time I neared him. Maybe I hadn't completely terrified him after all.

I paused in front of the mirror and studied the reflection. There was now a glow about me now. My skin looked light and smooth, even the old wakeboarding scar had faded. The image of my mother flickered in front of me, and I smiled, admiring the likeness we shared. Then thoughts of the life I'd never know filled my mind, and my expression fell as I bit back tears.

Gabe moved behind me, his arms snaking around my waist. He kissed my temple and rested his head on my shoulder. "You take my breath away, Gracie. I would be content to hold you this way forever, seeing a smile on your lips, enraptured by the way you look at me," he whispered in my ear, his gaze meeting mine in the mirror.

My lip trembled, and I pulled his arms tighter. His smile faltered.

"You're stronger than you know, Ashton. Remember that every time you see your reflection." Gabe brushed my hair away. "You won't be sad forever. I promise."

"Thank you."

"Ashton, before we go, I need you to know something," Gabe began and turned me to face him.

My shoulders fell as dread washed over me. "Yeah?"

"I adore you," he breathed, his eyes shining like the sun. "I didn't say anything last night for several reasons. One of which revolves around what might have happened had I stayed." He laughed once before his tone turned serious. "But more importantly, I would never want you to believe I said so simply out of obligation. I love you, Gracie," Gabe said, his lips brushing against mine. Our current hummed to life. My fears and hesitations melted away as warmth seeped through me.

I reveled in the silky-soft feel of his mouth before backing away. "I love you, too."

We packed the car, and Gabe offered to man the wheel again. My thoughts were running a thousand miles an hour; there was zero desire for my vehicle to follow that pattern.

The unexpected turn my life had taken over the past few days left me dumbfounded. The search for my identity, my desire to be a better person, and all the things I longed to find or become had begun falling into place. Regret settled in my stomach when I realized my father, and even my mother in a sense, would never know Gabe like this. They would never get to see our happiness together. But I had Harry. He'd always been an essential part of our family. The thought of the hurt he must be suffering wrenched my insides into knots.

"Is something wrong?" Gabe asked when my breath hitched.

"No, I'm just thinking about Harry."

"What about him?" he asked.

"This must be so hard," I said. "As far as I know, he's known Charlie since before I was born. They were like brothers. I can't imagine what this must be like for him, being alone right now."

Gabe nodded, his eyes flitting to me and back to the road. "Why do you call your father Charlie?"

"Because that's his name," I answered dryly.

Gabe's expression fell in apology.

"I'm sorry. I don't mean to be rude. The fact is, Charlie never felt like a dad to me as much as he did a benefactor. It was my way of keeping him where he belonged in my life — just another name." I stared at my hands, ashamed of my behavior.

Gabe let it go. "Tell me about Harry."

"He's clearly aged well." I laughed softly, thinking of the obvious signs I'd missed over the years. "Harry's wise, kind, and sympathetic. He's always been there for me."

"It seems like you're lucky to have such a great man around." Gabe's smile didn't quite reach his eyes. I noticed the subtle change in the way he sat a little straighter, his body no longer relaxed but angular and tense.

"What?" My head fell to one side.

"What does Harry look like anyway?"

I gauged the look on Gabe's face. Skepticism tight in his eyes, a crooked set to his mouth. I fought to hide the amused grin that tugged at my lips.

"Gabe, be serious," I began, trying to keep a straight-face. "Harry? Eeeyuw."

"I don't know what you mean." His tone turned defensive.

I swept my fingers the length of his jaw.

Gabe shivered and glanced out of the corner of his eye. "You didn't answer my question."

He couldn't be serious. Of all people to get jealous over, he chooses Harry. True, Harry was exceptionally attractive. He had thick blonde hair and eyes the color of faded denim; his smile was to die for, and all of my girlfriends had crushes on him at one time or another, but that wasn't anything I wanted to share with Gabe. Likewise, my father was handsome as well. That had zero affect on the creepy factor.

"Aside from the fact that thought is way beyond disturbing, Harry is literally like family. Besides that, no one has ever made me feel the way you do." I blushed and looked down.

"Fair enough." He smiled.

"On another matter, I've been thinking," I began. "If Naiads are water beings, what is your deal with the Willows? They're trees."

"Yes, but they're one of the few trees that Dryads can't use. In fact, they're toxic to them," Gabe explained. "Willows need moist soil to thrive, and their bark contains salicin, better known as salicylic acid."

"That's the stuff in face cleanser, right?"

"Among other things, yes. While it's beneficial for our kind, it's quite harmful to them. So Willows are an inside joke for my family."

"Makes sense, I guess," I said. I couldn't put my finger on it, but there seemed to be more to the story.

A sharp curve in the highway set my attention on the double yellow lines. I stayed quiet for the remainder of the trip. The winding roads in conjunction with the escalating stress did unpleasant things to my stomach.

Gray-green clouds layered the sky. The wind whipped through the trees as we climbed a steep hill to the cemetery. Goosebumps raised the fine hair on my arms, and I swallowed against the rising panic, forcing a calming breath through my mouth.

The cemetery sat along a ridge of the mountain. Trees surrounded the perimeter, casting the outer edge in shadows. Stone grave-markers dotted the thick grass, some recent, but most so aged the dates were indiscernible. It bared a striking resemblance to the cemetery in my dream.

Gabe pulled the car beneath a ceiling of low hanging branches. I climbed out wobbly-legged and gasped at the sea of people in attendance. Parents carried children in their arms, many wearing badges on their shirts that read, 'Charlie Blake saved my life.' I couldn't even begin to imagine what those meant.

Prominent individuals and officials were in attendance, as well as the everyday locals. Harry stood in their midst, speaking with a solemn-looking man with white hair and a navy suit. Harry's shoulders slumped, his hands in his pockets. Dark circles stained the skin beneath his eyes, and his cheeks sank in. Charlie's death had affected him more than I'd realized.

I chafed my hands against my arms as a breeze licked at the exposed flesh. Gabe's anxious gaze fixed on me as we cut through the crowd toward Harry.

"Hey, kid," he greeted, his voice breaking. "I'm relieved to find you made it safely."

Harry pulled me into a too tight hug. My heart began to ache for our loss as the embrace lingered in an almost desperate way. I should've already been here for him. While I had Gabe behind me, Harry'd lost his best friend and suffered it alone. Guilt weighed heavy on my conscience. I swallowed against the tears and pulled away, shivering at the emptiness.

Harry sat next to me in the front row of the crowd. He shrugged out of his jacket and placed it around my shoulders. I nodded in appreciation but avoided meeting his eyes. Gabe stood behind me, one hand resting at the base of my neck. He shifted restlessly from foot to foot. I stared at the ring on my finger, trying to concentrate on the distinct color, but it was lost to the chaos that warred within.

I ignored the minister's delivery. What did he know about my father? Certain it was just a generic spiel about his life and success, I trained my eyes on the swaying trees in the background. Gabe's grip suddenly tightened when Harry released my hand and stood up. Harry stooped down and whispered something about trying to speak to me sooner, adding an apology, and told me not to take off.

I frowned as he strode forward to take the minister's place beside the ominous wooden box. He stepped up to the makeshift podium and began to speak about someone I'd never known.

"Charlie Blake was a man you all knew," he began. "That's why you're here today, to show your love and support for Ashton and your respect and admiration for such a wonderful man.

"Some of you grew up with Charlie, you helped raise him yourselves." Harry smiled. "He loved this place. It hurt him to have to be away, but Charlie left to make something of himself, to leave his mark on the world. He had plans to retire here someday, but first he had to meet that special somebody and start his family. And let's face it, we're all related to each other around here anyway, right?" Harry teased lightly, inciting a soft chuckle from his audience.

I shook my head trying to reason out what I was hearing. This was my father's hometown? He grew up here? Why didn't I know this?

"Charlie worked hard for the tri-city area, determined to bring it back to its former glory and beyond. He didn't want later generations to have to leave for work and college. He wanted them to have a hope of staying without sacrificing their futures or having limited options.

"Charlie founded Families of Miners to assist families who had lost their income due to the death or disability of their loved ones resulting from coal mining accidents. He funded the new expansion in the Appalachian Regional Hospital, as well as offered the backing needed to attract new and promising doctors to the area. His college scholarship is offered throughout the country to children of small towns so they might have an opportunity to further themselves..."

Harry's voice faded into the background. I never knew the man he spoke of. A man who was selfless, generous, and kind.

My breakfast threatened to come back up, but the lump in my throat kept it at bay. I tugged Harry's jacket off and slipped out from under Gabe's hand. A few curious bystanders eyed me understandingly as I squeezed through them, making my way to the back of the crowd.

I didn't know where to go, but I had to get away from the absurdity Harry offered the masses. A ribbon of trail wound up a hill between the trees. My escape. I pushed my legs as hard and as fast as they would go, trying to outrun the anger and grief. I didn't hear anyone on the path behind me, but by the time I stopped, Gabe was there pulling me into him. He said nothing as we stood in the woods, my sobbing the only sound.

"Nothing in my life makes sense," I said, choking back more tears.

"I know, love. This has all been so confusing. I wish I could say something that would make it all better. I would give anything I had to fix it." Gabe swept his fingers beneath my eyes, wiping away the tears. His love and support meant more to me than I could say.

"I guess we need to get back." I sighed as he held my face in his hands.

"It can wait. You don't have to placate anyone."

"I know, but they came to pay their respects." I sniffled. "They've lost someone too. I should go meet them." My voice sounded stronger as I thought of all of the people that came to show their love and gratitude.

In the cemetery, Harry shook hands and offered condolences. Gabe and I made our way through a sea of support. The two men locked eyes as Gabe led me to take my position beside Harry. I dutifully received hugs and well wishes for the next hour before the last mourner retreated.

Thankfully, I missed the eulogy and dismissal. I didn't want to say my goodbyes in front of an audience. My eyes shifted to the shadowed opening where the casket had been lowered, and

Gabe sighed. Entwining our fingers, I pulled him behind me as I inched forward to stand in front of the large marble headstone that marked my father's permanent dwelling. For a passing moment, I wondered where my mother was buried. Couples tended to be laid to rest in the same place, but her marker was nowhere to be seen.

Gabe stood quietly behind me with his hands on my shoulders. There was no emotion left inside of me. My eyes drifted over the inscription chiseled across the glossy black stone.

Charlie Winton Blake

June 8th 1961 — July 1st 2011

"There's more to life than meets the eye."

I lifted a single white calla lily out of my bag and dropped it onto the casket covered with various flowers, not the least of which, plum-colored tulips. An utter barrenness filled my chest as everything closed in on me. Maybe my tears were gone. Maybe the revelation of my life — the troubling past, the strange present, and the unsettling future — overwhelmed any other emotion. But I could do no more than stare at the emptiness in front of me while I pondered the emptiness inside.

Gabe's arms wrapped around the tops of my shoulders, and he kissed the back of my hair. "Little mourned I for the parted gladness, for the vacant nest and silent song – Hope was there, and laughed me out of sadness; Whispering, 'Winter will not linger long.'"

"Emily Brontë." I sighed, not wanting to stay there with the nothingness, but struggled to remove myself from the fleeting presence that lingered with my father's remains. Gabe laced his fingers through mine once more as I drew a deep breath and walked away.

We stopped in front of Harry. I turned toward Gabe and stood still in his arms, pressing my cheek against his chest. Harry eyed our embrace in speculation.

"Harry," I began, peering around the grounds, "this is Gabe Willoughby. Gabe, this is my father's attorney and our dearest friend, Harry Waterford."

"Mr. Waterford." Gabe emphasized Harry's last name and extended his hand.

Harry grasped Gabe's hand and shook it firmly, offering an inflection of his own as he lifted a dark-blonde eyebrow. I wondered if he suspected that Gabe shared more with him than unusually youthful looking skin.

"It's a pleasure, Gabe." Harry smiled. "How do you know our sweet Ashton?"

Yep. He knew. I bit back the urge to grimace, and sighed.

"Ashton and I go a long way back," Gabe responded. An odd notion when I thought about it.

"Do you now? That is interesting," Harry spoke with disbelief.

He started to continue but Gabe interrupted him. "Mr. Waterford—"

"Please, call me Harry."

"Sure, Harry." Gabe nodded. "We would very much like to speak privately with you about several matters — some more pressing than others."

"Yes." Harry's eye flickered to my wary expression. "I didn't expect their need to arise quite so soon."

Harry was still unaware of the extent of my knowledge, though I sensed there was more than I was being told.

"Harry, is there somewhere else we can go? Do you have a hotel or someplace you're staying?" I felt exposed outside, even among the trees — especially among the trees.

"Yes, of course. Please forgive my thoughtlessness. I'm sure you're quite tired." Harry pulled a set of keys from his pocket. "I've been staying at your father's house. It's not too far from here, just outside of town. You can follow me if you'd like."

I nodded quickly, eager to be away from the woods.

By the time we reached Charlie's, I was grateful again that Gabe had driven. The mountain roads here were high on my things-I-despise list. My stomach turned as I mentally relived the winding highway.

"How are you feeling?" Gabe stroked my face, wiping the sheen of sweat from my forehead.

"I've been better, but it's starting to lighten up." I shifted on the gold-patterned loveseat in the parlor.

"How about some sweet tea?" Harry gave a knowing grin as he carried a silver tray with a crystal pitcher and several glasses into the sitting room. The ice cubes chimed against the decanter as he placed it on the coffee table. The sound soothed my frazzled nerves.

"That'd be perfect." I reclined, feeling some relief.

"I haven't been through Kentucky in a long time," Gabe spoke as if he were making small talk, though we all knew better. "I'd forgotten just how mountainous it is."

"Indeed," Harry said on a slight frown. "It is heavily forested."

"Like Ashton, I much prefer water and open areas myself," Gabe said, implication heavy in his tone.

"You're not likely to find much open water near Cumberland," Harry replied.

"Yeah, yeah, everyone's a freaky nymph," I joked. "Can we stop beating around the bush here and cut to the chase." My sentence fell away as I saw Harry's expression darken in fury at Gabe.

"Are you insane?" Harry spoke through gritted teeth, his voice low. "Do you want her dead?"

"Harry, I would never do anything to endanger Ashton." Gabe pulled me into an embrace that was more than a friendly gesture.

"What?" Harry's face twisted in a mix of pure rage and complete bewilderment. "Ashton, what's going on here?"

"Harry, please," Gabe soothed. "Let us explain."

"What us?" Harry looked between Gabe and I. "There is no us here!"

"Please," Gabe entreated once more and held out his hand toward the armchair.

Harry resigned with a growl and sat down hard. "Well? Go on."

"Yes, Ashton knows," Gabe said, "but please allow me to explain before you speak. I didn't tell her just to tell her, though it would've been for the best if I had."

Harry inched further toward the back of his chair though his posture remained rigid, a deep scowl carved in his forehead.

By the time Gabe finished our brief history, explaining the things such as his arm and finding the attic, Harry wore a blank expression. He leaned back in his armchair, shaking his head and mumbling to himself. I couldn't understand anymore than hearing something about complicating things. The room went silent for a long minute as Harry rubbed his face in thought.

"You said it would've been for the best to have told Ashton, even if those things hadn't happened." Harry inched forward. "Why?"

Gabe's jaw tensed. He spoke one word, simple yet full of hate. "Oren."

"You had a run-in with him? When?" Harry asked, the vein in his forehead throbbing under his skin.

"He was in a hotel outside of Flagstaff where I stayed. We haven't seen or heard anything from him since," I assured.

Harry pulled a handkerchief out of his jacket pocket and mopped it across his wet forehead. "That works to our advantage then. Bringing you here wasn't a mistake."

Gabe edged closer in thought. "That's what I hoped you had in mind."

"Why would they want her now though? We'll have to hide her," Harry mumbled, smoothing his sandy-colored hair back in thought. "Maybe keep her in the mountains. They might not think of that. Of course, they have no idea that she knows any of this, so perhaps we should keep near the water; we unquestionably have the upper hand there. If only she had the ability..."

"You know, Harry, that reminds me." Gabe looked back toward me, his eyebrows raised. "Ashton has shown some changes lately."

"Changes?" Harry echoed in question as he stared at Gabe and wiped his forehead again. "In what way?"

"She's craving water and her senses are heightened," Gabe said, grinning when I sighed.

"Unbelievable." Harry shook his head, his eyes focused on mine. "You're changing?"

"I don't know." I hesitated. "It looks that way, I guess. You've seen this happen before?"

Harry nodded solemnly. "And so have you."

I thought for a moment. "Oh!" I gasped. Harry looked at me expectantly. "You don't mean ... Allie?"

He nodded in apology but with a sense of relief.

I fell back against the loveseat, pressing my palms to my temples. Allie was a nymph? How was that possible?

"Who is Allie?" Gabe asked, his expression worried.

"Allie Taylor was the daughter of Ashton's childhood nanny," Harry began. "They grew up together like sisters until the Taylors left rather abruptly when Ashton was fourteen. I don't know the whole story, but needless to say, Allie was like us."

"I see. They disappeared, didn't they?" Gabe eyed me with regret.

"Was that why they left? Did it have to do with ... the incident?" I asked.

"Yes, to the extent of my knowledge," Harry continued. "After the episode in the woods, it became imperative. Unlike yours, Allie's symptoms came about abruptly and very pronounced. She shouldn't have changed so early."

"That makes sense, I guess." I risked a glance at Gabe's face. It was full of nothing but concern for me. "You're wondering what we mean?"

"I don't want you to talk about anything that makes you uncomfortable." He rubbed my hands between his.

I so wanted to take that as a promise. I wondered selfishly if he'd offer me a rain check.

"No, it's okay. Now that I know, it's a little easier to not feel so..." I started to say guilty, but I couldn't imagine anything erasing that emotion. "Would you like to hear about Allie?"

Chapter Twelve
What We Found There

"Growing up, I was surrounded by people who saw me as an obligation. Even though Allie's mom worked for us, she never treated me differently, and Allie and I were best friends." I smiled remembering the way Allie's sapphire eyes twinkled when she laughed. Gabe and Harry stared intently as I began my story. Harry was no stranger to my childhood but much more occurred than he knew.

"Lynn Taylor, Allie's mom, was my nanny of sorts. She had taken care of me from as early as I can remember, and I loved Miss Lynn as much as I could imagine any child loving her parent.

"Allie and I grew up like sisters. We'd ride horse-back and explore for hours. The only place Charlie forbade us to go was the easternmost point of the property that was lined with a high stone wall. It wasn't until I turned fourteen that I started to question the rule, and I took trying to find a way around the wall as a challenge."

Gabe and Harry chuckled, and I lifted an eyebrow.

"One morning, we overheard Charlie say he was leaving for the day," I continued. "Allie and I had been trying to figure out what was so special that Charlie would build a fortress to keep us out. I figured there was no better time to find out."

I stood and walked over to the window. Dropping my head against the pane, I stared over the little river that curved behind the house. I imagined a gust of muggy Louisiana air heating my skin as the memory played full force.

"We waited until Miss Lynn went inside, and then we snuck along the border of the tall grass near the water's edge. It took the better part of a half hour to make it across the lake, but one breath carried us the whole way.

"Allie took a few steps onto the shore, trying to follow me, and then she collapsed. I tried to shake her, to wake her up, but..." I drew a shaky breath. "I pulled her back into the water and swam us home, screaming for Miss Lynn as the shore came into view. I'll never forget the look on her face as she ran from the house." My voice broke as I swiped at a tear.

"After Miss Lynn put Allie in a tepid bath, she demanded to know if we'd gone beyond the wall. I couldn't even look at her." I shook my head. 'You must never go into the lake again!' she said. 'It's too soon for...' But the sounds of footsteps cut her off.

"Charlie stopped when he saw my wet clothes and that I was crying. 'Go to your room,' he said. But I'll never forget how he wouldn't even look at me." I took a deep breath. "When I woke up the next morning, Allie was gone. I never even got the chance to say goodbye. Charlie, as he'd become to me that day, never mentioned them again."

I turned away from the outside world and back to my own. Gabe stood behind me, staring at the floor. His breathing was slow and deliberate. An emotion I had yet to see settled on his face.

"I don't know how he could just make them leave like that." My lip quivered. "Did I make him that angry?"

"Ashton, none of that was your fault. You have to know that." Gabe met my eyes. "This is why humans can't be involved in our world. The heartache, the seeming betrayal." He looked away, his expression pained. "It's a part of our nature, love. We often act on impulse or direction without appreciating the consequences. Choosing to involve ourselves in human life, with no regard for how it will end, only hurts those we wish to love. The Taylors would've vanished either way."

I shook my head and sniffled.

"I certainly didn't help matters by showing up and telling you to pack your things, did I?" Harry asked, his tone low.

I gave him a halfhearted smile.

"What happened that day, Ash?" Harry asked.

"That was the day I stopped caring about anyone but myself." I took a deep breath and turned to face him. "I promised myself I'd go back to try and find answers. Since Charlie never replaced Miss Lynn, I was alone most days. The day you showed up, I decided it was my last chance to find out what really happened to Allie."

"You found your way back into the woods?" Harry asked.

I nodded. "The walled section closest to the house was covered with vines and weeds. It took me forever to find the gate, but the lock had been broken off. So, I tugged on the door until it broke free."

Harry's gaze turned questioning but he didn't say anything.

"What was it like there?" Gabe asked, his expression curious. "What made it so special or different that Charlie didn't want you to see?"

"It was like another world — one where nothing was tainted or spoiled; a place where time stood still." I laughed once. "The trees were bright and vivid. Even in the coolness of winter, it was comfortable.

"There was an odd scent in the air. It was sweet, like apple blossom but stronger, as if it had rained recently. I don't know why, but it messed with my emotion. It was like the smell of firewood in winter; there was a feeling of excitement tied to it because of the memories associated with that smell. In that one moment, I felt perfectly at peace," I explained, remembering the feeling as if I lived it all over again.

"There was a small pool there between two trees. The branches curved over the path, forming an archway." I motioned with my hands. "When I pushed them away, I saw it was actually part of a large pond. There was a giant willow there, larger than any I'd ever seen, and it hung over the water." I smiled at Gabe, thinking of his connection to willows.

"Underneath the tree, there was a wooden bench barely big enough for two people. I sat down and leaned back for a long while, enjoying the peace and quiet for a change. But eventually, the sun crept behind the trees, and the air turned cool. I knew I needed to find my way back before it got dark.

"I remember I was looking at the ground as I walked. Something glimmering in the grass caught my eye. I bent down and picked it up. It was cold and wet. My necklace. The charm was a mariner's compass. Ms. Lynn had given it to me the Christmas before."

My finger swept below the collar of my shirt and locked onto a thin chain. I gazed at the same necklace. "She said it was a reminder that no matter where in the world I would ever be, to remember that we were all under the same sky, and it would lead me to my place in life. I haven't taken it off since that day, though I don't know why. It doesn't even work."

"May I?" Gabe asked eyeing the silver trinket. I nodded, and he took possession of the charm. He studied the compass's erratic movement as I continued.

"I found the gate and passed back into reality. That was the last visit I made to the other side of the wall because we left the next day — leaving my new paradise and my old heart behind."

Gabe pulled me into his chest. "Thank you for sharing your story with us. You shouldn't have been forced to go through that to begin with."

"I don't understand though. What did I do?" I dropped my head against his shoulder. "Why does everyone I love end up leaving me? Am I that big of a pain?"

"Ashton," Gabe whispered, backing away.

"Ashton, look at me." Harry stood beside us. "Look at me."

I turned my face enough to see his pale-blue eyes boring into mine.

"You don't know what you're saying. The incident with Allie would've happened one way or the other. It wasn't your fault it occurred too early. Trust me. Few things about our existence are normal."

"It doesn't change anything," I murmured. "I'm cursed to live alone apparently."

"That's not true. You have me ... and Gabe. You must understand. After your mom was gone, something happened to Charlie. It was like he died with her loss." Harry walked away and came back with a single framed picture of me as a child.

"This is great, Harry." I shrugged as I looked over the image. "But it doesn't mean much. If anything, it tends to prove the fact that I'm little more than a nuisance. I don't even see one of me in this room with Charlie."

"Open the back." Harry pointed.

I flipped the frame over and loosened the velvet backing. A lone picture lay hidden behind the original. Charlie beamed with pride, his arms filled with a newborn. My mother sat on the arm of the chair, her hand resting on his shoulder as she looked down at us. Her expression held one of complete and utter devotion. Tears stung my eyes, wishing that I could have experienced a lifetime of knowing her … of knowing them.

"See, there? He was crazy about you," Harry said on a smile. "They both were. That never changed, even if he did."

"Could you guys just give me a minute, please?" I asked, my eyes locked on thc picture.

"Sure, love." Gabe stood and kissed my forehead. "I'll be outside if you need me." He and Harry turned to leave.

I stared at the photo for a minute longer. My mother was so beautiful it was hard to look away. My eyes, her eyes. They were identical in shape and color. Sky blue. We shared the same slightly upturned nose and pouty mouth. She of course was beautiful in a way that was more than human. Her golden hair, the opposite of my Charlie-colored brown, billowed down to her waist, shining like satin in the sun.

My gaze lingered a moment more before I stood to put it away. I smiled at a framed image of Harry and me at a swim meet that sat on the desk. I lifted it up, but it slipped through my fingers and clanged to the floor. Glass splintered and crunched as it made contact with the wood.

"Nice hands, Ash," I grumbled and lifted the frame. Fractures of glass streaked from the center, outward. I tapped the front of the metal against a trash bin to loosen the pieces. Shards fell into the can, the picture behind them.

Confusion struck when I saw two photos on top of the mess. I looked on the desk to be sure I hadn't knocked off the one with my parents. Reaching in, I lifted the papers out. The top was the original photograph; the bottom scrap was upside down with handwriting on the back. I recognized the script immediately. I had seen it once before and not even in English, but I knew it to be my mother's.

"Ruarc and me. Texas. June nineteen ninety-two," I read aloud and turned the photo over.

My gaze fixed onto the face of the man with his arm slung over my mother's shoulder. He wore a happy grin, white teeth against tan skin. A lock of dark-bronze hair curled into his eyes. Gabe stared back at me.

I flipped the paper over once more to read the label.

Ruarc. Not Gabe. Ruarc.

Chapter Thirteen
Responsibility

"That's where that photograph was hiding." Gabe paused in the doorway. I jumped and turned to face him. He focused on the image in my hand. "Edlyn was clever, wasn't she? And it's pronounced Roar-k."

"What?" I shook my head. "Ruarc? I don't understand."

Gabe took the picture from me. His eyes grew tender. "I changed my name when I decided to live among the humans."

"But why?"

"It's a long story, and one I'd rather not get into at the moment," he said, his eyes searching mine. "Does it matter?"

"Do you love me?"

"With every part of my being." His palms swept around my cheeks.

"Then it doesn't matter." I sighed at his touch and smiled. He returned the gesture, but it didn't meet his eyes.

"Why do you look sad?"

"Ash," he started to speak but an unexpected grin flashed across my face, interrupting his sentence.

His eyebrows pulled down. "What?"

Gabe never called me anything but Ashton and the occasional Grace or Gracie. I didn't know why it moved me, but I loved it.

"I just love you," I said.

He locked his gaze on my upturned mouth. Squeezing me tighter, he lifted my chin and touched his lips to mine. A moment longer, and he gently pushed my face away. I conceded with a defeated pout. He grinned at my predictable reaction.

"Let's get some fresh air, shall we?" he asked. I gestured for him to lead the way.

Gabe led me around a wishing well and beyond a towering sycamore. We eased down the hillside to a place where the river cut through the mountain. Gabe picked a flat boulder jutting out into the water and sat down. I curled up into his side and sat in silence as he hummed a familiar tune.

"What has you so quiet?" Gabe murmured against my hair as the song came to an end. "Still contemplating my name change, I imagine?"

I hesitated, not sure I wanted to say anything.

"You don't want me to know?" I finally asked.

"It isn't that I don't want you to know," Gabe wavered. "I only wonder if it will ... upset you."

"What do you mean?" I looked up at him.

"Would my past, my prior motives or intentions, influence your opinion of me?"

A barrage of potential scenarios flooded my mind. But deep down I knew nothing he could say would affect my love — though plenty that could cause me any amount of heartache.

"Don't worry, love." Gabe squeezed my tight shoulder. "It's nothing too devastating," he teased, but there was a note of uncertainty in his eyes.

"Gabe," I spoke confidently. "It doesn't matter who you were or what you did, my feelings for you are absolute. I can't love people in slices. You, who you are in here—" my fingers swept across his heart "—that's the Gabe, or whatever name you choose, that I adore. And as long as you want me, that's all I care about."

"Thank you," Gabe offered, his eyes crinkling into a smile.

"Well, you look better," Harry interrupted, pausing at the top of the hill.

"You think?" I responded playfully as Gabe helped me to my feet.

"Most certainly, I'd say you're pretty much back to normal."

"She's dealing with everything exceptionally well, wouldn't you say, Harry?" Gabe brushed the back of his hand down my cheek. My heart fluttered, and I blushed.

"Yeah," Harry muttered, the line of his mouth hardening. "I'm going to head inside and scrounge us up something for dinner tonight."

"Do you need any help?" Gabe offered, shielding his eyes as a gust of wind whipped the leaves from the trees and thunder rumbled in the distance.

Harry paused, pivoting to meet Gabe. "Nope." He smiled peculiarly. "I've got this just about all wrapped up."

I glanced at Gabe, trying to get a read on their bizarre exchange, but he seemed as baffled as me.

∽ ∽ ∽

After dinner, Gabe and I lingered on the covered veranda. The sun nestled behind the mountains, abandoning the sky to ominous clouds. I snuggled beneath Gabe's arm as we sat on the wooden porch swing, soothing folk music humming in the background over the falling rain.

"Just coming to check on you, Ash." Harry emerged from the shadowed archway leading from the house. "I'm retiring to my study for the evening, but I'll be awake for a while if you need anything."

I stood, and Harry kissed my cheek.

"I'm fine, thanks." I hugged him.

"I'll keep an eye and ear on everything tonight." Harry turned to Gabe when he stood beside me. "I trust Ashton explained your room is on the third floor?" He shook Gabe's hand and clapped him on the shoulder, still wearing an expression I couldn't make sense of, though I thought I saw a hint of fatherly-like caution there.

Gabe nodded, apparently sensing the warning. "Yes, she did. Thank you again for everything."

"You take good care of me." I smiled at Harry.

"I don't know about that." He shifted an appraising glance toward Gabe. "I guess we'll see. Good night, you two."

I stared into the crackling fire burning on the outdoor hearth and relished in my small piece of near perfection. Two smooth arms wrapped around my waist as a pair of lips brushed back and forth against the curve of my shoulder.

"Hi." Gabe's warm breath tickled my skin.

I turned to face him, my arms curling around his neck. Even in the faint glow of the dimming flames, his eyes smoldered. My pulse quickened, carrying the heat to my skin. Gabe's hand rested lightly on my face, his thumb stroking the blush that colored my cheeks.

"Breathe," he murmured with a smile, reminding me that it was a necessity. I drew in a quick breath hoping to alleviate the spinning.

Gabe backed away, pulling me toward the source of the music, never breaking our gaze. I shivered as he drew me into his chest. His fingers slid down my arm, leaving a trail of heat along the way. Warmth spread from the place where his hand pressed just above my jeans, his fingers grazing the skin at the small of my back. An almost painful ache drummed inside my chest. I looked away, trying to lessen the pull that encouraged us to close the distance.

"Is something wrong?" Gabe's lips brushed against the curve of my ear, his voice a whisper.

"I can't get enough of you," I whispered. "I always need more." I dropped my forehead to his chest, feeling his rapid pulse beneath the cotton. Gabe's warm scent filled my lungs. I nuzzled into his neck and drew a slow breath. His fingers tightened around the fabric at my back as I rose on my toes, my wandering lips dancing toward his.

"I think we should sit down now," he murmured against my mouth, his tone contradictory to his words. My lips stilled, but I allowed them to linger, pressing myself into him. Gabe's breathing hitched. His hands knotted in my hair as he pulled me closer, but hesitated, his eyes closed.

My hands trailed down the front of his shirt. I paused for a moment before catching the top button then flipped it open. Gabe sighed as I traced the open seam down his smooth skin to the next button.

"Stop," he huffed, his hands over mine.

"Why?" I whispered and tried to close the gap he'd made between us. His hands moved to my waist. Confusion set in as he pushed me away.

"Harry is just inside, love." Gabe took another step back, his mind made up.

My shoulders slumped, and I sulked back to the corner.

Gabe laughed at my diplomatic surrender. "Thank you, nonetheless, for being gracious about it." He peeked down at me from the corner of his eye. "I'm in no frame of thought for negotiations." He settled into the swing and opened his arms in an irresistible invitation.

I sighed, disappointment warring with desire, but curled up in his side. The music continued softly in the background as we swung. Several verses later, my pulse slowed, and I began to yawn. At last, I drifted off, barely noticing the melancholy notes that'd begun in the background.

❧   ❧   ❧

The dawn brought with it an air of excitement. Today was brand new and unpredictable. That thought had me smiling when Harry wandered out to the veranda where I sat under a blanket, drinking a glass of sweet tea and relaxing in the same swing as last night.

"Well, you're up early." He moved the quilt aside and sat down beside me.

"I guess I am," I chimed, and bit down on my lip to keep the dopey grin off my face.

"You seem especially cheerful this morning. Sleep well?" He lifted an eyebrow and sipped at his coffee.

"Yeah, I did. There's something about this place." I sighed, my focus on the light angling though the trees. "Must be the mountain air."

"Or Gabe," he stated bluntly. I ignored his gaze and kept my attention on the rustling leaves.

"That's another possibility," I said through a smile. "I guess you're wondering about that, huh?"

"Does Kevin know?" His question hung heavy in the morning mist.

My smile fell away as I pulled the blanket around me a little tighter. "I haven't spoken to him since I left."

How was I supposed to broach that subject?

"Do you want to go back to California when everything is settled?" Harry looked at me from the corner of his eye. I considered his question and slumped against the back of the swing.

"I hadn't thought about it." I sighed. "I really don't know what to do."

"Putting it off won't help the situation. This is all yours now." Harry gestured around the area "It would be relatively simple to—"

"Mine?" I jerked my head up. "What do you mean it's mine? This house?"

"This house and the countless other properties your dad owned. Everything belongs to you now." He took a deep breath. "And Kevin would know what to do with it. His family comes from a long line of successful businessmen, after all. He can help you take care of everything. And you never know how he might take the news of your ... nature. With his connections, he can help hide you."

I scowled at the trees at a loss for how to think or react. What was I supposed to do with Charlie's properties, his company? I couldn't run things; I hadn't even gone to college. And Kevin? I didn't want to spend my life in hiding with Kevin. I didn't want any kind of life with him. Kevin's capabilities ended at anger and control.

Harry stared at the ground, thinking. "Ash, I don't mean to intrude, but are you certain you're making the best choice by Gabe? Are you sure he's who you belong with?"

The muscles in the back of my neck tensed. I drew a breath to answer, but Harry continued. "Gabe is a good guy, but being with him, you're choosing a whole new world. You haven't any idea what that entails."

"That world chose me, Harry, with or without Gabe." My tone came out sharper than I meant. "I know it probably doesn't make sense to you, but I love him. He's different than anyone I've ever known. I'm sure it has something to do with our being alike, but more so he's just different. He cares about me and what I want. It's not like Kevin ever asked."

Harry sighed. "I can appreciate that. But so much has changed this past week; don't you think this is all kind of fast?"

"I know how it looks. Believe me. But what Gabe and I share is special, something I could never have with anyone else. And not just because we aren't exactly human," I added, sensing an accusation. "There's more there. Something that ties us together."

"You're binding yourself to a man, and you have no idea who he is."

I scoffed. "Binding myself? We aren't walking down the aisle, Harry. We're not even living together. I'm barely eighteen." He lifted an eyebrow and started to speak, but I cut him off. "Look, I know Gabe, inside and out. I know his heart and his intentions. Learning someone's history, their interests or pastimes, it doesn't change who they are, just what they like."

Harry sighed again. "I'm not trying to tell you what to do. Things would just be much simpler if you would reconsider what you're doing — or thinking about doing. There are some things that can't be undone, if you know what I mean."

"Harry! It's not like that." I blushed.

He sighed in relief.

"Gabe and I have no permanent plans. We're just taking things one day at a time."

"Permanent means something different in this world than it does in the nymph. You can't ... There are rules, Ashton. Boundaries you can't step outside of. If Gabe wants to keep you safe, he'll respect that." Harry drew a breath. His face carried the familiar expression of trying to monitor his words. "Could you just not write Kevin off? Please. He can protect you from the Naiad's rules. Take some time, don't do anything rash, and consider the life you're giving up. You're still young — much younger than Gabe. There's a lot you don't know."

"Then please tell me, Harry." I threw my hands up. "Tell me what I don't know! Tell me why choosing your soul mate is somehow operating under flawed judgment?"

Harry's eyes fell. He swirled the coffee around in his mug and took a slow sip, his silence speaking volumes. "Look, I apologize. I don't mean to come down on you and make it seem as if I don't like Gabe," he said, and I scoffed. "I'm telling you the truth, Ashton. I just want what's best. There's so much to learn about life and keeping yourself safe. Throw in Charlie's wishes for you here, and it gets sticky."

My thoughts blurred with thoughts of nymphs and humans, businesses and employees. Panic swept around me, nearly taking my breath away. "I can't do this, Harry. I don't know anything about running a company. I can't even balance a checkbook. I don't fit it anywhere. I'm a mythical half-Naiad destined to live the rest of my life in hiding!"

"Time-out, kid! I'm going to keep everything on the level. The business, I can manage for the time being. We'll work around the half-Naiad/hiding part. Trust me. I know exactly what I'm doing." His mouth curled into an assured smile.

I took a deep breath. "You're right. You can handle the business and the properties. I'm safe here. You and Gabe know how to keep me out of trouble." I looked up and smiled ruefully. "I know you'll take care of it."

Harry wrapped an arm around my shoulders and gave a squeeze. "It's all going to work out beautifully. Just wait and see. This time next week, everything will look different."

I nodded.

"What's on your agenda then?" Harry asked, but I didn't get a chance to answer.

Gabe rounded the corner of the veranda and jogged up the stairs.

"Good morning, Gracie." Gabe kissed the back of my hand before turning his attention to Harry beside me. "Harry."

Harry nodded by way of greeting.

"Well, I guess I'd better get a move on. A lot to do today and it seems I have a few phone calls to make." Harry stood and ambled to the stairs. "Think about what I said, Ashton. You have more authority now. Apply it wisely."

Gabe claimed the space next to me and wrapped his arm around my shoulder. He pushed off on the ground, setting the swing in motion. "What was that about?"

I hesitated, not wanting to share Harry's recommendation of dumping Gabe. "He was just notifying me of my new responsibility as the sole owner of Charlie's company, investments, assets, you name it." I looked up with a playful expression. "You're now holding a very powerful girl."

Gabe smiled and ran his finger the length of my jaw. "Yes, I am. Though it has absolutely nothing to do with your capital or your corporations," he whispered, his lips lightly brushing back and forth across the skin of my throat.

I drew a tremulous breath. I definitely wasn't the most powerful person in this scenario. "So you say," I teased. "You're just using me for my money, aren't you?"

"Money is fleeting." He began another pass across my neck. "I have little need for funds … but lots of need for you."

I tried to think about that, but his mouth was working its way upward. The spinning made it all but impossible for my brain to form thoughts outside of my desire for him. Finally, I tucked my hands around his face and brought it to mine. The turquoise of his eyes was lost to dilated pupils. Our lips met and for that brief moment, nothing else mattered. Not Harry or anything he'd said, not my newfound wealth or responsibility. Nothing was important outside of Gabe and the passion he stirred inside of me.

My hands slid along his muscled chest, gripping the fabric there in a worthless attempt to control their ventures. Gabe's hand slid down my ribcage, tracing over my hip, and settled along my thigh. I gasped as his fingers wrapped behind my knee, and he pulled one leg over his. Our breath intermingled, his intoxicating scent sending me spiraling into a logic-deprived longing.

My palms slid beneath the fabric of Gabe's shirt, exploring rise and fall of firm muscle. He shivered and pulled me onto his lap. I moaned as his teeth grazed my bottom lip and tried to pull the quilt away, but Gabe caught my wrists.

"Not now, love," he mumbled weakly and began to distance himself.

My arms snaked around his neck, and I leaned forward to press my lips beneath his jaw. "I wasn't doing anything," I whispered, my mouth skimming his ear. "Just being friendly."

Gabe's quick breaths fanned against my shoulder. His steady grip squeezed around my ribs, somewhere between the motion of pushing me away or pulling me closer. Gabe's fingers tightened, and I anticipated the victory. To my surprise, he pushed me back.

"Not now," he repeated with more commitment. I huffed and fell against the swing, a frown etched in my face.

"I wasn't going to do anything, Gabe," I spouted. "We're on the stupid porch, in broad daylight for crying out loud."

An entertained grin played around his flushed lips. "You're cute when you're frustrated."

I rolled my eyes, not sharing his sentiment. I wasn't feeling cute by any means.

"Ash, it gets harder and harder to say no to you."

"Then why bother?" I crossed my arms.

Gabe leveled a disapproving expression. "We have all the time in the world, love. I can't coerce you into binding yourself to me. There's other stuff to take care of."

What was with all this binding nonsense?

Harry appeared at the back door and looked our way. "Ashton," he called, capturing my attention. "Breakfast is on the table."

"Come on." I sighed on a smile. "Nothing fun to do out here, we might as well head inside."

Gabe stood and pulled me to him. He tucked a stray curl behind my ear, his hand lingering as he leaned in, his voice low. "I'd love nothing more than to demonstrate the many ways you're mistaken," he began. I felt his lips curve into a smile as he nipped my earlobe. "But I don't think that would be a wise decision at the moment."

Gabe backed away on a wink then pulled me toward the kitchen.

After breakfast, Harry left to take care of some business. Gabe and I wandered through Charlie's palatial three-story house, exploring rooms long since visited and uncovering more of what my life could have been like had we been a normal family.

"Gabe?" I began as we roamed through the library. "What was my mother like?"

His hand paused on an overflowing shelf near the window, and he turned to face me. "She was very much like you," he said and then gave me a playful smile. "Though slightly less stubborn."

I stuck my tongue out, and Gabe laughed.

"What do you remember most about her?" I asked.

"Everything for that matter," he said. "Nymphs never forget. But the thing I appreciated the most was her laughter. She lived as if she didn't have a care in the world. Edlyn saw the best in people." His eyebrows lowered. "That was both her most noble quality and her downfall. She chose to live as if everyone had some redeeming trait, and it only took the love of one person to bring it out."

"Finding the best in someone is a bad thing?"

"Of course not. Searching out the best is never wrong. One can never be entirely good, but I'm not so sure they can't be entirely bad. All the world has shadows, but there are some places the light simply can't reach. Edlyn's fault lay in her believing otherwise." Gabe drew a breath and met my eyes. "Do you think that's the wrong mindset?"

I considered his question. Everyone had faults; Gabe was right about that. But can a person be beyond saving?

"I don't know," I answered honestly. "I'd like to think there's a measure of good to everyone, but I haven't seen what you have. I haven't lived through it."

Gabe's mouth pulled into a soft smile. "If I learned anything from Edlyn, it's the same lesson you teach me as well: Have compassion for all and grow from experience."

I laughed without humor. "I can hardly teach anyone about compassion or growing. Or has the impossible happened, and you've forgotten my story about Allie?" Thoughts of my behavior toward Charlie and the trouble I'd caused in the past filed through my head like a suspect lineup.

"Don't be so hard on yourself, Gracie." Gabe's hands settled around my waist. "You have every right to be upset with what's happened in your life. To make matters more complicated, you've recently discovered you're not human and of all the things expected of you. But you aren't bitter and resentful. You take what life's handed you, and you make it work. That's what I admire most about you."

"Thank you." I smiled and stretched up on my tiptoes to meet his lips.

Gabe and I spent the remainder of the day lounging inside the house, passing the time with trivial stories about my life up till our meeting — leaving out the bits about Kevin. Guilt gnawed at my insides for not broaching the matter given the opportunity, but I had no idea what to say, and honestly, I was just too chicken either way. By the time bedtime rolled around, my stomach felt like I'd swallowed a broken glass.

"Are you feeling well?" Gabe asked as he walked me to my room. "You've been quiet since we talked."

"Sure. I'm fine. Just tired, I guess." I paused with my hand on the knob and met his worried gaze. The shame amplified.

Gabe nodded and pressed a kiss to my forehead. "If you need me, you know where I'll be." He smiled softly. "Goodnight, Gracie."

Chapter Fourteen
Taken

I wrestled with sleep that night. Images of gray eyes and wicked smiles filled my dreams. Finally, I gave up and switched on the bedside lamp. The clock over the mantle chimed five-thirty in the morning. With a sigh, I slipped into a bath robe and crept downstairs.

The double doors to Charlie's office stood open. Soft light from various electronics blinked on his hutch. The smell of pipe tobacco and peppermint lingered in the room, setting my heart aching. A studded leather chair rested behind his desk, the material faded and worn with age. Stepping through the doorway, I turned a lamp on and caught sight of a laptop.

Taking a seat behind the desk, I opened the lid and connected to the internet. I clicked on Kevin's address. I needed to let him know what was going on before he did something drastic. A cruel smile touched my lips at the thought of simply typing "It's over" in the subject line. The smile slipped from my face imagining of the reaction that would cause. I couldn't do that. I needed to confront him face-to-face.

Hey, I'll be gone another week, but we need to talk when I get back, I typed, leaving out any formalities.

My shoulders tensed as I read the message several times to be sure I didn't leave a window for any misunderstanding. The last thing I needed was for Kevin to show up here. I clicked the send button before I could change my mind, and flipped back to the inbox. A half-dozen emails from Kyle filled the upper half, all with similar messages in the subject line.

Checking in.
Hey, Monet. Any new news?

Where are you?
Is everything okay?
Seriously, I'm getting worried.
Ashton, call me, please!

I needed to call him today. Kyle was such a worry wart. I should've contacted him as soon as we got here, but I didn't want to draw Gabe's attention to that situation. Kyle didn't deserve to stress over me.

A new message popped up in my inbox. I held my breath then frowned. It was from Kevin. I glanced at the time. What was he doing sitting by the computer? It was 3 AM in California. My hands shook as I clicked on his reply.

We will have a discussion. You can be sure of that.

Heat flooded my face as adrenaline kicked in. How on earth had I let it come to this?

"Morning, love. What are you doing up so early?" Gabe's voice sounded from behind me. I reflexively slammed the laptop closed. I swiveled around in my seat, and his eyes narrowed as I stood up quickly.

"Are you all right?" Gabe studied my expression, his eyes falling on my flushed cheeks.

"Yeah, I'm fine. You scared me, that's all." I hurried from the office, trying to distract him from the computer. Gabe followed me into the kitchen and propped himself against the counter. He crossed his arms and studied my harried movement.

"You want some breakfast?" I rummaged through the cabinets in search of a skillet.

"Ashton?" He continued to watch me.

I ignored him and opened the pantry door, hoping to hide behind it.

"Ashton." The door closed firmly, Gabe's hand pinning it to the frame. "Would you please stop flitting around and look at me."

I drew a quiet breath and forced a smile. "Yeah?"

"What's going on?" His eyes searched mine.

"Nothing is..." I paused, not wanting to lie. "I'm just feeling a little strapped right now. You know?"

"If there's something you need to tell me, you should do it now." He sounded suspicious. Or maybe my guilt made him sound that way to me. "Is there anything you want to share?"

I hesitated. I didn't mean to, but it was enough to give me away despite my words. "Nope. There's nothing I want to share."

His hand fell and he backed away, hurt clear in his eyes. Seeing the pain I caused him, guilt swelled inside. I stared through the window, willing the truth about Kevin to be told whether I wanted it or not.

"Okay, yeah, I do need—" My sentence cut short as I caught sight of Harry walking toward the mailbox. What was he doing out there at sunrise?

Gabe stood at the next window down, staring toward Harry like me. I looked at him with question before turning my gaze back outside. The sound of an engine racing pulled our attention to a black SUV screaming down the street. Tires squealed to a stop next to Harry. Panic rose up, and I banged on the glass.

"Harry!" I yelled, but he didn't turn.

Two large men dressed in black hoodies jumped from the SUV and grabbed him. One of the men wrapped a white cloth over Harry's nose and mouth and pulled him into their truck before peeling out of sight.

"Harry!" I screamed and stumbled around the table. "Gabe!"

"Stay inside!" he commanded, already out the front door.

I hurried to the porch overlooking the now empty street. The acrid smell of burnt rubber stung my nose. Gabe, like the SUV, was nowhere to be seen. I paced the cobblestone around the side of the house, anxiety suffocating me. I didn't know what to do. I couldn't call the cops, not if it was something more than human going on.

Without thinking, I set off on foot down the hill to the main highway, each step more frantic than the last. "Gabe?" I called as I crossed a bridge. I stopped on the other side, listening for any sign.

"Here!" Someone whispered from the tree line.

"Gabe, is that you?" I inched toward the forest, searching the shadows.

"Shh, come on. This way," the whisper said.

I scanned the empty town behind me. Not a car or person in sight.

The dense mountains swallowed me in a matter of seconds as I entered the trees. Dew soaked through my socks, and the smell of wet moss and rotting bark wafted through the chilled morning air.

"Where are you?" I searched the darkness, an unease beginning to grow inside. I turned to look for the road, and fear enveloped me like the morning fog. It wasn't there. My breathing spiked as I took a step back, nearly tripping over a fallen log, then set off in a sprint the way I'd come.

Sunlight flickered through the wind-blown branches and sliced across the forest floor. Thistles and thorns tore at my arms and legs as I fought my way through the heavy branches and dense undergrowth. Where was the road? Was I even running the right way?

Rustling footsteps sounded behind me. I bit back a panicked whimper and pushed my muscles harder. The sound grew louder, accompanied by a frustrated grunt. This time, I couldn't bite back my fear. Something brushed my back, and I let out a cry before racing blindly ahead.

The sounds of the river flowing pulled my focus back. I pushed my legs with everything in me toward the water. Whoever, or whatever, was behind me had better know how to swim.

My lungs ached for the air I couldn't pull in fast enough, and my legs felt like boiled rubber, but I pushed them on. Finally, a faint light shone in the distance. My feet skidded across the wet grass as I came to sudden stop, twenty feet above the river. I looked over the edge and back toward the shadows. There was no knowing if the water was deep enough, but I didn't have time to debate my options.

My sharp cry pierced the morning air before the rush of the river filled my ears. The slick rocky bottom skimmed my feet as I pushed off and kicked toward the air. A brief sense of relief washed over me that I hadn't broken my legs.

Breaking the surface, I stared toward the rising sun to see the broad silhouette of a hooded man against the forest. He made no attempt to follow as I swam to the opposite bank, but his hostility radiated through me. Climbing ashore, I peered around and realized I'd circled the woods behind Charlie's house. I wrestled my socks off and clamored over the back wall, hurrying up the stairs beside the veranda.

"Ashton!" Gabe rushed from the sitting room, wrapping his arms around me. "Thank God you're safe."

I nodded and let him pull me closer.

"I told you not to leave the house." Gabe backed away, really taking me in for the first time. His eyebrows lowered as he studied my wet clothes, breathlessness, and various scrapes and bruises.

"What happened?" Fear and anger burned in his voice.

My eyes filled with tears. I bit down on my lip to stop the quivering. "Someone chased me. I thought it was you out there."

Gabe pulled me into him, his embrace tight and protective. "I'm sorry. I shouldn't have left you here. I don't know what I was thinking."

"Harry." My voice broke as I choked back a sob.

"Don't worry." Gabe's shoulders tensed. "We'll figure something out."

"Gabe—"

"I know, love." He sighed. "Let's get you some dry clothes and clean up these cuts."

I followed him upstairs. Gabe flipped the switch on in my bedroom and froze in the doorway.

"What?" I pushed past him and saw a piece of yellowed paper lying on the pillow of my recently made bed. My body suddenly went cold.

Gabe reached around me and lifted the note, his eyes frantically scanning the words.

"What is it?" I asked, dread filling my tone.

The skin over his knuckles whitened as the paper crunched inside his fist. "It's them. They found us."

I yanked the note from Gabe's hand, trying to steady my own enough to make out the writing.

Dearest Ashton and 'Gabe,'

I regret to inform you that you are too late. However, I commend you on your efforts. Ashton, I have taken your uncle as means of ensuring payment to my debtors. My apologies, Ruarc, for luring you into this chaos. Nothing personal, it just seems that you're always in the wrong place at the wrong time — or in times past, the right place at the wrong time.

In the meantime, Ruarc, I expect that you will be compliant with our demands. Seeing how much you typically love the women in your life, I'm sure you will.

I have enclosed a map for Ashton to follow. It is the forest after all, I'm sure you both will keep that in mind; you do have quite a long way to travel. I anticipate your arrival, Ashton. Do not keep us waiting.

Until we meet again,
Leith

"Leith? My mother's uncle who betrayed our family? What do we do?" My fingers ached with the viselike grip I had around Gabe's arm.

"We do nothing. I'm going after Harry. Alone."

"No, you're not." I squared my shoulders.

"Ashton, you cannot come with me." A muscle worked in his jaw.

"I'm not letting you go alone," I spouted. "They want me. I can end this."

"And what, you think I should just lead you to the lion's den?" he demanded sharply.

"They have Harry. They won't let you get away with this. It's ridiculous to think there's any hope if you go alone. I can't lose you like that. I won't!" I could see the logic working on him, but he still fought it.

"This isn't just about you," I spoke, trying to sound calmer than I felt. "In fact, it has little to nothing to do with you. Leith told me to come. I won't let Harry suffer over something that is all my fault."

All my fault, I thought. It's always my fault.

The walls and furniture around me contorted. I dropped to the bed with my head in my hands. Gabe sat beside me, his arms around my shoulders as I blubbered about my seeming curse.

"This is not your fault," Gabe said. "You can't fix everything, love. There's nothing you did to cause it or anything you could've done to prevent it. Things happen all the time. In our world there or in our world here." He lifted my chin to look me in the eye. "You cannot blame yourself for something you had no hand in. This started even before your mother's time."

"It doesn't change anything." I huffed. "They still want me. It's irrelevant who started it. What's important is that I can end it."

"I can't let you go." His fingers tightened around my arms.

"You have to. It's the only way," I spoke firmly.

A plague of emotion flashed across his face. Fear of what could happen if he agreed to my demand. Dread of what would happen if he attempted this by himself. And finally, a tiny shred of uncertain hope of what might happen if we worked together.

His determination wavered. "If you're going with me you will have to agree to trust me and do whatever I ask without question. Will you do that? Or rather, I should ask can you do that?" he amended, understanding the way I function all too well.

I peered back at him, cautious to consent to such a hefty demand. I had no doubts that he would do what he thought was best for me. But would his idea of what's best really be the best?

"I trust you," I said without painting myself into a corner.

Gabe lifted my chin and eyed me. I tried to look away but he wasn't having that. "Ashton, I'm serious about this. You don't know..."

"Know what?"

"Why all of this is happening. You have no idea who Leith truly is or why he would even take Harry to get to you."

I swallowed hard and shook my head.

"Aren't you wondering why any of this matters if your family is gone, and you aren't human enough for it to make a difference that you know? Why Leith wants you and no one else?"

"Well, yeah, but there's just been so much going on," I said, trying to excuse my shortsightedness. I had never asked myself why I seemed to be doomed to calamity, I simply accepted the fact that I was.

Why?

Charlie was gone. It had to have something to do with Oren, Leith, my mother and Darach. Their names looped through my mind over and over as Gabe paced my room, grabbing anything he deemed useful and shoved it in a bag. How did they tie in? What was the connection?

Gabe paused in front of me, his expression torn. "Do you remember what I told you about rules, laws, and how those things have an order in our world, especially regarding the royal families?"

"Yes."

"You remember what I said about Edlyn being next in line." This wasn't a question.

He never finished the story of my mother's intended fate. I never asked.

"But you said Oren didn't want to kill me, just that he needs me."

"She was next in line," he repeated once more, his voice gruff.

"In line for what?" The question hung heavy in the air.

Gabe's eyes finally met mine. "To marry."

Chapter Fifteen
The Truth

"I'm supposed to marry him?"

Gabe nodded, confirming a destiny that would outshadow death by an immeasurable margin. "If you join the Dryads, they will be effectively marrying into the most powerful family in the Naiad realm. That would result in a great deal of influence, which is exactly what Darach wants most. Power."

"No." I shook my head firmly. "I will have a say in my future, Gabe. And I'll marry who I want. I'm not a political pawn in some world I've never known. Aside from Harry, it's obvious none of my nymph family cared one way or the other."

"Ash," he began.

"You aren't responsible for me. This is my choice. I get to pick my life, not them."

Gabe closed his eyes, grief lingering in the lines of his forehead.

"No more." I backed away, resolved. "I can't let you agonize over this. I'll do what you ask me without question, but I have to go. It will be a catastrophe if you show up alone. You won't even get the opportunity to see Harry." I sighed. My commitment made, I couldn't withdraw the words if I wanted to — and I was confident the moment would come that I would want to do just that.

"You have to listen to me, Ashton. If I think for even a second you're trying something, I'll take you away myself. I want to save Harry, but I love you. I'll always choose you. Do you understand?"

I nodded.

"Let's get going then. We're wasting daylight." Gabe sighed.

After I changed, we hurried outside. Gabe opened the passenger door on the BMW for me then loaded the car. He sprinted around the front, climbed in, and fastened his seat belt. The smell of burnt rubber filled the car as we tore out of the driveway.

Broken stoplights swung in the breeze as we hit Main Street. I tried to avoid thoughts of Harry or the future and focused my attention outside. We flew through the tiny barren town full of antiquated buildings and boarded up storefronts. The emptiness seemed fitting somehow.

"Where are we headed now?" I asked, lifting the unfamiliar map to study the diagram.

"Southern Tennessee." Gabe rounded the corner and picked up the pace on the main highway. "We'll get as close as we can before we have to take to the water."

"What do you mean?"

"It's the safest way to travel. We'll swim downstream until we get close to the cave on the map."

We drove most of the afternoon, only stopping for gas and water. Turning off the highway, the side road grew rocky under the tires. We dipped and slid our way into unfamiliar woods, my sleek sports car no match for Mother Nature. Gabe groaned under his breath as we hit something solid and lunged to a stop.

"It looks like we go on foot from here." He climbed out, grabbed a few items from the trunk, and stuffed them in his cargo pockets. "We need to put in some distance before dark. Would you hand me the letter?"

I offered him everything, and he stretched the map across the hood. I looked over his shoulder but couldn't read the words. They were sketched in the same language as the writing on the jewelry. The handwriting was different though, more erratic.

"So, where is this place?" I asked.

He positioned the map and studied the detailed diagram. "That way." He gestured upstream where a small river flowed from between two peaks. "There's a cave. The map says the second marker is there."

He zipped the paper into a waterproof pouch with the other items then stuffed them into his pockets as we made for the river. Gabe pulled his ragged thermal shirt off and knotted it around his belt. "Are you ready?"

I sucked in a deep breath as the light glistened off his sun-kissed skin. "Not in the slightest."

"Let's go then." His smile turned to tentative excitement, and he dove into the river.

I followed Gabe's lead and made an eager leap toward him. The water caressed my skin like rose petals, drawing a satisfied moan from me. Gabe watched me closely, an eyebrow raised and a mischievous smile on his face.

"We'll stay well below the surface," he explained. "We don't want to risk being seen. Wearing the backpacks will make moving tougher. I don't know how swimming will play out for you, so stay behind me. I'll keep an eye out for any signs of trouble."

I nodded, trying to listen over the delightful sensation surrounding me.

Gabe sank twenty feet beneath the water. Pulling in a lungful of oxygen, I fought against my backpack to follow him. He moved easily, swimming a body length in front of me. I admired the fluency of his action, each movement efficient and productive. I floundered after him, taken by the feel around me and my ability to see him clearly through the murk.

Gabe reminded me of a dolphin as he swam. He twisted and spun through the water, like a fish at play. Fear of getting tangled in some fisherman's line or looking like a floundering idiot kept me moving at a steady pace.

The river hummed with life. Vibrations of things above and below assaulted my senses. I tried to focus, but so many things demanded my attention. A rhythmic splash above pulled my eyes upward. A pair of red and yellow kayaks paddled overhead. The slice of oars cut through the water in the opposite direction, the raucous laughter of the boaters drumming below the surface.

Noisy humans.

My mind didn't boggle at the term now the way I thought it should have. It seemed almost normal somehow, appropriate. A sense of pride swelled in me, feeling like maybe I'd finally found my place in life.

Hours into the swim, the filtered light gradually gave way to shadows. Gabe paused below a bridge and motioned for me to surface with him. His face lit up as I closed the distance.

"What is it?" I whispered just loud enough for him to hear.

"You did so well, love. How do you feel?"

"I feel great. Do we have more swimming tonight?" I asked, enthused at the thought of testing my limitations.

"I don't think that would be wise with the weather." Gabe's eyes searched the graying sky then wrestled his shirt over his chest. "Feels like a storm is going to hit."

Thunder rumbled in the distance, and the smell of rain loomed on the horizon. It seemed Gabe was right. He led us to a narrow tributary leading into the bank of the river. I kept slipping on the rocks and slowing us down. One deep place in particular caught me by surprise as I sank to my chest without warning then toppled over.

"Steady there, Gracie." Gabe fished me out of the deep end using the strap of my bag. I grunted and slid on something slimy.

Gabe bit back a chuckle as I muttered under my breath and wrestled the snarled mop of hair from my eyes.

"It's not funny." I half scowled. "I can't move around like you do. The whole river bottom is a deathtrap. I liked swimming."

Gabe looked on as I struggled through a muddy area, his mouth flirting with a smile. Finally, my foot went into the mud and didn't come out.

"I'm stuck," I said on a sigh, trying very hard not to grumble. Gabe kept his expression level as he bent down to extract my shoe from beneath the muck. His fingers slid down my calf, to my ankle. My breathing hitched as his free hand rested on my hip for support. The heat of his palm warmed the skin beneath my shorts, causing me to forget about our predicament.

He gave a stiff tug, and my foot came loose with smack, sending us both tumbling toward the bank. Gabe hit the grass with me on top of him, arms and legs tangled. I tried to stand, but my wet clothes and heavy backpack threw me off balance, leaving me to thrash about uselessly.

I looked to Gabe for help, but his arm locked around my waist, pinning my muddy body to his. The hungry look in his eyes caught me off guard. His other hand fell slowly, tracing the lines of my neck and shoulder, sliding to my ribs and down to my waist. I sucked in a breath as it paused on the small of my back and drew me tighter. Gabe shifted his weight, pulling his bag over his shoulder, and moved over me. He leaned in, his mouth so close I could feel the heat.

"Ashton," he whispered against my lips, almost a plea, and I was lost.

The kiss moved from gentle to needy. His lips parted, and the scent of him filled my lungs. My arms wound around his neck, fingers weaving into his hair as his hands roamed the length of my body. Warm lips blazed across my neck, exploring every curve of soft skin there. His hand swept around my leg, hitching it over his thigh as he shifted us to a sitting position.

Gabe's mouth traveled back to mine, and I pulled myself higher. I couldn't fathom how we could be any closer than we were, but I struggled to accomplish it. Gabe lifted me off the ground, my legs wrapped around his waist. Our lips never disjoining, I realized we were moving but couldn't find it in me to acknowledge why.

Something soft and springy sank beneath me, Gabe hovering just above. My hands trailed down the hard muscle of his arms, tracing the ridges along his stomach, and slid beneath the fabric of his shirt. In one swift motion, the material disappeared leaving me breathless. A peal of thunder roared through the air at the same time a bolt of lightning cracked like a whip.

"Mmm," Gabe moaned as my fingers danced over his bare chest. I toyed with the catch on my shirt, and his hands moved over mine.

"Stop," he breathed. I shook my head and pulled him back to me, holding him close with every part of my being.

"Ashton, please," he pleaded. "I ... I need you to stop."

I stilled my lips and clenched my hands into fists, willing my body to let him go.

Gabe moved away, breathing deeply as he pushed his back against a wall.

Another roll of thunder rumbled through unseen clouds.

"We're inside?" I struggled to figure out how we'd gotten here.

"It started raining." Gabe half-smiled, his posture still restrained as he looked away from me.

"You'd think I would've noticed that."

"Perhaps, but you were occupied otherwise."

"This is true." I gazed longingly at Gabe before forcing myself upright. "Should we keep moving?"

"We need to wait out the storm for now. Besides that, it's late and you should sleep. We're safe for tonight."

"But what if they come looking for us here?" My teeth sank into my lip.

"They won't look for us, love. We're going to them. Besides that, this isn't the cave. See?" He lifted a flashlight from the waterproof pouch and shone it around the space. The walls glistened black under the beam. I was no cave expert, but it appeared we were in an abandoned coalmine.

"Amazing, isn't it?" Gabe's voice echoed off the chiseled walls. "It's fascinating how humans can excavate something like this. Can you imagine working inside a mountain all day? And not just inside, but miles inside."

I swallowed hard and unconsciously edged back toward the mouth of the mine. The thought of being closed up, trapped by the hillside, sent me into arrhythmias.

Gabe moved behind me, wrapping his arms around my waist. "You should try and rest, love."

I laughed once and dropped the back of my head against his chest. Sleep was the furthest thing from my mind. Frustration crept back in as I thought about Gabe ending our moment too soon.

"Don't I do anything to you at all?" I huffed.

Gabe's fingers curled into the hem of my shirt, and his lips brushed across the back of my neck. "You have no idea." He backed away with a moan.

I turned around, my hands on my hips. "Liar."

"Am I?" he challenged, arching a brow.

"You're the one who said stop." I rolled my eyes.

"Simply because I'm not going to do anything tonight — not that I don't want to," Gabe clarified. "There's a substantial difference."

My expression remained unchanged as Gabe moved to stand in front of me. He tilted his head to the side, meeting my gaze. His eyes looked like the ocean on fire. How was that possible?

"Don't look at me like that," I complained. "You know it's not fair."

My teeth captured my lip, and Gabe sighed.

"Don't you want to be with me?" My finger traced a path down his chiseled torso. His breaths came quicker.

"Yes." He held my face between his hands, refusing to let me escape his gaze. "You drive me crazy."

"Then what?" I asked.

"I want you in every way imaginable," he said, his words more caress than a whisper. "But things need to be in order."

"Order?" I echoed.

"Ashton, you don't understand what you've done to me." He sighed, his scent swirling around me once more. "Everything has changed now. I've never felt this way before. You overwhelm me."

Passion stirred inside me, warring with reason and responsibility. Gabe's turquoise eyes burned into mine, swaying my resolve, till finally I gave way to what I knew we both wanted.

My breath came in a gasp as my arms wound around his neck, and I kissed him. Gabe pulled me into his body. My palms roved over his smooth skin, exploring, testing boundaries I wasn't sure were there. Gabe's hands slid along the outside of my hips. He lifted me off the floor, wrapping my legs around his bare waist, and pressed me into the wall.

My head spun with desire to have more, to be closer. Gabe's fingers knotted in them hem of my shirt, waiting for the slightest invitation as his mouth roamed freely over my collarbone.

"I want you," I murmured against his ear. "More than I've ever wanted anything. I want to be yours."

Gabe's hands slid beneath the cotton of my shirt, pausing on my ribcage. "I love you." His lips trembled against my shoulder, working their way upward. "I didn't know it could be like this."

I undid the first few buttons on my shirt, my heart racing so loud I thought he must hear it.

"Have you ever been in love before?" Gabe murmured against my ear.

My fingers stilled, and I stopped breathing.

"Ash?" Gabe paused immediately. He took a step back, his eyes worried, and his breathing still ragged. "What's wrong?"

"N-nothing," I stuttered, my skin growing cold.

Gabe searched my face as guilt washed over me like the river. His eyes narrowed into slits. "You're lying," he panted. Hurt sank in his expression more deeply than I'd ever seen.

"No! Nothing's wrong. I ... I got carried away, and I don't want to rush into this and us regret it later."

Gabe's mouth opened like he was going to say something, but he closed it again. The storm raging outside the mine paled in comparison to the one in it. Silence stretched on, cracking louder than the fiercest bolt of lightning.

"What are you hiding from me?" Gabe spoke through his teeth, his voice tight with wavering control.

"I've never been in love before, if that's what you're wondering." My mind raced with demands of honesty. I sucked in a breath. "But I was once in love with the idea of someone."

"What does that even mean?" He scraped his shirt off the floor and yanked it on. "Does this have something to do with the computer and this morning?"

Don't lie. Don't lie. Don't lie. I tried to say something, but my silence said more than I ever could.

"Are you with someone?" His tone twisted in disbelief.

"It's complicated." I rubbed my forehead.

"Complicated?" His mouth hardened. "Are you with someone else or not?"

"He hasn't officially asked me to marry him, but I didn't—"

"You're engaged?" Gabe's body went rigid.

"No! Well, sort of. I ... I don't know." My eyes brimmed with tears. "I don't love him, Gabe!"

"Have you been with him?" Gabe's skin paled.

"No. I could never be with a guy I didn't love!"

He scoffed. "Of course not. You'd only marry one."

I flinched at his tone.

"I would've never gone through with it." I took a step toward him, but he backed away. "Things have been bad lately." My fingers absentmindedly covered the all but faded bruise on my arm.

"He did this to you?" His voice grew low.

The tears spilled over, and I nodded. "We fought when I left California. Look, I made a stupid and desperate decision. But I swear to you, I don't love him. He doesn't love me. And I've never been with anyone else that way. Before you, I never wanted to. I don't want to lie to you. I know I have already in some sense, but he was a mistake." My voice broke. "I didn't want to lose you, but I didn't know what to say."

Gabe's eyebrows lowered, and he blew out a sigh. "I'm sorry. I shouldn't have snapped at you like that. But I need some time, Ash. We need to calm down. Take a step back. Harry needs us to focus right now. We can discuss this later."

"Okay. I understand." My heart sank.

"You should rest. We have a long day ahead of us tomorrow." Gabe pulled an inflatable pillow from his pocket and blew air into it.

"Sorry about the accommodations. I know it's not the most comfortable." He laid the pillow out for me, but avoided my gaze as I sat down on the mossy area. He walked toward the mouth of the mine.

"Where are you going?" I asked, doubt pulling at my heart.

"I need to check on things. Try and rest." He forced a grim smile.

"Do you need any help?"

"No." His eyes flashed to mine, the effort to calm his voice warring in his expression. "Thank you though. I'll be back soon. Don't wander about. Please."

I lifted an unsure eyebrow.

"It's too easy to get lost or hurt around here." His sad gaze lingered a moment more then he set off into the rain.

I folded myself on the ground. The moon threatened to peak above the trees as the rain slowed to a mist. The minutes ticked by at a painful rate, and still no sign of Gabe. I stood and began pacing. Images of Gabe's reaction to the news of Kevin replayed in my head. What if he couldn't get over this? What if he left now and never came back?

My unease increased with the silence. The clicking cicadas droned in my ears, echoing off the mine walls. Shadows danced in the tree line. My pacing turned frantic. A tall figure moved just at my peripheral vision. I froze as yellow streaked through the darkness. It was too tall to be Gabe and the color was wrong for his eyes. A bear? What if it was mountain lion? I concentrated through the blackness. Nothing there. My imagination was getting away with me.

A sharp crack of snapping underbrush sounded from the nearby fringe of the forest. My vision blurred with fear. Heart pounding, I whipped around to search the woods. Gabe strode between two trees, his eyes twinkling in the darkness. I blew out a sigh and smiled to myself.

Gabe hesitated when he neared me. His right hand tapped anxiously against his leg, breaking rhythm as he brushed his forearm against his mouth in a wiping motion. Gabe gingerly tucked his right elbow into his ribs, moving uncomfortably. In his left hand, he carried a gallon of water.

He didn't say anything as he sat down to my right a couple of feet away and offered me the jug. I took a long drink.

"Where did you find this?" I asked as I handed him the remaining water.

He extended his right hand — the anxious, tapping one — to retrieve the container. His eyebrows rose suddenly, and he tried to pull it back but not before I caught sight of a recent injury swathing the front of his fingers. My mouth fell open. The wounds were still an alarming shade of red. His skin was pleated in odd shapes across his knuckles. Gabe noted my wide-eyes and drew it behind his back.

"What happened?" I gasped and reached for his wounded hand. I pulled his arm toward me. His body turned, revealing more injuries. A long gash marred his left eyebrow, and a contusion had his cheekbone dark and swollen. Blood caked over a split running his lower lip, top to bottom.

"Gabe..." Shock froze me mid-sentence.

"It's nothing really. I just h-hit it." His tongue absentmindedly swept across the inside of his cheek.

"On what?" I pried his arm from behind his back and pulled his chin around. "It looks like you got into a fight with a tree." I brushed dirt and flecks of bark from his hair.

He scoffed, a scowl etched in his forehead.

Gabe tensed as I lifted his hand to my face and brushed my lips across the healing wounds. Warmth colored his expression for a moment before a blank mask settled in its place.

"It's already almost healed." He stood and drew his hand away.

Confusion and heartbreak filled the empty space left when he walked away.

Gabe fashioned a fire pit out of stones, stacking them in a shallow circle, and built a tepee near the opening using the material. I watched as he worked in silence, never allowing more than a fleeting glance in my direction, not even long enough to see the timid smile I offered each time.

Gabe pulled two flint rocks from his pocket and ignited the fire. We sat in grim silence, my eyes flickering to his face as he stared, sometimes glared, into the blaze. An odd fascination encased him as he watched the bits and pieces of trees burn.

I wrapped my arms around my knees and shivered.

"Are you cold?" he asked, his focus fixed straight ahead.

I flinched at the chill in his voice. "I'm fine."

He tossed me his shirt and laid another branch on the fire before going back to glaring at the flame. I wanted to say something, to ask him what he was thinking, why he was so distant, but I pressed my lips together and tried not to upset him any further.

My stomach grumbled, inciting a listless but welcomed response from Gabe. He dipped his hand into his pocket and pulled out a granola bar. I looked with hope that this subtle change in atmosphere would close the distance between us in some way, *any* way. He met my eager eyes for a fleeting second, offered an apology for the lack of a better meal, and tossed the snack to me. I made no attempt to catch it, and it landed at my feet with a soft thud.

An insidious panic began to creep in. The crack of wind howling through the trees carried through me. I tightened Gabe's shirt around my shoulders. His vacant stare flickered toward me. I still didn't know if he could hear my heartbeat — which was battering like a helicopter's rotors — or the short rapid breaths that spiraled me into hyperventilation, but it caught his attention.

"Ash, I'm—" Gabe's mouth froze in an open expression. He searched my expression before dropping his gaze, defeat simmering beneath.

"Please, what's wrong?" Tears prickled in my eyes. "What happened earlier, I ... I should've told you about that before. But it's over with him. Can't you forgive me?"

Gabe hesitated, a cold resolve settling around him. "What's to forgive, right?"

I watched in stunned heartbreak as he backed away and returned to his former position.

"Please, sleep now," he said on a sigh, his tone torn between pleading and exhausted.

I balled up on my side and turned my face away to hide the tears streaking silently down my cheek. The fire crackled, warming my back, but I still felt cold inside.

"It wasn't supposed to happen this way," he murmured.

That was an understatement. How could this happen? Why would fate bring us together only to tear us apart by something so easily fixed? How could things fall into place so effortlessly only to be completely lost? No, I wouldn't let that happen. I wouldn't lose the best part of me to some stupid choice I made.

I thought love could conquer all...

"Gabe?" I tried to keep my voice steady. "Do you think love is ever enough?"

"Enough for what?" he murmured.

"Enough for ... us?"

He scarcely breathed before answering. "Who ever said that love's enough?"

I felt what seemed like should've been an audible splintering in my chest, but my heart continued to throb.

"I'll be outside keeping watch." Gabe's voice echoed from the mine opening before he turned and vanished into the shadows.

The darkness of the moonless night filled the space around me. I tried to reason though Gabe's feelings and behavior, but he wasn't the one keeping secrets. Guilt joined the emptiness and they danced across my soul. Gabe had every right to be angry, but that wasn't what I felt from him.

My mindless worrying finally gave way to exhaustion and I fell asleep, the sounds of a raging tempest filling my dreams.

Chapter Sixteen
Confrontation

A bead of sweat trickled down my neck, tickling my skin. Muggy summer air filled my lungs as light flickered across my eyelids. The sound of echoing footsteps caused me to turn. Gabe stood at the mine opening, staring into the misty forest. My heart ached inside my chest, longing to connect with him. Even now amidst the heat, I felt cold and void.

"We need to get going. You should eat something," Gabe spoke up, his tone somber. Fish hung from a skewer over the makeshift fire. Tears pooled in my eyes, but I turned and started picking at the meal, allowing more to fall to the ground than I placed in my mouth.

We packed up and headed out after eating. The last few miles to the base of the mountain weren't especially difficult as far as the terrain was concerned — the wretched silence was another issue altogether. Gabe only offered to speak or touch when it was required, but the contact never lingered. The stressful minutes ticked away into hours, each one bringing us closer to a place neither of us wanted to be.

The imposing mountain which seemed so far away this morning, now stood at our feet. Gabe found a stony path winding up the side.

"We'll need to climb from here," he said, wiping his palms against his shorts.

I stared toward the peak stretching impossibly high into the sky. "I can't climb that. It's too tall." I shook my head. "You know I don't do so well with heights."

Gabe peered upward, his eyes narrowing in thought. Finally, he sighed and squatted down. "Climb on my back. I can carry you easily enough."

I hesitated. What if I was too heavy? One slip was all it'd take. Gabe turned his face, peeking at me from the corner of his eye. I drew a steadying breath and climbed on, wrapping my arms and legs around him.

Strong fingers found a firm grip on the mountain, and we began to ascend quicker than I imaged possible. Gabe's hands and feet moved at a perfect pace, carrying us smoothly up the rock face. I glanced over my shoulder and gasped. My arms tightened around his torso, my chest hard against his back. Gabe sucked in a breath, and slowed as he turned an ear toward me.

"Are you all right?" he asked, his voice strained.

"Yeah, we're just really high." I breathed against his cheek. He shivered once and returned his focus to climbing. I buried my nose in the crook of his neck and concentrated on the strong scent of warm cedar and rain.

A symphony of crickets and tree frogs echoed throughout the woods as we reached the entrance to the cave. Gabe pulled me from his back, and we stood against the mountain face, stretching our stiff and tired bodies. I craned my neck to see over the ledge and swallowed hard.

"Thanks for carrying me," I said, my voice shaky.

"You're welcome." He gave me a weak smile and turned away. I battled fear and heartache as the weight of the mountain settled on my chest.

Gabe stood to the left of a boulder taller than himself and twice as wide, resting near the mouth of the shadowy opening. With the jarring groan, the boulder rolled and covered the small gap in front of me.

My eyes shifted in question back to Gabe.

"Most people won't climb this high, but just in case. The other opening—" he pointed to the hole he had just covered "—only goes about thirty yards before it dead-ends."

Gabe lifted one of the waterproof pouches from his side pocket and pulled out the two flashlights. He switched them on and handed one to me. "Let's go."

I stepped inside and walked a few feet forward, allowing Gabe to make his entrance. My light glowed to life and washed over the chiseled rock wall. A grating scrape followed by a thud reverberated through the space, causing me to jump. I whipped around to see Gabe sealing off the mouth of the cave.

"What are you doing?" I rushed back and shoved against the boulder.

"We have to seal it up. We can't allow anyone to follow us in here. No one knows about this place."

Cold sweat seeped through my shirt. The air sat heavy in my chest, dusty and choking, causing my eyes to water. I placed my hands on my knees and tried not to pass out.

"Shh. It's all right." Gabe tried to calm me.

"No, it's not. Nothing is all right." My stomach churned, and the raspy breath moving through my lungs came too fast. The emptiness around me began to mingle with the emptiness inside, leaving fear to take over.

Gabe pulled me to his chest. I took a deep breath and leaned into his body. The slight shift caused him to stiffen.

"Please, Gabe. What's wrong?" My voice wavered. "Can't we talk about what happened before? I can't take the silence of you and the cave."

"Later maybe, but not now." He held me at arm's length. "Let's just focus on Harry."

I felt the heartache in my expression as his eyes met mine.

"I have to concentrate on what we're doing. There's a goal and I can't let emotion get in the way of that. I will keep you safe," he vowed, but somehow with remorse.

"That's not what I'm afraid of," I muttered.

Gabe didn't respond. I bit my tongue and continued forward into the unknown.

"Do you know how far it is until the next marker? How will you see it?" I whispered, risking a glance his way.

"I don't know about the distance, but we won't miss it," he said, bitterness seeping into his tone.

The deeper we moved into the mountain, the colder and bleaker the atmosphere became. It hugged me like hopelessness, whispering threats and promises of sorrow. I wrapped my arms together, my palms chafing the bare skin beneath my shoulder.

Gabe untied the gray thermal from his waist and slipped it over my head.

"What's that smell?" I asked minutes later, scrunching my nose.

"What? Do you smell something unusual?" he questioned cautiously.

"Yeah, don't you?" Surely if I could tell something was different, Gabe could have a mile ago. But he shook his head, a troubled look on his previously emotionally-frozen face.

"Describe it for me," he said.

"It's vivid and earthy … distinctive." I frowned into the darkness.

His eyes narrowed. "How?"

I closed my eyes, and inhaled slowly through my nose. My heart sped at the scent. "It's like the sun, leaves, and moss maybe … pine, newly turned soil, wet rock, fruit." My gaze found his once more. "And it's getting stronger. Do you know what it is?"

He avoided my eyes. "Who is it, would be the more appropriate question."

My heart felt like it dropped into my stomach before leaping into my throat. "Who is it?"

"Do you recognize the scent?" he asked.

I shook my head. "It's familiar somehow, but I can't quite place it."

The scent reminded me of times past when I had emotion tied to certain smells, even if I couldn't remember what they meant.

"It could be more than one person then. Their scents could be blending together."

My fingers dug into Gabe's arm. "Darach?" The lump tightened in my throat at the sound of his name.

"I wouldn't think so. I doubt he would come here to meet you, or us." His eyes darted away from mine. "He would stay somewhere safer for now. Royalty, you know."

"How close do you think he, or she maybe, is?" I asked.

"With my sense of smell, I can usually detect something a couple of miles away in the air. Of course, I have nothing to judge it against with yours. I would think it should be comparable — maybe another mile or better than mine."

Without warning, the smell of the cavern shifted. I sucked in a breath. "I smell water."

"The second marker." His voice fell to a whisper.

We rounded a bend in the tunnel. The air cooled as the sound of a waterfall echoed around the space. The falls surged through a deep gully near the roof and into a seemingly bottomless fissure. A halo of light circled fifty feet overhead. The sun played off the water, dancing over the walls in a thousand rainbows.

I breathed in the scent of our surroundings, my mind warring with my senses. Gabe's narrowed eyes scanned the outer lying darkness then he motioned for me to move toward the falls.

Just as I took the first step, Gabe grabbed my wrist and yanked me behind his body. The smell of a forest filled the open space. The fingers of my free hand curled around his bicep. His arm stiffened, and he stood motionless except for the hand that flexed around my arm. I stepped to his side, determined to show my loyalty.

Shadows loomed before us, pausing at the fringe of the darkness just ahead, their upper bodies hidden in the shade. Two cloaked individuals flanked the leader, a third behind him — of course, the blend of scents. I shouldn't have been surprised by their presence, but I was.

"Ruarc, I'm relieved to see you again so soon," the closest shadow spoke, his voice saturated with arrogance and unnervingly familiar.

Gabe's teeth came together with a snap. Hostility rolled off him in waves as his eyes burned with hatred.

"Perhaps my soon-to-be sister-in-law will be a bit nicer," the voice mocked. Gabe's arm tightened around me as his lip curled up into a snarl. The man stepped further into the sunlight as he spoke, illuminating his face. "Good to see you again, Ashton."

I recoiled from his advance, squeezing my body into Gabe's side, hoping to make myself disappear entirely. "Oren."

"I hope you had an interesting trip," he continued in a contemptuous tone.

"That's enough, Oren," Gabe spit through his teeth. "We're here. You can refrain from the pleasantries now."

Oren tsk'd. "So touchy. I was just making conversation, Ruarc. But you're probably right," he paused and eyed Gabe deviously. "I know Darach is quite tired of waiting for his prize — or wife. Thanks for the delivery." Oren grinned as Gabe's face hardened. "You made good on your end of the bargain. I told them you would."

Bargain?

A sick dread washed over me. "Gabe, what's he talking about?"

Gabe's eyes stayed fixed on Oren, hatred etched in his every feature.

"The rest has been taken care of, as agreed," Oren added.

Tears flooded my vision as I stared at Gabe's profile. "He's telling the truth?"

Gabe grimaced.

"What? He didn't tell you?" Oren sneered. "Oh, this is good! His job was as simple as mine. That's why he was sent to find you in the first place. And you thought you meant more to him than a means to an end." His laughter rang with malicious pleasure. "You are way too trusting, Princess."

Gabe pulled me closer to Oren. I dug my heels in and fought to yank my arm away.

"Ashton." Oren took a step forward, one hand extended.

"I'm not going anywhere with you," I spoke through gritted teeth.

Gabe looked back at me. "It's not your choice, Gracie."

I jerked my hand out of his grip. "Don't call me that." My chin quivered, but I held my head high.

Gabe's eyes flashed with hurt before being smothered once again with cold resolve. "Remember your promise."

Tears slid down my cheeks as Gabe backed further away, Oren taking his place beside me.

"Go," Gabe ordered, meeting my eyes with severity.

"No." I swiped at the tears streaming down my face. "That wasn't the deal."

Gabe looked away for minute, and then turned his gaze back to mine. His eyes were bitter, remote … dead. "This ends here," he whispered, though I knew everyone could hear him. "You have to go where you belong, and you belong to Darach."

"I don't believe you." I tugged against Oren's grip. "Not like this. You said—"

"It was an act, Ashton," he snapped, his tone calloused. "You were a job. I told you I was in acquisitions. You were the biggest target yet. I did my part, and now it's over, so go."

The air rushed out of me. A painfully-clear detachment covered Gabe's entire demeanor but more evident and powerful than I had ever seen. It was like I wasn't even there. Pain overwhelmed every other sense. I reached for him, and he shot me a daunting glare.

"Don't," he ordered, a never before seen hatred in his eyes. The color fell from my face. "It's never been enough and will never be."

His words bit like a scorpion's sting, their meaning perfectly clear. The duplicity ran to my core. He turned his back on me and walked away.

"Gabe, no!" My voice echoed off the cavern walls.

His shoulders tensed, and he paused for a moment then rounded a bend, never looking back.

I fought against the thick arms wrapped around my waist, clawing and kicking, trying to escape. A white cloth appeared from behind me and tightened around my nose and mouth. The rock walls swirled as a sweet chemical smell filled my lungs. I didn't fight the blackness that teetered so near; I welcomed it, hoping it would devour me absolutely.

Gabe betrayed me.

Chapter Seventeen
Desperation

Light danced across my eyelids as I floated in and out of consciousness. I tried to reason through the impossible motion around me before finally concluding I was being carried. Muted voices drifted through the darkness, drown out like I was back in the river.

"Clearly you were mistaken." A deep voice close to my ear swam into focus, sounding unimpressed.

"I'm never wrong," a second man said, the rumble of his tone loud against my ear resting on his chest.

"Spare me your overconfidence. No one is that good of an actor." The first sighed.

"I think you're both idiots." Oren's voice sounded near my head.

Hot hands brushed across my face. Disgust coursed through me; I didn't want to be touched. It felt more intimate than it should have.

"How is she?" someone whispered.

"Still no change. Guess we used too much chloroform." Oren laughed.

A frustrated sigh blew my hair across my face.

"I'll let you know when she starts to stir," the man carrying me assured.

My throat felt like sandpaper when I tried to swallow back emotion.

"Gabe," I rasped. My heart ached as I thought about him leaving me. A tear trickled down the side of my face.

"Hey," the one carrying me spoke up. "She's starting to come around. Ashton? Can you hear me?"

"Mmmm," I moaned. My reluctant lids opened into slits. A flood of sunlight blinded me at the same time the warm hand slipped away. Someone moved to stand over me, casting a welcomed shadow over my stinging eyes. I squinted through the brightness, trying to make out faces.

Sturdy arms lowered me to the ground. I lifted my head and swayed, feeling groggy. The thick arm supporting me, shifted to help me stay upright. I cupped my hands around my throbbing skull and squeezed against what felt like a giant crack down the center, hoping to hold the two halves together.

"Hand me the canteen," Oren said. "Here, drink this. If you go dying, Darach might want to kill me. Again." He laughed.

For a second I thought about pouring the water on the ground, but the sloshing sounds overpowered my resolve. I tipped it up and emptied it to the last drop.

Wiping my mouth, I peered around at the enveloping forest and the beings that seemed as big as the trees. The man supporting me studied my expression when I looked back to him.

"I'm Pearse," he said. "If you need anything, you can ask Elon or me." His brows pulled up in the middle as his honey-tinted eyes flickered to the man who stood at his side. The guy at my feet rolled his eyes and gave a dramatic sigh. I got the feeling Elon wasn't especially excited about the arrangement.

A shrouded figure at the outskirts of the trees drew my attention. He was the only one with his hood still up. His body stiffened when he caught me staring, and he turned away.

"Don't mind him. He's quite the wet blanket these days." Pearse shook his head. A stray lock of dark-brown hair drooped over his forehead, and he brushed it back.

"She awake?" Oren's booming voice echoed throughout the forest. Dread seized me as I openly recoiled from the source. "Can she walk?"

"I don't know. She seems pretty weak." Pearse helped me to my feet. My legs felt like Jell-O. Suddenly, my knees gave out, and I toppled backwards. Oren's arms whisked under me, and he held me to his chest with more of an embrace than I liked.

"Hey there, gorgeous." He winked and began walking forward. "How are you feeling?"

I scowled and made a show of pinching my lips together.

"Aw, don't be like that now, darlin'. See, I told you." Oren looked up at the sunny sky. "No rain on our date, 'course it seems you've grown somewhat fond of the water." His nose turned up, his expression accusing. "I guess that's to be expected with you going through the change. Though I'm sure that experience left a bad taste in your mouth, huh?"

A sharp pain constricted in my chest, but there was a hollowness there now — a void where the pain seemed to flood in and settle, smothering and drowning as heaviness pooled inside. I stared forward, fighting the grief that followed the truth.

"That's what I thought." Oren grinned smugly, his stride lengthening as he picked up the pace.

"You hungry?" Oren asked. I didn't respond. "Oh, come on, you gotta be starving. It's been at least two days since you had anything."

Had I been out for two days? I was famished of course but refused to openly admit it. My stomach on the other hand, was in a traitor kind of mood and rumbled loudly, giving me away.

"Right again. Trust me. I'm a lot better than you give me credit." He winked.

"Not likely," I murmured under my breath and glowered toward the blurred wall of trees.

We ran in silence for the better part of the day. The Dryads' speed and agility bothered yet amazed me. They never seemed out of breath. Their knack for running on land was equal to mine in moving through the water, possibly better.

I bit down on my lip and considered the situation. Now that I was here, had they let Harry go? What if the Dryads still held him captive? ...Maybe I was going about this the wrong way. Maybe I should change my tactic, get some information. I might even gain enough knowledge and trust to escape. A wave of desperation engulfed me as I thought about the step following my freedom.

There wasn't one.

I didn't have anything to go back to. My family was gone. I had no idea if my presence meant Harry was going to be freed. And Gabe was … he gave me up.

Thinking of everything brought a sickened frown to my face.

Oren caught my expression and grinned. "What's the matter? Finally realizing I'm right?"

My notion resurfaced. I didn't know if being alone was worthwhile, but anything had to be better than being stuck here. "What if I am?"

His stride faltered. "You trying to be funny?"

A glimmer of arrogant anticipation shone in his ash-gray eyes. I offered Oren a coy smile, hoping it appeared genuine.

"I don't know." I attempted to flirt in spite of my gag reflex. "Maybe you're better than I'm giving you credit for."

He might have been good but he was either A) not perceptive, which was very likely regardless, or B) so narcissistic that he believed everyone would fall into wanting him, which was quite probable, because he was eating this up.

"Maybe I am." He arched an eyebrow.

My lips pursed as I studied him, pretending to consider his statement. Oren stared at my expressive mouth.

"Hmm," he interrupted my thinking with a smile. "I can see where that would be tempting."

A short gasp slipped out as I understood his meaning. The intimate scene between Gabe and me in the forest on the way here filled my memories. My façade quickly fell in horror.

"Guess you'll never know," I murmured through a tight throat.

Oren stopped running and glanced over his shoulder, a wicked expression curving his mouth upward. He lifted me higher and tilted his head down. My pulse shot into the realm of hysteric as his breath fanned across my face.

Laughter rumbled through his chest. "Sorry, didn't mean to get your hopes up."

"Your loss," I whispered, sounding like a fraud even to myself.

"Hey, you never know. Maybe Darach met someone. He's been waiting a really long time for you," Oren hinted. "I might get that chance after all."

The stiff sound of a throat clearing growled behind us.

"Hey, he's alive after all," Oren retorted. His sarcasm was met with silence.

Surprisingly, the narcissist didn't speak again. I risked a fleeting glance at Oren's face. He stared straight forward, all traces of humor removed.

Intriguing.

Time passed by in silence till the low setting sun warranted a break.

"We should make camp for the night," Oren suggested but looked to the cloaked man for approval. He was met with a nod.

Oren left me on the ground in an oak grove clearing. "Don't you move now," he directed with a wink. "We'll rustle up something to eat."

His ego was back. Wonderful.

Oren, Pearse, and Elon dashed off into the woods, leaving me alone with my unknown captor. He reclined against one of the mossy trees, the steady rise and fall of his chest the only movement. The hood of a long dark cloak shielded his face, but his unseen gaze burned a hole through me. His rigid posture hinted that his focus was in my direction, though his body wasn't turned toward me.

My stiff but weak limbs ached to move. I struggled to my feet and arched my back, stretching my arms overhead. A wave of dizziness blurred my vision, and I lost my balance before staggering forward. Two hot hands wrapped around my waist and lifted me up before placing me beneath the tree again.

"You can let go now," I said gruffly, surprised by his speed. I hadn't even seen him move.

He scoffed and let out an irritated sigh.

"Am I bothering you?" A smile tugged at the corners of my mouth.

The man hesitated then shook his head.

I studied him for a moment trying to gain an ounce of understanding before he shifted to turn his back to me. Sitting up, I crossed my legs. My eyes stayed on the mystery man's back as he stared over the clearing, his hands clenched at his sides.

"Why won't you speak to me?" I asked.

His head turned sideways as if he was peeking at me from the corner of his eye. He couldn't see me anymore than I could him. Apparently, this bothered him. He swiveled around once more, his disquietingly thick arms folding across his chest, the hard muscle of his forearms tensing.

A new course of action worked its way through my mind.

"You won't tell me your name?" I asked.

He exhaled gruffly and shook his head once more.

"Would you like me to be quiet then?" I pressed, almost enjoying his discomfort.

To my complete surprise, he shook his head again.

My eyebrows rose in speculation, his action throwing me for a moment. "If you don't want me to be quiet, you're going to have to talk. It's hard to carry on a single-sided conversation. Monologues aren't really my specialty," I harped. "I wouldn't have the slightest idea what to say to you or what to even talk about in general so unless you just want me to—"

The cloaked figure took a deliberate step forward and huffed as he jerked his hood back. "You could've fooled me," he boomed, his beautifully recognizable face annoyed.

Chapter Eighteen
Traitor

"Kyle?" I gasped and shuffled backwards, wedging my back against the trunk of the tree.

"All this time, you can't be quiet for more than five minutes, even when you're irate … especially when you're irate." He threw his hands up and shook his head like he couldn't believe the girl sitting in front of him.

"Wh-what are you…? H-How did…?"

"Really, Ash?" Kyle spoke. "How could you not notice?" He smiled without humor. "Never mind."

My arms wrapped around my knees as I battled with the impossibility that stood in front of me.

"Well, you wanted to talk. Talk. Have at it. I'd just love to hear what you have to say right about now," he almost growled, waving his hand in front of me when I kept quiet.

The silence stretched on with my back pressed into the tree. What was I supposed to say?

Kyle stared at me, his black brows low over his eyes. "Fine, I'll start," he said, running his fingers through his thick hair, his mouth set in a hard line. "You don't seem entirely clueless about all of this. You've been with him though, so I imagine some minimal information has been passed along not that most of it wasn't fabricated."

Kyle stared at me with accusation, and my eyes fell to a patch of daisies behind him. He sat down in front of me, an olive-toned arm resting across the top of his knee, the other falling along the ground. He began tugging at a piece of grass with his free hand.

"Before I tell you anything, answer me this." One brow rose. "What exactly happened with him?"

The tempo of my heart increased, and I held my breath. My lip quivered, and Kyle looked away.

"Can't ever get you to be quiet at home and now you won't even speak to me." Hurt touched his expression. "You should've talked me about this before, Ash. You know you can trust—" His face fell.

My guilt and confusion unnerved me. I discreetly wiped a tear away before Kyle could see it.

Kyle forced a smile. "Kev won't know what to think. I bet he doesn't even recognize you by the time we get there."

"Kevin?" I choked. Why would he be with the Dryads? Did he have something to do with everything happening? I swallowed against the growing panic and prayed my notions were wrong.

"What? You're surprised? Where is your head?" He paused for a split second before scrunching his nose in distaste. "Stupid question. But really, you haven't put two and two together?"

"You're here to save me?" I guessed, knowing I was wrong.

"As if that were option. Kevin is his human name," he murmured, resentment thick in his tone.

"What?" A hollow ringing echoed in my ears. The trees began to sway and blur as blackness teetered on the fringe of my vision. Kyle pushed my head between my knees and ordered me to breathe. Defeat swelled and enveloped my oxygen. I sucked in short bursts of air on the verge of losing it.

This whole time I'd been with Darach? How could I be so stupid? Hot tears streamed down my cheeks.

"Don't cry." Kyle's voice turned pained as he backed away.

"Don't cry?" I whispered, putting my forehead on my knees. "My dad is dead, Gabe left me, my entire life has been one elaborate setup, and now I have to deal with this? What other reaction would you expect from me?"

Kyle scooted a little closer, but didn't touch me. "I'm sorry about Charlie, Ash. I know there's nothing I can say to fix that or anything else, but I've talked with the others. We've agreed not to mention your friend to Kevin." He grimaced. "Nothing's changed as far as he's concerned."

"I love him, Kyle." My voice broke. "That changes everything."

His eyes flickered with pain before they turned cold. "He doesn't love you, Ash. He never did. The sooner you accept that, the better off you'll be."

Kyle's words knifed through me, and the tears subsided, replaced with a bone deep sadness.

"It's for the best, Ash," Kyle said, his tone gruff. "You know Kevin's temper. The rules aren't the same here. Kev would act first and ask questions later, and I'd rather not have a potential war on our hands if we can help it."

The threat in Kyle's words turned my blood cold. "Would Kevin really start a war over me?" My hand slid to cover the last place Kevin marked in his rage. Kyle's eyes followed my movement and hardened.

"Your people mean little to him aside from having you. You're all he wants … and he's used to getting what he wants." Kyle looked away.

The other three reappeared from the woods, their arms full of a variety of fruit, roots, and some unknown meat.

"What's with the sudden indiscretion?" Pearse asked with a mouth full of apple and dropped a few beside me.

"Don't worry about it." Kyle's gruff tone grabbed everyone's attention.

Pearse glanced at my sniveling and back to Kyle who yanked his hood up and stalked to the edge of the clearing. He got a fire going then settled down against a tree further away from me than the others.

The smell of cooked meat wafted through the air as three guys laughed around the fire. Each positioned themselves so that they could see me, but Kyle stayed at the fringes of the clearing, his back to everyone.

Oren ripped the flesh off of a bone with his teeth then grinned at my expression.

"Want a bite?" he asked, a chunk of something falling from his mouth. My lip curled in disgust, and I looked down.

Pearse left the fire and plopped down a few feet away from me. He stuck out his hand, offering me some beef jerky. "It's not so bad there, you know. Home. You'll like it," he insisted. I sighed and concentrated on the ground. "It's a beautiful place. And everyone's excited you're finally coming."

"I'm sure it'll be a delightful prison sentence, thank you," I sneered. The voices around the fire silenced, and Kyle's body shifted, his hood now pointing toward me. I looked away, rubbing the faded bruise on my forearm.

"How long until we get there?" My voice cracked, dread seeping through.

Pearse glanced at Kyle before looking at me again. "Tomorrow."

I turned my body from Pearse. He sighed and reclaimed his spot by the others.

As dusk turned to darkness, the only visible light was from the crackling fire. Oren, Pearse, and Elon pulled rough looking blankets from their rucksacks and spread them across the ground. When no one had thought to bring an extra blanket, Kyle carried his over and laid it out for me.

A gray lump of cloth landed in a heap at my feet. "I couldn't quite wash the stink out of this, but it'll keep you warm tonight," Kyle muttered under his breath then turned and retreated into the shadows.

I lifted the material and my heart churned in my chest. The faint scent of Gabe lingered in the thermal shirt he'd given me in the cave. Slipping my arms through the sleeves, I couldn't help but draw in a breath and wade through painful memories of warm cedar and rain.

I stared at the uninviting pallet Kyle laid out and briefly deliberated its position before towing it away from the fire and everyone around it. Balling up on my side, I wrapped my arms around my legs, longing for more cover. But I wasn't about to give them the satisfaction of anything. It might have been childish, but it felt like surrender to try to be comfortable in any way.

Warm tears streamed freely, leaving enticing paths for the crisp air to sting my cheeks. Sniffling and shivering, I dozed in and out of consciousness. My shoulders finally relaxed when someone placed a cover over top of me, their hands lingering at my back for a brief moment then I surrendered to the warmth.

ॐ ॐ ॐ

The morning sun beat down, roasting me beneath the makeshift blanket. I sat up, sore and rigid from the all the nights of painful accommodations, and stretched. Things popped and cracked loudly into place.

"Oh, perfect!" Kyle grumbled, his ire marred with sleep. "Which one of you slackers dozed off during his shift?"

I smiled a little to myself at being a cause of dissention. I had zero intentions of making things easy for them.

"Psh, take it down a notch, Warden," Oren grumbled. He stood and stretched with a loud yawn. "She wasn't going to do anything. Even if she wanted to, where's she going to go?"

Ouch. My smile melted into a glower. Thanks, Oren.

"Yeah?" Kyle snapped, unusually agitated. "You want to explain to Kev why we lost her? Again." He looked pointedly at Oren as he spoke, standing frighteningly close to his irritated cohort.

"Oh, come on, like you would've done any better! You're the one who wouldn't screw her car up to begin with," Oren accused.

Kyle's eyes flashed to mine then he looked away.

"That stupid hotel didn't even have a valet service, so that wasn't my fault," Oren continued. "And don't even try and peg the parking lot on me!"

I gasped, but Pearse spoke before I could form an intelligible sentence.

"Ah, brotherly love," he teased, deliberately fueling the fire.

"Shut up, Pearse!" Kyle and Oren shouted at the same time.

"Whoa, hang on," I interrupted. "The four of you are brothers?"

Everyone stopped and stared.

Oren stepped forward, a smirk on his face. "No, the five of us are brothers." His gaze fixed on the play of emotion crossing my expression.

Kyle sniffed and muttered something unintelligible.

The light bulb of my reasoning flickered to life. Kevin would be the fifth. "There are five of you?" My tone shot up. "How is that possible? I thought males were uncommon enough, but five in one family?"

"You see how this is a big deal then?" Kyle eyed me, the silent message in them obvious.

Hatred and bitterness washed through me, hardening my expression. I'd lost Gabe, my freedom, my sanity, and possibly Harry all because of the Dryads.

"No, I don't! This is my life, Kyle. I shouldn't be responsible for someone else's selfish decisions or mistakes. It shouldn't fall on my shoulders. How is that fair?" I yanked the cloak off and heaved it in Kyle's face then stormed into the foggy woods.

"Let her go, Elon," Kyle commanded, his voice weary as it faded into the background.

A fine mist floated through the air, enhancing the smell of wet ferns and leaves. I loped aimlessly through the thick undergrowth until my grief caught up with my anger. Curling up against an old mossy log, I let the anguish have me. The hollow space in my chest echoed the grief found in memories of Gabe — his piercing eyes, the scent of him filling every part of me, the way his lips felt against my skin.

I dropped my head against the dead tree beside me and stared into the murky vacant woods, lost in my own bleakness. The smell of the shallow creek winding through the trees encouraged me up. I walked over and bent down to scoop up a mouthful and splash my face. I pushed the long sleeves of Gabe's shirt up and washed the best I could. The crisp water helped to sooth my weary heart.

Suddenly, a soft cool hand snaked around my mouth from behind, silencing my cry.

Chapter Nineteen
Unexpected Company

My heart beat frantically as I tried to jerk away, clawing at the hand covering my face.

"Shh, stop," the hushed soprano voice encouraged. "I'm not going to hurt you. Hopefully, I'm here to help."

I tried to pivot.

"Don't turn around," she warned. "There's no time for explanations. I'm going to try and help you though. We just have to bide our time and wait for an opportunity. I don't know how soon that'll come, so just relax and wait, okay?"

I nodded breathlessly and listened. The girl released her grip, but I didn't turn.

"Play along but don't be easy. Be yourself." She laughed once. "We don't want them looking for anything; that wouldn't do at all."

"Okay," I whispered quickly, trying to figure out who would be here to help me.

"Don't get up yet. Wait a few minutes and let the scent die down. And remember, be patient."

The leaves rustled as a gentle breeze swept through, the girl with it. As quietly as she appeared, she disappeared. I stood up, wading though the disbelief, but remained by the water, heeding her warning. A hint of a smile pulled my mouth up. An unexpected release washed over me with the thought of my mysterious ally. That tiny flicker of hope was all I needed to keep going ... for now.

I stood and made my way back for fear the Dryads might pick up the stranger's scent. It suddenly dawned on me. I couldn't smell her either. Was I losing my ability? I pulled in a long breath. Each of the Dryads scents stood out. What was it that made her different?

"Good thing you didn't try to run." Oren shook out his blanket and packed it away. "Though I do enjoy the hunt."

I rolled my eyes and watched Kyle in my peripheral vision. His eyes lingered on me as everyone broke camp, but I refused to meet his gaze. While losing Gabe scarred me in a way I couldn't even comprehend, having my best friend betray me was just as bad — maybe worse in some ways.

We left the camp, heading south. My mind raced over the conversation with the girl from the woods. I watched the trees, wondering who she was and how she could possibly get me out of this mess.

"Are you walking backwards?" Oren spoke, pulling me from my thinking. "I'd like to move a little faster than a glacial pace."

I tugged Gabe's shirt over my head and tied it around my waist. "If you want to go so bad, why don't you take off," I suggested with a sarcastic smile. "I'd be happy to help any way I can."

"And lose my head? No thanks, Princess. Your wrath is a little less intimidating than Darach's." Oren swept me up and onto his back before I could even blink, let alone oppose. With that, we set off at a frightening speed. Oren smiled over his shoulder when my grip tightened.

The brothers ran till the sun was well past overhead, never pausing or breaking stride. They moved nimbly around the trees, hopping over boulders as if they were no more that bricks in their way. And despite their enormous size, they ran with grace, never making a sound.

A jolt of fear shot through me when we came to an abrupt halt, fearing they had seen or heard someone. Oren's sudden movement slammed my face into his shoulder. I moaned as pain seared through my mouth, and the coppery tang of blood assaulted my taste buds. I ran my tongue over my bottom lip, nursing the gash caused by my teeth.

"What is wrong with you?" Kyle snapped at his brother. He lifted my chin. "You all right?"

I jerked my face away and swallowed against the metallic flavor. "I'm fine."

"Yes, you are," Oren jived. "I think that's the appeal. Now, if you could just learn to be quiet."

"I feel sorry for your mother," I quipped.

"Funny," Oren said then looked to Kyle. "So, should we blindfold her?"

"You know what Oren..." Kyle began, but resigned himself with an exasperated huff. "Nevermind. And no, she doesn't need a blindfold now."

Oren opened his mouth to argue, but Kyle's glare silenced him.

I wasn't used to seeing Kyle angry and resentful. It set my heart aching, missing the light-hearted friend I'd left in California. What could've possibly happened to change him so drastically? And why did he act like I was somehow at fault in this picture?

The sun blazed against my back and the heat from Oren smothered my front. My gritty sweat-soaked shirt clung to my torso and chafed against Oren and my temper. A faint rumble of a waterfall crashed in the distance making my agitation worse. My insides gnawed for the water like an empty stomach.

"It's not too much farther now," Kyle spoke beside me, his eyes on my expression.

The thought of water was like a jolt of electricity to my system. It took all my willpower not to fight Oren's grip and run headlong toward the inviting sound. My legs twitched, and I sighed as the fragrance filled my senses.

Rounding the mountainside, I caught sight of my proverbial unicorn. A towering waterfall cascaded down a sharp precipice into a river below. Sunlight cut through the mist, as it hovered near the base.

Seeing the pool renewed my hope; I might get that chance to escape after all.

Our pace didn't slow as we neared the falls, though Oren's grip tightened around my wrists. Understandable. This was the one place I could get away, even a dolt like Oren could see that.

"Um, we're running out of path," I offered as if they hadn't noticed.

"Thank you, Dr. Obvious. I think I know where I'm going." Oren scoffed.

"Could've fooled me." I threw back at him just to be spiteful.

"She's going to fit in nicely," Pearse teased, casting me a sideways grin.

That shut me up.

Oren slowed as we inched toward the cascade. The edge of the water flowed just a few feet away, leaving nowhere left to go. I peered at Kyle, sure he would answer my question, but he just nodded toward the waterfall.

"Now, Elon," Kyle spoke as we stopped beside the cliff. Elon pulled his backpack off and opened it. He handed Kyle a length of rope and a red strip of cloth.

"What's all this?" I asked as Kyle pulled his pack off and passed it to Oren.

"I can't have you trying to take off." Kyle pulled me from Oren's back to his. "Be good. Don't make this difficult for either of us."

Oren walked around Kyle, grabbed my wrists, and bound them together around Kyle's neck. He wrapped the red cloth around my eyes, securing it with a knot in the back.

"What am I going to do now that I wouldn't have done before, Kyle?" I demanded, provoked by the sudden security.

"I don't want you killing us both," he murmured.

"Oh, well thanks for clearing that up. It's nice to finally understand something for a change." The blindfold was getting to me. I couldn't watch for an opportunity if I couldn't see.

"Please cooperate," Kyle said, holding my arms against his chest.

"Look, I'm not going to know where we are anymore than I already do now. I don't need the blindfold."

"It's to keep me safe. Not you," Kyle said, already beginning to move.

"What? What are you talking about?" I barked. "I swear, Kyle, you make absolutely no sense whatsoever. Why can't you just give me a straight answer, for once?"

Someone huffed beside me. Even blinded, I inclined my head toward the sound, a scowl on my face.

"Geez, man," Oren grumbled. "Now I see what you guys mean about her not being quiet. She seriously won't quit, will she?"

"Shut up, Oren!" I growled. His booming laugh carried over the thunderous roar of the waterfall.

After a minute of silent movement I realized why I had been bound and blinded — we were climbing. I'd have an open view of the landscape, and I imagined the Dryads didn't want me having any clue where we were. At least something made sense, even if it was a bit extreme.

Kyle's arms continued to lift and flex overhead as if I were no more than a human-sized backpack. I shuddered at the thought of Dryad's strength and speed. No one could ever outmatch them on land.

"Something wrong?" Kyle asked, his breath fanning over his shoulder. He wasn't even winded. Who were these people?

"You mean aside from the obvious?" I harped. He stopped moving.

"Monet..." Kyle's voice softened and my throat went tight. The Kyle I'd known and loved for the past eighteen months bled through — the one who'd been my best friend and confidant. The one I hadn't seen since leaving him bewildered in Malibu.

"How could you, Kyle?" My voice broke, but the blindfold caught the renegade tears.

"It wasn't my call, Ash," he murmured. "It's never been mine."

"And you thought acting like a jerk to me would make it all better? I needed you." I dropped my forehead against the back of his neck. "I still need you. I'm all alone in this, Kyle. I can't deal with losing Gabe and you."

His shoulders tensed. "You'll do better not to mention that name anymore."

"Because that'll change anything that's happened?" I scoffed. "I'm not going to pretend like everything's okay, and I'll just get over it with time. I'm not the same flighty girl that fell for your brother."

Kyle sighed. "I don't expect you to put up a front, Ash. But if you don't want to fuel the furnace, you'll keep your memories of what's happened to yourself."

I swallowed hard. "Right.

I felt Kyle's head fall to one side.

"Or until we're alone at the very least," he added with a sigh.

"What's the problem, big brother?" Oren called from above us. "Is her nagging sucking all the oxygen out around you? I can come get her if you want."

"Idiot," Kyle groaned and began moving again.

We finally came to a rest and he squatted down, lifting my numb arms over his head. I wobbled as he set my feet on the ground. My legs were numb but tingly from being bent up for however many hours I'd been carried today. Being blinded certainly didn't help my cause.

"Careful." Kyle steadied me and tugged the blindfold off. After blinking a few times, I looked around and groaned.

"Ugh. I hate caves." My voice echoed in the rocky entrance.

Kyle's mouth turned up. "We're just cutting through. It isn't far."

"Long enough." I glanced longingly over my shoulder toward water.

"Don't even think about it." Kyle lifted a suspecting eyebrow.

"What?" I demanded, crossing my arms.

"You know what. I'm not stupid, Ash." Kyle moved to mimic my action. We stood, identical postures, measuring the other for a beat before everyone else got annoyed.

"Let's go. The sooner we get through here, the sooner this will all be over." Pearse walked toward the blackness. I considered chucking a rock at the back of his head — turn for turn after his snarky comment about fitting in with his family.

Kyle gripped my wrist. For a second I thought he must've seen my rock hurling idea, but he merely grasped the rope, and with one quick motion, my hands were free.

"I don't want to restrain you like that anymore, so be good," he said, his eyes falling to the ring on my index finger.

I tucked my hands in my pockets and nodded.

Firelight flickered off the damp rock, reflecting in the pooling water along the stone floor. Stray drops of condensation fell from the ceiling and tickled down my bare shoulders. The smell of musty air and wet limestone filled the tunnel, settling on the back of my tongue.

Kyle's warmth heated my side as we walked. His closeness wasn't in a guarded way like he was concerned I would run, but almost protective, as if he were trying to keep me from some unseen harm.

"We'll go ahead and prepare everyone for her highness's arrival." Oren winked at me before bounding off with Elon and Pearse.

"Idiot," Kyle and I spoke in unison. He smiled halfheartedly and motioned for me to sit down.

"I'll stand." I shoved my hands in my pockets, not in any mood to bother with politeness. "I may never regain full use of my legs after the past two days."

Kyle smiled even though my frostiness. "I think you'll make a recovery. But I'm sorry about that."

He glanced over his shoulder, his expression torn.

"Why do you look sad?" I asked despite myself.

"I didn't want this for you, Ash. None of it," he began slowly. "You're right. You don't deserve this. You have every right to be happy with the person and life you choose. For what it's worth, I would change it if I could."

I dropped to my knees in front of him. "Then help me," I begged, shameless tears of desperation in my eyes. "Talk to them — talk to Kevin. Tell him to let me go."

"I can't, Ash. There's nothing I can do," he said in defeat. "I've argued my point from every imaginable angle. You were in too deep from the beginning. Then you and Kev actually got together. They won't let you leave now. You're here forever."

"No, not forever," I whispered, "just as long as I live. I hear being miserable shortens your lifespan considerably. What's that leave me? Fifty years? Sixty at most." I contemplated the idea both encouraged and disgusted at the same time.

Kyle stared at me as if I had a terminal illness.

"What?" I asked, dread in my tone.

"You know, right?"

I shook my head.

Kyle appraised my reaction. "Haven't you ever wondered how we've all known each other so long? Why Kev is marrying you now, instead of your m—" He paused. "Well, why you're next in line and he's not old, like he should be?"

A cold sweat beaded over my skin. It all became painfully obvious, no one was aging. Or more appropriately, no one was dying.

"No," I whispered in a crushing defeat. "Maybe it's not for me. I mean, I'm only half ... nymph. I can't be immortal."

"Ash—"

"Don't speak," I ordered. "Don't tell me how sorry you are when you aren't going to do a thing to fix it. Just leave me alone."

I stood up and stormed through the tunnel. Kyle followed silently behind me, allowing my frustration to play itself out. Neither of us spoke until a faint brightness glowed ahead. Kyle caught up to me and grabbed my wrist.

"Sorry." He stepped in front, towing me behind him. I scoffed. "It's not you. I just have to look responsible."

"Whatever, Kyle." My voice echoed my life now, bleak and hollow. "Let's just get this over with. Maybe if I provoke Kevin enough, he'll just kill me himself. That'd probably be fairly easy to pull off given the fact he has a history of hating the women in my family." I grimaced, finishing my thought in a whisper, "There's no one left to care one way or another now anyway."

Kyle jerked me to him and pinned my back against the cave wall, bowing it along the curving rocks. His infuriated face, inches from mine, burned with resentment.

"None of that!" he growled. "Don't you give up. You..." He blew a heavy breath through clenched teeth, his woodsy scent fanning across my face.

Kyle moved a step back but made no attempt to let me go. A new pleading tone painted his voice, "Ash, please, give it some time. Maybe things will change. Maybe it'll be different." He sighed wearily. "Will you please just be good?"

"Be good? You want me to just roll over and—"

Kyle's hand covered my mouth. His eyes bored into me, begging me to understand. "I can't help you if anyone suspects something is wrong," he whispered, his hand falling away.

"I don't promise you anything," I answered roughly, but something about Kyle's words and sudden emotion reminded me of my former optimism. Maybe things could change. One thing had to. "But I refuse to marry your brother. I will promise you that."

Kyle scoffed. "Guess I can't hold you to that, can I?"

"What?"

"Nothing," he said. "Don't worry about it. But you'll be good? You promise that much for now?"

"For now," I agreed, still taken aback by his sudden intensity.

He nodded. His fingers tightened around the shirt at my waist, and he pulled Gabe's thermal off. I reached for him, and he caught my hand.

"Don't worry, I'll give it back," he said sarcastically then shoved it into his rucksack.

Something peculiar shone in his eyes and the way he looked at me. It almost seemed familiar. I tried to identify the emotion he now struggled to conceal.

"Let's go then." He encouraged me forward.

Chapter Twenty
The Valley

Kyle stooped through the mouth of the cave, towing me behind him. Two guards stood on either side of the doorway, their focus fixed ahead as we emerged from the darkness. I shielded my eyes against the sunlight to take in the scene. My breath caught in a gasp.

Walls of the mountain rose up, forming a protective bowl around the expansive vale. The tops of the endless trees covered the valley floor so thickly it looked like you could walk across them. And green. Everything glowed with it.

"Not what you expected, huh?" Kyle grinned.

I looked back at the perfection of The Valley. It was gorgeous though I'd never admit it. But that wasn't enough. Even in all its splendor, it was empty, just like me. Maybe I did belong here.

We followed the narrow stone pathway that wound down the mountain. Wildflowers fanned out across the rock, their sweet fragrance flooding the air around me. A wall of trees sprouting from the cliff-face cast welcomed shadows, cooling the summer air beneath them.

As we neared the base of the trail, I saw what lay underneath the thick mantle. Try as I may, I couldn't stop my mouth before it fell open. Various trees stood about, their low branches laced throughout with lavender and sage colored ribbon. The scent of black current and citrus wafted through the breeze.

Kyle caught my surprise and smiled enticingly. "They're welcoming you," he whispered, knowing that my favorite sights, sounds, and of course scents were being influenced.

"Strange reception." I scoffed. "Did they think I'd be happy about this?"

"As a matter of fact, yes," Kyle stated. "You are with Kevin. And remember, your promise."

"That's not what I meant." I frowned. He rolled his eyes and shook his head.

The music grew louder as we headed into the forest. Sunlight filtered through the dogwoods overhead, casting the forest in a pinkish glow. The ground sank beneath my feet, soft and yielding. Kyle slipped his boots off, stepped onto the silky looking grass and sighed.

"Go ahead." He inclined his head in my direction and motioned for me to remove my shoes as well.

My mouth quirked to the side. "I'm fine thanks."

"Come on," he encouraged with a grin. "I promise you, your feet will thank you for it."

I started to protest but decided it wasn't worth the effort. Slipping out of my flip-flops, I stared at the luscious patch of green for a moment then took a tentative step. The soles of my feet relaxed against the coolness. The blades laced between my toes and tickled my ankles. Warmth spread from my heels up. I gasped at the feeling, not caring that Kyle smiled beside me.

"See? What'd I tell you?" Kyle bounced on his toes, his hands in his pockets.

I refused to agree, but I didn't argue; he was right. My feet felt rejuvenated. The soreness, calluses, and blisters from days of trudging through the wilderness, literally faded away.

"How did it do that?" I asked staring at my unblemished skin.

"It's a secret." He winked. "It works on everything too, not just your feet."

"Is it the grass that does it?"

Kyle shrugged his shoulders. "Pretty much."

Intrigued, I bent down to examine it more closely. While standing upright, it looked like regular grass — green individual blades, very nondescript — but upon closer inspection, I noticed it was something entirely other. The blades were a similar design — long and thin, tapering toward the end — but unlike grass the texture was soft in both directions, like silk.

"We should keep going. Everyone is expecting us." Kyle nudged me.

I sighed and stood. "Who's everyone?"

Kyle pursed his lips. "It varies from time to time. Some are able to travel freely, but the royal family stays put for the most part."

My heart sank. Being a future royal, I wouldn't be leaving The Valley anytime soon. If ever again. If Gabe and I were together, that'd be fine. But the perfection of the forest and seemingly magical grass were nowhere near a consolation prize for an eternal prison sentence.

"Cottages." Kyle gestured to the small houses dotting the woods as we entered the thickest part.

I looked at each of the flawless stone chalets staggered throughout the forest. Brightly colored roses climbed along the trellises as delicate white petals of orange blossoms fluttered in the breeze. Fields of lavender ran between houses and bordered the pathways, filling the air with their delicious fragrance. Trumpet vines sprouted over and around the cottage windows. A pair of squirrels settled above us, chattering back and forth before they scuttled to the next branch in a playful chase.

"A few clearings." Kyle pointed to the west as we turned the opposite direction. "And that continues on to the palace."

"Palace?" I asked. "How do you manage that? Wouldn't it be visible from the sky?"

"Nah, the magic keeps planes away." He shrugged, his hands in his pockets

"You have magic?" My eyes widened.

Kyle laughed. "You're so gullible. You'll believe anything."

This coming from a mythical wood nymph, I thought.

A cardinal whistled over head as we rounded a bend in the trail. The outline of an ancient oak dominated the landscape. My eyebrows rose as I slowly scanned the tree from the roots till it disappeared above the canopy. A natural archway grew through the center, leaving a tunnel to the other side.

"Wow, I've never seen a tree grow like this before," I murmured and brushed my fingers over the green fuzzy trunk as we passed through.

"Neat, huh?" Kyle winked.

"I guess." I dropped my hand.

Nestled in the trees at the end of the path stood a two-story home. Ivy weaved through the stone and snaked around the large windows. An elegant cedar pergola stood at the corner, heavy with fragrant wisteria. A rainbow of flowers grew along the ground and cased the archway leading to the front door. Kyle opened the anterior gate and ushered me to the small porch.

"Well?" Kyle grinned, his face alive with expectation.

"Well, what?"

"What do you think?" He gestured across the property

"It's fine." I shrugged, dismissing the most perfect house I'd ever seen.

Kyle laughed once. "It's yours."

"Mine?" My voice rose. I studied the attention to detail. Memories of Gabe and the life I had planned flashed through my mind. Suddenly, the beautiful home took on the appearance of an ornamental cage.

"Yeah. Don't you like it?" His shoulders slumped.

"It's unbelievable, Kyle, just like everything else," I said, my tone in contrast with my words.

"Doesn't change anything though, right?" Kyle frowned at the ground. "You should get cleaned up now. I'll be back for you in an hour."

"You're leaving me?"

"We aren't going to hold you prisoner here. You're free to go wherever you like in The Valley."

In The Valley, I thought bitterly.

"Be back in an hour," Kyle called tentatively as I slipped inside.

I pressed my back to the door and gazed around the room.

"Wow." I mouthed now that Kyle could see me.

Heavy wooden beams formed peaks atop the vaulted ceiling. Familiar paintings hung in assorted shapes and sizes across the walls, each having a water theme. Fresh flowers decorated the tables, a vase of crimson calla lilies on the coffee table.

The hall led through the sitting room. An unlit fireplace stood against the north wall, flanked on either side with built in bookcases constructed from a deep chocolate wood. Every shelf was lined with an array of books and trinkets.

Following the grooved planks of the hallway, I drifted into the cozy kitchen. The open-front cabinets were stacked with simple white dishes. A breakfast nook sat in the corner with an oval table surrounded by six chairs and a wide view of the forest.

The hallway wound back toward the front of the house — a tasteful half-bath, a lavish dining room, and a well-stocked library on the way. I reluctantly climbed the staircase behind the front door. The only room I hadn't seen was the bedroom meant for me … and Kevin. I strongly desired to keep it that way.

An unexpected number of doors lined the corridor, each one pulled together, blocking my view of the inside. I walked to the second room from the last, guessing those at the ends of the house would be the largest and likely the master.

With a nervous breath, I turned the iron handle and pushed the door open.

Bedroom. Thankfully, it wasn't the one I feared. Still as beautiful as the rest of the home, this room held two single beds resting on either side of an oblong floor-length window. It boasted high ceilings with peaked beams like the ones downstairs. The walls were a warm golden-straw color. I glanced around briefly, searching for a bathroom, but only found a closet. Anxiety mingled with my relief as I shut the door and moved on to the next.

Five doors, and a disconcerting number of bedrooms later, two doors remained at each end of the hall. Fending off the panic that bubbled so close to the surface, I eased to the southernmost room and paused with my hand on the knob.

Just do it and get it over with, I ordered myself, eyes shut.

I forced my defiant hand to turn the knob. The door creaked open, causing me to flinch. One unsure eye opened and my body froze as comprehension plowed over me like a freight train. The door I had so fervently wished against seemed a joy compared to this.

Chapter Twenty-One
Transition

Light strained through layers of delicate organza. A rocker sat in the corner, enveloped in a soft glow. A carved royal crest hung on the golden walls between the windows. Sweat beaded on my brow, the colors swirling and blurring as my eyes locked on the hand-carved crib in the center of the room.

I quickly shut the door, my heart pounding in my ears, and stumbled down the stairs. The backdoor banged on its hinges as I tore out, heading into the forest behind the house. There wasn't a goal; I just pushed my legs as far and as fast as they could carry me. I ran, trying to escape the anguish that endlessly awaited me at every turn. It seemed like I was destined for a perpetual carousel of misery.

The panic delivered me to a large pond beyond the house. My knees buckled at the water's edge beneath a flowering willow tree. I stared longingly into the pool and watched my reflection ripple through the lilies, hoping that at any moment I might possibly wake from this nightmare to find myself back in Gabe's arms.

"Ashton?" As if mockingly, another set of arms wrapped around my shoulders, but for the first time, I didn't retreat from the embrace. In one swift motion, I turned and pulled myself closer to Kyle who knelt behind me. I wept into his chest, fighting against desiring things that could never be.

"I don't understand," I mumbled. "How could this happen? I'm not a part of this world. I never wanted to be."

Kyle's hand made gentle passes over my spine. "I know. It isn't fair, and you don't deserve what Gabe did or what Kev's trying to do. But I'm still here, Monet. I won't ever leave you."

"I saw the nursery," I croaked, hoarse from crying.

"There's not much I can say about that, is there? You have a few months before the ... ceremony. Just wait a little while. Please," he begged, his sincerity bleeding through.

"Kyle?"

"Yeah?" he whispered, his voice unsteady.

"Thank you," I said, understanding now. Kyle was saving me the best way he knew how, the only way he could. He was being the friend I so desperately needed.

Kyle shook his head. "I haven't done anything but hide things from you. You're my best friend, and you couldn't even trust me."

"It's not your fault." I stared at my hands on the front of his chest.

"I'm so sorry—" he began, before I interrupted him.

"No." I lifted my fingers to touch his lips. "Don't. I'm sorry. Sorry that I've taken it out on you. It's not your fault. You're doing more for me than anyone here, anyone anywhere, could ever do. It doesn't take away from what Gabe did or how he left me, but knowing you're here makes all the difference. I don't know what I'd do without you, but I hope you aren't mad at me anymore."

A peculiar look crossed his face. His eyes flashed with a strange fire as he met mine. I recognized the familiar smoldering that lay beneath. I'd seen it before but never in him. The sound of a soprano voice calling his name broke his concentration.

"We have to go," he breathed, but his eyes stayed fixed on mine.

"Okay." I relaxed my aching fingers from his shirtfront.

Kyle's jaw tensed as he rose and lifted me to my feet. "We need to get you changed. Everyone's waiting."

He took my hand and led me toward the house.

"Can't I be excused from everything for a while? Can you just tell them I'm sick or something? I can't deal with this right now." I rubbed my head with my free hand.

"It's not possible," he said.

"Why? They won't believe you?"

"No, it's not that. It just isn't feasible. No one here is ever sick, not for long anyway," Kyle said, ushering me through the front door.

I paused at the top of the stairs, Kyle at my heels. "What do you mean?"

"You remember I told you about the grass?" he began. "Well, it can cure anything. If you have an injury, it can be mixed into a paste to cover it. If someone is ill, it's made into a tea and so on. There's never been a time when it hasn't worked. But take your time, as much as you need, really. I'll be downstairs when you're ready"

Hopelessness enveloped me, and I turned and walked through the door I'd been avoiding. It didn't matter now. Nothing was worse than the thought of being a brood mare for the throne.

The shower was all too short, the warm water running out well before my tension. A white armoire stood against the wall. I opened the doors and chose the first thing I came to: a long beige skirt with beads sewn across and a darker peasant shirt. After dressing myself in a daze, I pulled my still-damp hair back into a loose knot, ignoring my reflection as I passed the mirror to leave.

Kyle stood when I made my way into the sitting room, his eyes scanning me from head to toe. "You look ... awful. I can't take you anywhere like this."

I didn't say anything.

"Sit down for a minute. I'll be right back." He disappeared through the front door.

Sometime later, Kyle peeked his head back in. "Hey, someone is here to see you, so don't freak out." He paused, waiting for the response I didn't offer, and then shifted his focus outside. "Well, she's ready, I guess."

A striking woman flitted through the doorway, grabbing my attention. "Hello, Ashton," she spoke in a musical voice. "I'm Aurelia."

"She's my little sister." Kyle smiled tentatively as he stepped back into the room. "She's just going to help you acclimate."

I looked over her. She had a different tone to her skin than Kyle. Aurelia's was warm, with a coffee-and-cream undertone instead of olive, much like Pearse and Elon. Shimmering bronze hair billowed to her waist, several tones deeper than that of her almost incandescent irises. They were the clearest shade of brown I'd ever seen. She wore a gentle smile as she stopped in front of me, studying me with a kindness I hadn't expected.

"She looks exhausted, Kyle. Really, what did you guys do to her?" Her delicate eyebrows pulled down at her brother. His expression turned guilty.

Aurelia encouraged me to my feet and led me back upstairs. She sat me in a makeshift salon chair then fluffed, teased, and managed my wavy hair quickly. This was followed with a vigorous but refreshing scrub to my face before applying what I assumed was some kind of make-up, though it was no more than a mint-scented cream. After my simple makeover, she danced to the double doors of the armoire and rifled around. Seconds later, she pulled out something lavender and flowing to replace my dull brown ensemble.

"There now, much better." She smiled. "But something is missing. Hmm. Ah, I see." Aurelia reached over, touched my lips with her fingertip, and tugged the corner upward. I smiled unenthusiastically, but it seemed to placate her. "There we are. Perfect."

"One more thing." Aurelia floated across the room, towing me behind her. "Look." She grabbed the tops of my shoulders and spun me around to face the mirror beside the armoire. "What do you think?"

I sighed and forced my eyes up. Gabe's voiced whispered through my memory. "Look at yourself, Ashton. You're stronger than you know. Remember that every time you see your reflection. You won't be sad forever. I promise."

I lifted my fingers to brush away the tear sliding down my cheek and caught sight of Gabe's ring.

"Is something wrong?" she asked.

"No," I muttered and looked away.

"Kyle," Aurelia called for her brother in no more than a conversational tone.

Sharp footsteps raced up the stairs. Before it seemed possible, he burst through the door almost snapping it off the hinges. "What's wrong? Is Ashton—" Kyle froze midsentence, his eyes locked on my silhouette. "Oh, wow. You look ... incredible." His face reddened.

"You'd better watch that." Aurelia smiled and tapped his crimson cheek with her fingertip. She spun around and opened the closet doors to replace the unused outfit. "I don't think Kevin would appreciate his little brother ogling his almost-wife," she concluded from inside.

Her words hit me at the same time as the scent. The closet was lined with cedar.

Kyle winced at his sister's untimely reminder. He wouldn't have recognized the scent, but he could read my face. I dropped my head and squeezed between them with a gruff pardon.

"Is she all right?" Aurelia whispered.

"Sure, it's just nerves, you know. This is a lot to deal with all at once," Kyle replied. His echoing footsteps followed me down the stairs. "Thanks Aurelia, we'll be there shortly."

I paced the backyard, with my hands on my hips. I heard the door click shut and turned to see Kyle.

"Hey," he whispered, his eyes full of concern. "I'm sorry about that."

I shook my head. "They're going to think I'm crazy here. Maybe I am. I don't know anymore."

Kyle led me to a bench overlooking a small Koi pond and encouraged me to sit. He took the spot next to me, waiting quietly with my hand in his till they stopped shaking. Sounds from the welcoming party carried through the trees, and the setting sun told me more about the time than Kyle. I stood, ready to finish the evening so I could be left alone to mourn in solitude.

"Let's get this over with, please," I mumbled.

Kyle offered his arm and a grim smile then we set off into the dimming forest.

Torches burned alongside the paths, the flickering warring with the shadows. I smoothed my fingers along my forehead, trying to rub away the stress — surely my eyes were puffy and swollen. There wasn't much I could do about Kyle's tension.

"Everything is fine." His thumb rubbed over mine, my temperature falling with the stress.

After a mile of fireflies and ribbon-laced trees, the path opened to a perfectly-cut circle in the woods. Lanterns surrounded the perimeter, and a large fire blazed in the center. The scent of wood burning and roasted meat filled the air. Cheers and happy music erupted as we entered the clearing. Hundreds of kinsmen bowed to one knee, and my gripped tightened around Kyle's arm.

"What are they doing?" I whispered. "Is this for you?"

"No, it's for you. You're practically their princess. Smile and nod." He glanced at me while we made our way to the receiving line. I stopped in front of him, ignoring the countless eyes on me ... all except two.

Kevin glanced up to see Kyle and I enter the clearing. His cold indifference stopped me in place. Flashes of lies and betrayal blurred my vision, and he simply stared at me with as much consideration as he might give an old shoe. An angry knot settled in my stomach like a hot brick. How could this happen? How could he repeatedly destroy so many lives and not even blink? Resentment rolled off me in waves.

Kyle's hand slid over mine once more as he gently shushed me. I drew a deep breath. He was right. I couldn't let Kevin get to me. Not here.

"Nice to see you finally made it, brother. Cutting the time a bit short, aren't you?" Kevin chided then took my hand from Kyle's arm. His steely eyes locked on Kyle before rebounding to mine. "Ashton, I trust you had an uneventful trip?"

"It was fine," I answered, my voice strained.

Kevin lifted a brow and looked to his brother. Kyle shrugged and took a step back to stand behind me.

Music continued in the background as I shook hands with countless people — all of whom genuinely seemed pleased to meet me. Until that moment, I hadn't understood the gravity of the situation. Their kingdom, their way of life, depended on this treaty. It didn't matter if I loved Kevin or even if I were happy. Their future was on my shoulders.

"What did you think of the house?" Kevin's voice interrupted my thoughts when the last in line kissed my hand and moved on.

"I will," I said my thoughts a thousand miles away. Kevin narrowed his eyes in question. "I mean … what did you say?"

"We need some time together. Would you like to get out of here?" Kevin's voice grew husky, and my stomach flipped.

"Could you get me a drink first?" I nodded toward the table across the clearing.

"Sure, then we'll head home." Kevin dropped his arm and hurried to the table across the way.

Kyle stood at my heels, his eyes darting around the clearing.

"What's wrong?" I sensed he was searching for something — or someone.

He frowned. "Nothing yet, but I didn't get a chance to talk to you before we came here."

"Talk about what?"

Kyle cleared his throat and smiled across the way to Aurelia who was chatting with Kevin. They both looked in my direction before Kevin began to make his way back.

"Talk about what, Kyle?" I asked.

Kyle turned his face away from Kevin. "About Harry," he whispered, his mouth hidden beneath his hand.

My temperature dropped, and I looked to Kevin. He was close, maybe thirty yards away. I didn't know if he could hear us over the roar of people and music, but I was about to risk it.

"I thought he left. I thought Oren let him go." I panicked.

"There's more to it than that," Kyle said quickly. "It's not what you think."

"Is he hurt?" I spoke louder, not caring that Kevin and several others could hear.

Kyle plastered on a smile and shushed me but shook his head.

I couldn't think straight. The day in the cave, Oren said everything was set. My presence meant Harry's freedom. What if they hadn't let him go? What if he lied? What if Harry was hurt or worse?

"Ashton?" Kevin nudged me when I didn't respond. He offered a silver cup filled with a dark liquid. "Are you ready to go home?"

"I guess." I took a sip of the sweet drink then set it aside. There wasn't anywhere else in this place I wanted to be more than alone.

"See you in the morning, little brother," Kevin murmured with a smile, not turning his eyes away from me. "Kyle?"

"What?" Kyle responded blankly.

"Ash and I are going home now," Kevin said. "Take care of closing the party."

"Right." Kyle bid us a sullen good night before loping off into the darkness.

Kevin held my hand as we walked, allowing me to set a casual pace. I was anxious to get back, but I had no idea if being there meant being alone.

"You should've told me about Charlie." Kevin broke the silence.

"Why would I?" I asked, trying to keep my tone in check. "Nothing you could do about it."

"That doesn't give you the right to run around as you see fit. You should've had an escort," he said coldly, as if I'd simply left on an unannounced vacation.

Blood rose in my cheeks, and I ground my teeth together trying not to snap.

We passed through the oak tunnel and turned at the path leading to the house. It seemed so surreal to stand beside Kevin now. He once held a mystique, almost like a drug, but now he just irritated me. The real Kevin shone through like a shadowed beacon, leading me to an eternal punishment.

I sighed.

"You seem different," he said, his tone put out. "Is it because of the whole change thing?"

I bit back what I really wanted to say and just shrugged.

"I'm at a loss for your behavior. You haven't asked me the first question. Has Kyle already filled you in on how things work here?"

I made a non-committal sound and gritted my teeth.

Kevin's hand ran possessively down my back, and I shuddered. He misread the signal, mistaking it for desire, and a smile spread across his lips. "Very soon, the ceremony will be over, and I'll have all of you to myself."

Kevin's eyes took on a hungry glint as they raked over my frame. He pulled me to him, his thumbs under my chin, and lowered his head.

My lips went pliant, and he huffed.

"What's with you? You used to whimper at my touch." His eyes narrowed. "What have you been up to?"

"It's all so much to take in, Kev. And I'm exhausted." For once, I didn't shield my feelings from him, allowing all the hopelessness to shine through my eyes, willing him to see how miserable I was. He didn't seem to care.

"Go to bed then. Maybe you'll be better tomorrow." He pulled me close again, his touch demanding a response. I fell into rhythm, but it was empty.

Kevin growled in frustration and backed away. "I'll see you in the morning."

Not yet ready to face the rooms upstairs, I waited until Kevin's scent faded into the night then headed toward the pond.

The light of the full moon glistened off the water, casting shimmering reflections against the trees. A gentle wind carried the fragrance of water lilies across the bank as cattails swayed along the shoreline. I skirted the fringe of the shore to the willow and inched my toes into the water.

The effect the water possessed was more powerful than ever before. Familiar scents comforted me as I waded out into the deep. The caress felt like satin against my skin, reaching into my very essence. It was part of me, something that would never change, that could never be taken away. My longing was more than simply a desire — it was a necessity, as required by me as eating or sleeping. Being here, it was almost like muting the chaos and heartbreak surrounding me. I couldn't turn it off, but I could turn it down.

For that one moment, I forgot about the nightmare that continued across the forest and the splintered heart's beat that persisted in my chest. I allowed the water to comfort me in a way nothing else could.

Wading into the shallows, I stared up at the stars till every emotion faded into the blackness.

Chapter Twenty-Two
Reflections

S oft pillows billowed round my head as the sun warmed my skin. I startled, bolting upright to find myself in my new bed, Gabe's thermal clenched in my hand. Memories of stars and lapping water floated through my mind. How did I get here?

I tucked the sweet smelling shirt into the deepest drawer at the bottom of the armoire and sighed. As I undressed for a shower, I looked down and blushed, feeling the satin nightgown brush across my thigh; I didn't remember changing. My stomach flipped at the thought of someone else undressing me as I was becoming more certain by the minute I hadn't done it. Only one other person had been at the pond with me before. With that realization, my blush reached my hairline.

After my shower, I reached into the drawer in the bathroom for a brush. The steamy mirror began to clear, and my disheveled appearance shone back.

You're stronger than you know... Gabe's voice whispered.

I dropped my towel and threw it over the reflection.

"I hate you," I muttered under my breath, not even sure who I meant. Slipping into a white sundress, I followed suit through the house, covering every reflective surface I could find. If someone else saw it and had me locked up, so be it.

I wandered into the library, waiting for someone to show up. My eyes flitted from title to title. "Brontë, Poe, Shakespeare, Hawthorne," I murmured to myself, running my hands along the spines. "Dickens, Carroll, Twain, Austen ... where did you come from?" Kevin didn't know about my love of poetry and the classics — he would've filled the room with fashion magazines — but row after row revealed my favorites.

I circled the room then turned to the items positioned on the mahogany desk: a few magazines, a leather-bound notebook, and a container of writing utensils. My heart stuttered as a familiar blue cover with gold trim stared back at me, a ragged copy of Tennyson's Poetical Works. I flipped the cover open. Pasted within the volume were clippings of poems from various works and Victorian-era pictures. I continued on to see Charlie's messy handwriting spanning the first page. My palm rested over the script, and I longed for the time when my dad was still here, when I could still dream of a life of my own.

I wandered through the hall to the sitting room. Finding the plush armchair near the fireplace, I opened my favorite book and scanned the pages. Each poem brought back memories of a different time or place in my life. Joy and sadness mingled together till my eyes fell on The Lady of Shalott. A memory I didn't want fought against my mental barrier. Seeing the words, my teeth ground together, and I slammed the cover shut.

A quick rap echoed through the foyer. I stood and cleared my throat before pulling the door back. Kyle stood at the threshold. His eyes rested on my face for a moment then shifted to the compilation in my hand.

"I see you found your book." His expression warmed. "I couldn't bear leaving it behind with it being your favorite and all."

"You did this?" I held up the volume, biting back the resentment of him taking it from Charlie's house in Cumberland to begin with.

"Yeah, I chose all the books." Kyle shrugged, weighing his words against my expression. "I know you love to read, and your shelves in California were full of the classics."

"Oh. Thanks."

Kyle took a step closer and eyebrows pulled down. "You look tired. Are you all right?"

"I'm trying to be. It's not exactly easy."

"No, I'd say not." Kyle looked away. His focus landed on the lavender towel hanging over the hall mirror. He glanced back at me with questions in his eyes but didn't say anything.

"I guess I should thank you for bringing me home," I said. Even if you overstepped a line.

His eyes met mine. "What are you talking about?"

"Last night when I went to the pond and fell asleep..." My voice drifted away when his eyes narrowed. "Never mind."

He started to say something then let it drop. "I thought you might like to go sightseeing today. Or if you're not up for that, I could take you to our museum. Show you some of our history."

I decided that it would probably be most beneficial to gather a lay of the land. I would need some perspective on that when my chance for escape came. Their history might come in handy at some point, but hopefully I wasn't in a position to plan a future here.

"Where's Kevin?" I asked as we hit the path.

Kyle's smile melted. He stuck his hands in his pockets and watched a blue-jay in the distance. "He's taking care of some business matters, but he expects you to join him for dinner."

I shuddered. At least I had the day without him.

We followed the tree-covered path to the west, Kyle growing more animated as he explained how the Dryads maintained their living with minimal aid from the outside world. "We have a variety of fowl and livestock," he said. "Everything from chickens and goats to peacocks and pigs." Cows bellowed in the distance, and the pungent smell of manure and hay saddled the air.

A herd of sheep crossed the road, bleating as dogs nipped at their heels. Their curly-haired shepherd grinned at me — his two front teeth missing — as he opened a pen and carried a lamb out. I gave him a tentative wave, and he offered a clumsy bow.

Kyle led me into one of the oversized barns. Spinning wheels piped along in the back. The women tipped their heads in respect as we passed but never met my gaze. The acrid smell of smoke and fermentation burned my eyes. I traced the scent to the center of the barn. Several vats hung over smoldering fires, each covered with a rough cloth. Beside the vats were vials of crushed leaves, seeds, and roots.

My nose turned up. "Dye?"

"Yep. That's weld, woad plant, and madder plant roots." He pointed to the different vials. "The ancient Egyptians helped us out on that. There's crushed shellfish, archil, and indigo as well."

"Ancient Egyptians?" I lifted a brow.

"They were very advanced." He grinned. "It still works well."

"How old are you?" I teased.

Kyle laughed. The pleasant throaty sound brought out a smile in me. "Me, I'm not that old. My family on the other hand has been around for quite a while." He tugged on my elbow. "Let's keep going."

As we approached the western wall, an odd formation angled from the mountain. I couldn't make out why until we closed in on the building. Traditional gothic architecture blended with contemporary accessories. It looked like a combination of ancient Petra and Notre Dame. Six circular columns stood across the front, supporting the overhang leading to the entranceway. Intricate stone carvings of nymphs lined the smooth mountain face. I shielded my eyes from the sun as I tried to decipher the story they told. They looked a lot like Egyptian hieroglyphs.

"What are you staring at?" Kyle nudged me, his mouth pulled into a grin.

I shook my head. "I can't believe the attention to detail. How you carved those things, it seems impossible. Hey, is that you up there?" I pointed to the carving that bared a striking resemblance. "I see your brothers. Who are the rest?"

Kyle tugged at my arm. "Lots of people. You ready to go?"

I frowned. "In a sec, I'm still looking. What's in there anyway?"

"It's just a factory. Very boring," he stated, his eyebrows pulled up in the middle, and I lifted mine.

"What's with the secrets, huh?" I inched toward the doorway.

Kyle's eyes darted around the area then he grabbed by hand. "It's nothing, really. Come on, we have a lot of ground to cover before dinner."

I sniffed at his lame excuse but let it go.

"I've been enlisted to educate you," he began as we walked. "All those questions I know you've been dying to ask, now is the time."

I smiled at his spot on comment. "I don't know where to start. I guess first of all, how are we different?" I passed my hand between us. "Like you can definitely run faster, but I think you'd acknowledge I'm a better swimmer."

Kyle rolled his eyes. "Yeah, you guys have us beat in the water — we swim about as well as a Volkswagen — but we're quicker on land. In general we tend to be bigger and stronger." He flexed the thick band of muscle around his bicep. A mischievous grin stretched across his face when my eyebrows rose.

"Our sense of smell is much better than yours. Out of water anyway. You guys have the upper hand in the covert department. Our size, while menacing, doesn't exactly promote quietness. Of course, we have other ways of blending in. We usually have a little darker complexion. Our skin, and sometimes our hair and eyes, tends to match the type of tree we're linked to. It helps us blend into our surroundings."

"The type of tree you're linked to?" My nose scrunched up. Kyle laughed and ran his finger down it, smoothing out the ridges in my skin. I lifted my hand to scratch my neck while surreptitiously pulling away from his touch.

Kyle's hand recoiled in an instant. He glanced around the woods as if he'd forgotten where we were. I saw the wheels turning in his head as he struggled to remember what we discussed.

"The trees," I reminded him as his face turned slightly panicked.

"Right." He exhaled heavily and shook his head. "We have preferences, as far as which trees we live near."

"Why is that?"

He paused. "You know how you need certain types of water? You can make do with what you have, but it's not really the best?"

I nodded, understanding completely.

"It's kind of like that but with more options." He picked an apple and tossed it to me.

I turned it over in my hands as I considered his statement. "Well, yeah, but why do you need trees at all? What do you gain from them? With water, I can soak in it and drink it. How can you drink a tree?"

Kyle smiled and looked down at me. "I guess that does sound a bit bizarre." An odd look came into his eyes as he scanned the area. "You don't have any knives, do you?"

He grabbed my hand and pulled me off the trail, deeper into the forest.

"Huh?" I followed behind, weaving around the blackberry bushes.

"I'll show you how we soak in trees, but I need you to not have anything sharp on you."

I shook my head.

"All right, there." We stopped in front of a well-aged tree. "My family uses oak trees mainly."

I nodded and took a bite of apple.

"Don't freak out on me. This is going to get a little weird." Kyle released my hand, quickly glancing around. He turned his back to the tree and leaned against it till every part of him touched the oak. His arms nestled alongside the trunk, and he molded himself to the length. A gentle groaning like the shifting of planks on a wooden ship then Kyle literally melted into the tree.

I gasped and choked on my apple. My eyes widened at the empty space where Kyle once stood. The oak remained unchanged less a slightly smoother area.

"Kyle!" I said in a strained tone. A ghostly chuckle whispered through the leaves.

He reappeared in an instant, a smile on his face. "Cool, huh?"

"What was that?" I asked.

"That's an example of why we need trees." Kyle's grin widened.

We started back toward the path. I didn't know what to say. It unnerved me and for more reasons than one. Not only was that a readily available source of reenergizing, it was a heck of a good hiding place.

"So you just dissolve into trees?" I sputtered.

"It's not that easy," he answered. "We can't just use any tree. Most of them that are local will work to an extent, though each of our families has preferences."

Kyle helped me over a tall tree root. "Gabe told me about that," I said absentmindedly. "You prefer oaks, so that would make you a Hamadryad, right?"

I turned when Kyle didn't answer. He stood still, irritation heavy in his expression.

"Yeah, that's about right," he murmured and stepped past me, out of the trees. "We choose oaks when it's an option, but most other trees will do in a pinch."

"Can I ask you a question?" I said, catching up to him.

"Depends on what it is."

"The day at the hotel, how did you know I was there?" I asked.

"We have our ways," Kyle muttered. His eyebrows pulled together.

"I'll bet," I said, my tone sarcastic. "Were you following me? Did Kevin know?"

"Yes, to both," he admitted after a moment.

"How did he—"

"That's enough for now." Kyle's tone kept me quiet as passed through the oak tunnel and headed toward the house.

Kevin waited at the front door, his arms crossed over his chest. "You can go now, Kyle," he spoke, his eyes never leaving me. Kyle's hands balled into fists before he shoved them in his pockets.

"Thanks, Kyle. I had fun today," I said as he turned to leave. He looked back with a nod then strode away.

"You shouldn't be rude to him. He's your brother and my only friend," I said.

Kevin's stared at me for a moment, rocking back on his heels. "I guess I can do that for you, Princess."

I frowned and shook my head. "Don't call me that."

"You'd better get used to the idea of being royalty." He inched forward and wrapped his hands around my waist. "We're the most powerful family in our world. After the wedding, and wedding night, we'll be the most powerful family in the realm of nymphs. Honor, respect, and loyalty above all else, Ashton. Don't forget that."

I fought the urge to tell him I'd more than violated all of those over the past few weeks.

"Why don't we finish your tour?" Kevin suggested. "Where have you been today?"

"Kyle showed me the western half of the valley." I glanced back in that direction.

"What exactly did he show you?" His grip tightened.

"Just the barn," I said quickly, wincing at his grip. "He explained about the dye."

His hands relaxed and the arrogant glint reappeared in his eyes.

"Well then, Princess," he began, smiling at my frown.

"Kevin," I interrupted.

"Maybe we should try Mrs. Hawthorne then?"

I bit my lip and turned my face away. I couldn't be Mrs. ... anything. I didn't want Kevin, and no one else wanted me.

"Could we swim, please?" Even in a whisper my voice sounded choked.

"I'd rather not." Kevin's lip curled up as I looked back.

"Like it or not, I actually need water." I thought for a second. "It helps with cravings and gives me energy."

"Now that is beneficial." A wicked smile pulled his mouth up. He swept me up and ran us to the pond faster than I realized what was happening.

Kevin forwent the dip, content to lounge on the grass with just his legs submerged to his calves. I sat crossed legged at the bottom of the glass-clear pond. My heart rate slowed as I watched different creatures swim by. Being underwater was like being inside a living snow globe. But even at the bottom, I would swear I could hear Kevin's impatient sighs. Staring toward the willow at the edge of the water, I saw him motion for me to resurface.

"How can you stand that? Doesn't it suffocate you?" he asked when I surfaced.

"No more than liquefying into a tree," I argued.

"So Kyle showed you that?"

"Briefly," I said and swam toward the bank.

"I am somewhat impressed. You haven't badgered me with questions." He stared me down for a long minute. "Still … something's off. I can't quite put my finger on it."

I didn't have a response to that.

"I'm sure you're adequately hydrated now." He sighed and stood to his feet, rolling the cuffs of his pants down. "Time to leave. We have dinner plans and being late isn't an option."

I climbed onto the bank, and we set off for the house. Kevin dropped me at the front door, leaving me with a wave since my clothes were wet, and heaven forbid he should get messy. Maybe I was onto something there.

Kyle had warned me that we were expected to have dinner with the family that evening. The entire family. It surprised me when I ambled inside to find him propped in the corner, his expression unreadable.

"Hey." His somber tone broke the silence.

"What's the matter?" I stepped toward him, searching his tight features.

"We need to talk."

"Sure," I said slowly.

Kyle drew a deep breath and stepped forward. "I don't really know how to tell you about this. I don't want to hurt you anymore than you already are, but I can't let you find out in the wrong way."

Every scenario imaginable raced through my mind. I bit down on my lip, fearing the worst. "You're worrying me here."

"It's the thing with Harry," Kyle said. My stomach dropped. "It's not what it seems."

"What are you talking about?" My jaw tightened. "What does that mean?"

Kyle drew a deep breath. "Harry was your mother's uncle. Everything that's happened from the beginning is his fault."

"I don't understand," I choked. "Harry's not related to my family at all. Why would you think that?"

His expression turned sorrowful. "Ash, Harry is Leith."

Chapter Twenty-Three
Family Ties

The ground moved under my feet. Kyle grabbed an arm to steady my swaying. "That can't be..." I struggled to stay upright. "If that were true..." I shook my head. If it was true, Harry had been playing me my whole life. Who would do something like that?

The seconds ticked by and the reality sank in. It was Harry. All this time. Harry knew everything because he had caused everything. It was probably the reason he hated Gabe. Why he was pushing for me to stay with Kevin.

My entire life was a lie.

"I'm so sorry," Kyle spoke after a moment. "I can only imagine what you're going through."

"I doubt that, Kyle." I bit my lip and pushed the thoughts of betrayal out of my head.

"Ash," he began.

"You'd better go," I spoke through a thick voice. "Kevin will be back soon."

Kyle walked to the door but hesitated in the archway. "Do you hate me, Monet?"

"No, how could I hate you?" I answered, and shook my head. "You're the only real thing in my life. You're my best friend."

"Yeah, I'm your friend." Kyle smiled sadly. He leaned in and kissed my forehead, his eyes darkening as he backed away. "See you in a bit."

෨ ෨ ෨

The wood floor creaked under my weight as I paced back and forth in front of the covered mirror. I wrung my hands together till my fingers ached and sighed for the umpteenth time. Meeting the Hawthorne family in its entirety was the stuff of nightmares. What if any of them had a gift like my grandfather Cowan? Would they see right through me? Would it ruin everything? What if Harry was there? I wasn't ready to confront him yet.

A sharp knock on the door jarred me out of my incessant worrying.

"Come in," I squeaked.

Kevin strolled through the archway wearing a pair of khaki slacks and a loose white shirt that laced at the top, emphasizing his muscular chest. A slow grin stretched across his face as he appraised my choice of clothing.

The silk ivory dress dipped and curved around my body in all the right places. The low cut back laced, crisscrossing with intricate beading that matched the delicate straps. Loose curls framed my face and spilled down my back the best I could manage without a mirror. And while I wanted to be convincing, perhaps I was overdoing it.

"Too much?" I asked.

"Hardly," Kevin assured, his eyes traveling the length of my body. "This is how a princess should look. I may need to bump up the wedding date and move in here." Kevin pulled me into his chest.

"You're just going to have to be patient, I guess." I tried to pull away but he held tight.

Kevin tsk'd. "I'm not so good at being patient." He lifted my chin to touch his lips to mine. Heat blazed from his skin as his fingers wound beneath the straps at the small of my back and worked their way up. The material slid off my shoulder, and I jumped away with a gasp.

Kevin shook his head and stepped back to appraise my silhouette once more. "You'd best get over this modesty problem. This used to be a non-issue."

I slid the strap back in place and followed Kevin outside.

As we walked, I thought about his comment regarding our current living arrangements. In California, Kevin had a house in Malibu, and my condo was in Pasadena about an hour away. When I was in school, I spent the week at home, but my weekends — and basically the last few months I'd been bumming around — were spent at his place. And while we occasionally shared a living space, I had been very strict about our physical relationship, despite Kevin's persistence. Still, I couldn't understand why he hadn't broached the subject of living with me in the stone house. It wasn't like him not to want to be close.

"Speaking of living arrangements," I began with caution. "Where are you staying?"

"Why? Are you lonely?" He smiled suggestively.

"Um, well, what I meant was just..." I stuttered, wishing I had kept my curiosity to myself.

"Are you considering rezoning your boundaries?" He lifted an eyebrow.

"No. I was just wondering why you weren't trying to weasel your way into my bed lately."

"My parents are very old fashioned, as you can imagine. My mother would not be fond of us shacking up, even if you are locked tighter than Fort Knox."

My blood pressure shot up. "Well, excuse me for having integrity, Kevin. Maybe you should find someone with looser morals."

He laughed. "So you set a moral standard, do you? Need I remind you of your junior year at Idyllwild? Or last spring when you had that run in with the state trooper, and I had to come clean it up at three o'clock in the morning?"

Or an almost incident in a coal mine? I sighed. "I guess not."

"Things have changed now, Ashton. It's time to grow up," Kevin said, his expression firm. "You have obligations to your people and to mine. More importantly, you have obligations to me."

"And what if I don't want this?" I stopped and met his gaze, anger bubbling up. "What if I want to choose another life?"

Kevin moved into me, grabbing my elbow. "You don't get that choice," he murmured in my ear.

I winced at the familiar words. His grip loosened as he glanced up to see the people milling around their homes.

"You see that child?" His eyes fell on a little girl who looked around four years-old. Her auburn curls bounced as she played with a small terrier. "Children are occurring less and less in both our kind. I refuse to let our numbers dwindle away. It would take so little to wipe out an entire race ... given the need," he said, his words thick with implication. My people, my family, would suffer the consequences if I didn't fulfill the treaty.

Hopelessness settled in my chest.

Kevin smiled at my expression. "I'll give you a life you never dreamed of, Ashton." He pulled my chin up to meet his gaze. "You need but to honor me."

I swallowed and looked away, refusing to let him see the emptiness growing inside.

"But you are mine, one way or another." His eyes hardened as he stared out over the landscape.

The sun skirted above the canopy of trees, casting the remainder of our walk in shadows. An owl hooted in the distance, and a chilled wind swept through the trees. I wrapped my arms around myself and shivered.

The face of the palace finally came into view, and my eyes widened. Much like the factory, the building spanned the mountain rim and moved inward like an immense monolith. Gray columns stretched toward the sky, protecting the statues of stunning beings perched on the ledge three stories high.

Our bare feet padded across a little stone bridge as we crossed over to his family's grounds. A full courtyard spanned the front. Box hedges framed a fountain large enough to rival an Olympic pool. Statues of a dazzling couple stood in the middle, a spray of water outlined them like a liquid umbrella. Waves of color swept over the lush grass. Flowers of every shade and design hugged the stone paths winding throughout. My eyes fell on a patch of plum-colored tulips, and I quickly looked away.

Kevin disregarded the beauty of the garden and hurried on. A pair of wooden doors, taller than any I'd ever seen, creaked open as we closed in on the palace. A pleasant looking girl with dark hair bowed and ushered us inside.

"Thank you," I offered, and the girl's skin paled.

Kevin jerked me to his side. "What are you thinking?" he hissed. "We don't speak to the help unless you have a request."

"Well, that's just rude." I turned back and smiled at her. She dropped her head and hurried through the foyer like a scolded dog.

I studied the walls in the entrance, intrigued by the structure of mirrors scattered about. A shaft stretching through the ceiling sent a ray of waning sunlight in and expertly reflected it throughout the foyer and hallways.

I glanced from room to room as we continued down a dimly lit corridor. Typical light fixtures adorned the walls on the interior side of the mountain. Kevin explained that the waterfall fueled their hydroelectric power, which was more than enough to run the entire Valley ten times over, but they preferred natural light during the daytime.

A pair of male servants opened the last set of doors on the eastern side of the house. The dining room held a table large enough to seat twenty on the other side. Heavy wooden armchairs surround the mahogany table, and to my surprise, each seat held a place setting.

The echo of doors closing at the opposite end of the room caused me to turn. A lovely couple, who I could only assume were Kevin's parents, walked toward us. I recognized their faces as those on the statues in the fountain. His mother broke from her husband and hurried to pull me into a hug.

"You must be Ashton," she said, her honey-tinted eyes sparkling with joy. "It is such a pleasure to meet you, my dear. I'm Ilana. You're even more beautiful than my son let on."

"Um, thank you," I murmured, caught off guard by her kindness and beauty.

"This is my husband, Aiken." Ilana smiled and wrapped her petite arm around the muscular waist of her towering mate. Easy to see where the Hawthorne brothers got their menacing size.

"Welcome to our home." Aiken's rich voice echoed over the marble floor, polite yet reserved.

"Thanks. It's great to finally meet you both," I said timidly.

Ilana relieved me of Kevin's grip and wound her arm through mine, leading me to the far side of the room. "The others will be here shortly. Tell me, how has my son been treating our future princess?"

Which son? I thought. "Everyone has been very welcoming. Thank you."

We paused at the end of the table, and Ilana met my eyes. "We're all delighted to have you here, dear. Please understand though, this is very new to most of our clan. It may take time for some to adjust."

Myself included. "Sure." I tried to smile. "Does your family get together often?"

"At least once a week. We're very close." She smiled and squeezed my shoulder. "Of course tonight is a special occasion."

The same doors Aiken and Ilana came through opened once more. A plethora of chattering family flowed into the dining room. Hugs and well wishes surrounded me as Kevin's countless siblings filed in. In total there were five boys, all of which I knew, and seven girls.

Aurelia fluttered to my side and kissed my cheek. "It's wonderful to see you again, Ashton. You're looking very well." She smiled, her eyes crinkling in the corners like her mother's.

"Thank you," I said and returned her smile, hoping I didn't seem panicked at the thought of the last time we'd spent together.

Aurelia pulled a female version of a younger looking Kyle over. "Ashton, this is our youngest sister, Adare."

"Nice to meet you," I offered, confused by her standoffish attitude.

"Right," she quipped with a sarcastic smile. "Excuse me."

She turned and stalked away.

"Don't mind Adare." Kyle's husky voice sounded through the mix. "She needs to learn she isn't the center of the universe."

Seeing Kyle calmed my nerves. The rigid muscles in the back of my neck began to unknot as we each took our places at the dinner table, Ilana insisting I sit across from her. Servants attended each family member and everyone dug in as they carried on, discussing everything from human politics and business to home design and fashion. I fell into simply trying to seem interested, though I couldn't help but feel like Ilana was watching me.

After dinner, Kevin led us to the sitting room. Ilana motioned for me to join her on a long sofa near the fireplace. I choked back the notion she could see through me and took my place beside her. She smiled as if she were trying to relieve my anxiety. I prayed she wrote it off as anything but what it was.

"How are you adjusting to things here?" she asked kindly.

"It's been ... interesting." I tried to put on a good face.

"I imagine it is a very complicated transition. I don't pretend to understand the difficulties this new life has put on you. I'm certain you feel pressured — especially with your changing — but I would offer you anything I can to help. We want you to be happy here."

Nice, I thought. It's going to be impossible to hate this woman.

"I appreciate that very much, Mrs. Hawthorne."

"Mrs. Hawthorne?" She trilled with laughter. "I'll have none of that. You call me Ilana. We're family now."

No, we're not. "Sure. Ilana."

I peered around for Kyle. I hadn't seen him since dinner and even then, he sat quietly at the opposite end of the table, but he was the one Hawthorne I couldn't find.

"Are you looking for someone?" Ilana questioned.

"Hmm?" I stalled, trying to drum up an explanation. "Um, no. I was just taking in the general beauty of everything. This place is amazing."

"Thank you." She laughed once, her eyes dropping to her hands in her lap as she toyed with a ring on her right hand.

"That's really beautiful," I said, gesturing to the quarter-sized emerald.

"Thank you, dear. I rather like your stone, as well." Her knowing eyes flitted to my face. I looked away from the blue-green rock on my index finger and tried to slow my breathing.

"Would you like to see the rest of the palace?" Ilana mentioned offhand.

"Sure, that sounds great," I said, hoping to mask my panic.

Ilana took my hand and pulled it through her arm again. She led us through the sitting room to an antechamber deeper into the mountain. A stone staircase spiraled upward, leading to the second floor.

Ilana guided me to the furthest door at the end of a seemingly endless hallway. She lifted a key from around her neck and inserted it through the lock. We stepped into an elegant parlor full of feminine touches.

"Raising twelve children could be tiresome at times. Aiken built this parlor for me shortly after Pearse and Elon were born. This became my place of solitude." She sighed as she glanced around the room.

Books lined two of the walls floor to ceiling while paintings of her family and various musical instruments covered the third. The wall against the windows held a high-back Victorian-era sofa.

"Please, make yourself comfortable." Ilana motioned for me to sit then she lifted something from one of the overflowing shelves.

I eyed the dark leather-bound book she cradled against her chest as she joined me. Her head tilted to the side in an attempt to gain my attention. When my gaze met hers, there was an air of expectancy about her. It felt as if she could see through my pretenses, like she suspected my real motives and feelings about everything.

I bit my lip and focused on the book.

"Did you know that I am not a Hamadryad?" she asked, taking an unexpected direction. "That's why I'm darker than my husband and some of my children. I am a Meliai, from the ash trees."

I nodded, unsure how to respond to her.

"You're wondering why this matters," she stated confidently. "It matters because, as you probably have not heard, the families of Dryads typically marry within their specific clan — a clan being the various types of Dryads. Hamadryad, Meliai,

Epimeliad and so forth, are all clans. It is a bit confusing at first." She smiled sympathetically at my wide eyes. "We do this in order to keep our bloodlines clean and strong."

Yeah, that one I'd heard.

"You see, the Hamadryads gain their strength from the oaks, as mine come from the ash. When you mingle our clans, you arrive at a being that is in between trees. On the one hand, you have a Dryad who can draw strength from two separate trees — on the other, you also have a Dryad who never reaches their full capacity because there is no ash-oak tree, you see?"

My mind reeled. I couldn't imagine Kyle, Oren and the rest, being at their full potential.

She laughed once. "Again, why does that matter, right?"

I smiled.

"It is a weakness," she stated. "Our kind does not want to appear weak, let alone have an actual weakness. Being Hawthornes, we have an even greater desire and need to be strong."

But even in my understanding, it didn't add up. Why would this happen, especially in a royal family? The Naiads certainly didn't seem to tolerate things like that.

Ilana didn't explain further, though she undoubtedly saw the questions shuffling through my mind. She laid the large volume across her lap and opened the cover of what turned out to be a photo album. I looked down at the first page. A breathtaking island stared back at me. It seemed to be suspended in endless blue, impossible to tell where the sky ended and the ocean began.

"There weren't cameras back then." She lovingly brushed her fingers across the painting. "This is my home. I left when I traveled here, and I've never returned."

For the first time this evening, Ilana's demeanor fell in sadness.

Whether it was from her sudden mood change or the possibility that she really didn't know what I was thinking, I had to ask the burning question in my mind. "Why?"

Her soft smile returned, but it held a hint of sadness. "I'm forbidden to return. I can never leave The Valley now."

Without thinking, I stretched my hand across the album to take hers in mine. "I'm sorry," I whispered. For whatever reason, she was stuck here, too. It brought me a small comfort knowing that, in one way or another, she understood my position.

"We live such complicated lives. Sometimes I wish things could just be simpler," Ilana said, speaking to herself more than to me. "You understand?"

I offered a sad smile. For once, I did know.

"Would you like to hear my story?" she asked.

"Very much," I said.

Ilana drew a deep breath and began. "This was my home," she repeated. "The Island was as close to paradise as one could get. Friends. Family. Love. Everything I had ever known was there."

Ilana paused then, seeing things I couldn't, lost in the memory of her former existence. "It was absolutely perfect. Nothing tainted by pollution or human touch. One of my favorite things there were the underwater caves. My best friend so enjoyed swimming and frequently wanted to explore them. As you know, our kind typically shies away from water, but he and I were always a bit strange." She smiled warmly. "No one else on The Island knew about the caves because they avoided swimming, so it was our secret place."

I lifted an eyebrow in question.

"He and I weren't permitted to spend time together. My family didn't approve of our friendship," she explained. Her tone turned bitter. "He was adopted in a sense — not a Meliai, to say the least.

"I had always known that he was special. It never mattered to me one way or the other. I didn't treat him differently than I would have anyone else, not because he was adopted, that is. He was so very unique. He had pale features — light-blonde hair and vivid green eyes; his skin was fairer than anyone else on The Island. And he could swim with amazing finesse."

She turned the sheet over, and my mouth fell open.

Ilana nodded her eyes locked on the beautiful face. "He was a Naiad."

My mind swirled with questions and confusion. How did a lone Naiad end up there? Why did he stay? Why would the Dryads even take care of him? My thoughts transformed into blatant disbelief in the fact that Ilana, a Dryad, was so obviously crazy about him.

Shaking her head, the smile returned and she continued. "As I was saying, there was a waterfall there in the center of The Island that poured into a large pool, and beneath the pool was the entrance."

She turned another page to reveal a tall mountain at the heart of The Island, a powerful waterfall cascading from the heart.

"Only the passageways were submerged," she continued, "the rest of the area was like any other cavern, except there was some natural light from openings in the ceiling."

I repressed a shiver at the sketches of the inside of the mountain on the opposite page. Caves would forever be a nightmare for me.

"On a day like any other, we agreed to meet in our cave, and as we swam, he professed his love for me. I was overjoyed for I too was in love with him ... more passionately than I could have ever imagined possible," she said on a smile. "We spent the next several hours discussing our future and hopes, speculating about the possibility of children and the places we could live."

She laughed, but there was an unmistakable edge to the sound. My hand tightened around hers.

"You must understand, things are done differently here. Commitments made among our kind are enough in themselves. We are unwaveringly devoted beings. So in that very place — the cave we held so dearly — we dedicated ourselves, our lives, to one another. Pledging with no greater a passion than would have set the world on fire, that we would spend our eternity together."

My own passion stirred inside, former dreams and memories overwhelming me. Ilana's eyes held a sadness I knew mirrored my own. She stroked the image of her breathtaking Naiad, her face a picture of steadfast adoration yet utter heartbreak.

"We held each other long into the evening, until it came well past time to leave. He walked me home, my hand in his, through the darkness. We agreed to speak with our families at first light and explain what we had done, that we had bound ourselves."

Ilana drew a steadying breath. "Neither of us realized that my eldest brother had been looking for me nor stood, not thirty feet away, hidden in the shadows. He watched as my forbidden friendship turned into something much more unthinkable. Little did I know he immediately told our parents."

The silence stretched on. I could imagine, all too well, the picture Ilana painted. My own shattered heart ached in my chest with the reminder of such a passion. It seemed she and I were both meant to live without a heart — a likeness I hadn't anticipated sharing with anyone, let alone the Dryad meant to be my mother-in-law.

"I didn't deny it when my father broached the subject," Ilana began and shook her head, tears welling in her eyes. "He lashed out at me, ranting about my thoughtlessness, writing my love off as childish and unrealistic. He stated that my marriage couldn't be real because I was too young, that I didn't know what I wanted or what I was doing. In his mind, I had been deceived or persuaded into marriage. I was forbidden to even leave the house until everything was ... dealt with."

I flinched at her wording, and the all too familiar lump knotted in my throat.

"I escaped in the middle of the night to warn him to leave and never return or they would..." She took an unsteady breath. "I forced him to go, promising we would find a way to be together again someday; I would find him. And then I watched him swim away."

My head spun. I realized I'd stopped breathing and drew a lungful of oxygen.

"What happened?" I asked, unable to stop myself.

Ilana wiped the moisture from her cheeks and sighed. "I left The Island to search for him, only to find that he had located his birth family." She laughed grimly. "As it turned out, he was part of royalty himself. We would never be together again. Now it was his family's turn to assure that that would never happen."

"But how did … you're with Aiken now," I pressed, wanting to understand but scared of overstepping a boundary.

"One day, while hunting in the forest, Aiken found me beside a pond, gazing into the water and crying. There was something so gentle about him. He was so different than my former love, but he loved me more than I deserved. Ignoring his family's wishes, Aiken married me and we have been happy together since."

"I can see that." I smiled when she patted my hand.

"Aiken accepted me as I was. When I married the first time, we committed wholly to it, you see?" Ilana searched for my understanding, and I responded with a nod. "Aiken and I were married quickly … so the child I'd brought with me from The Island was no more than a rumor after a time. He was sent to live with his father, bearing too much of a resemblance and likeness to his side of nature."

Child? She was forced to give up her heart and her baby?

She turned the page of her album, her fingers trembling. A baby as beautiful as a cherubic angel smiled back. Dark curly hair covered his head and he wore a smile that would melt your heart. The love in Ilana's eyes was scarred by heartbreak.

"I haven't seen him since he was just a few months old. You cannot imagine that kind of loss, Ashton. Every piece of me … gone." Her red-rimmed eyes brimmed and spilled over with fresh tears. She was right. The pain I'd experienced over losing the love of my existence was nothing compared to giving up my love and my child.

I leaned forward and wrapped my arm around her shoulders. She smiled and leaned her head against mine. "You're probably wondering why I shared my personal history with you."

Again, she was right on target.

"I loved my Naiad more than the stars combined." She smiled nostalgically. "But it could not be for us. Maybe if things had been different — a different time in our lives, a different place — things might have worked out, but it just couldn't in our circumstance. My point is, you may only have one heart, one time to offer it completely, but there is always love to be found.

"Aiken knew my life, where my heart lay, but still, he wanted me. And over these many years, though I have never regained the heart that longs for my Naiad, I have grown to love Aiken. He is more than I deserve, better than I'd ever been allowed to hope. ...And things aren't always the way they seem. Oftentimes a compromise can work better than one might ever imagine."

The story of Ilana's history replayed through my mind as we made our way back to her family. Without hesitation, she walked over to her husband and smiled before lighting the room with a loving kiss. I forced my gaze away from their intimate encounter, and caught a glimpse of Kyle as he rounded the corner on his way out.

The rest of the evening passed by quickly and with little required of me. I barely spoke more than a couple of sentences, only speaking at all when required to do so. Ilana's story replayed through my mind as she hugged me, expressing yet again her joy with my arrival. Kevin escorted me to the entrance of the palace as I bid everyone, except a missing Kyle, goodnight.

"Why are you so quiet?" Kevin asked. "Didn't you like my family?"

"You're family's great," I said. "Most of them anyway."

"Yes, my mother can be tiresome." He sighed. "Her life is all sunshine and rainbows. She wouldn't know what to do if something bad actually happened."

Disgust twisted through me, and I fought not to slap him. He had no idea what he was saying, and I guessed he really didn't care. "Your mother is one of the most amazing people I've ever met." *How she ever got stuck with a selfish and ungrateful son like you is beyond me.*

"Smiles never got anyone ahead. She's too much of a dreamer."

"So if someone isn't ruthless or selfish, they're inherently worthless? Looking for the best in people is a bad thing?" I asked for the second time in my life.

"It depends on who you ask — the person who's trusting or the person being trusted. I've always found that quality quite helpful in getting what I want." His smile turned callous.

It was all too much. Anger swelled inside and bubbled over. "Is that what you told my mother before you took matters into your own hands?" I spouted, tears cascading down my cheeks. "Did you tell her how stupid she was? Was that the last thing she ever heard before you killed her?"

"I never touched your mother," he said coldly. "I didn't have a reason to after your father ruined the situation. My hands are spotless … on her account, at least."

I froze, pulling my arm away from him. "Then what happened to her?"

"How should I know? Why don't you ask my brother? Kyle was the one sent to deal with it when Oren brought her back."

Kevin ushered me to the front door and hemmed me in the corner. My stomach rolled, and I fought the bile rising in my throat. Kevin didn't give me a chance to react.

"Now then, I'm not the villain, so you can end this crusade at being angry with me. Forget the past, Ashton. Your future is with me," Kevin murmured against my unyielding lips. He pulled me into his chest, his hands blazing against the small of my back. I closed my eyes and shut off my mind until I felt his mouth still, and he backed away.

"Your future is with me," he said again then retreated into the darkness.

I did the same but in a different manner. My darkness was inside, hiding in the emptiness that used to house my heart.

Chapter Twenty-Four
Acceptance

Relief seeped through my closed eyelids. The teabags made from the silky grass soothed my tired and swollen eyes. I sat at the kitchen table, a plum in hand, and relaxed my head against the chair as I chewed.

Someone tapped gently against the glass of the back door. I pulled the teabags off and opened it to Kyle.

"Morning." I said, confused.

"Morning, Monet." His smile faltered. "Why are you looking at me like that?"

"I was just wondering why you came to the back door."

"I heard you in here, so I figured I'd save you the trip." He looked down, shuffling his feet.

My eyes narrowed."Hmm."

"Oh, calm down, Ash. It's not like I hang out here all day and eavesdrop. I was just close."

"If you say so. So what's up?"

"We're going to the clearing for a while, and I hoped you'd come." Kyle shoved his hands in his pockets, his eyes hopeful.

"Who's going?" I really didn't want to put myself in Kevin's line of sight — or Adare's for that matter.

"Mostly my siblings," he said. "Kev's working today though."

"Sounds great to me then. Let's go!" I shrugged.

The sun shone brightly, warming me from the outside in as we walked. Kyle whistled an upbeat tune, his face as bright as the glow in the sky.

Figuring it would be a good time for more answers, I jumped in without warning. "So what's up with your eyes?"

"What do you mean?" His head fell to the side.

"Your eyes shine yellow. Some of the others here are reddish-orange, some are golden. Why is that?"

"Just like animals. Different animals have different eyeshine. Green, red, blue. I'm a Dryad and we have darker eyes, so warmer shades, I suppose. I don't think there's an exact science to it."

"That makes sense, I guess. Is it the same with scents then? Is that why you all smell like plants and fruit?" I asked.

Kyle's laughter bounced off the trees. "Yeah. Of course, I don't smell like fruit. Right?" He raised an eyebrow.

"No. You smell like sandalwood." I elbowed him. "What do I smell like?"

"Do you really want to know?" His nose scrunched up.

I rolled my eyes.

Kyle leaned down. His nose skimmed my jaw, and he took a long slow breath. He exhaled, sending a shiver down my spine.

"You smell like Monet." Kyle's voice grew husky as his breath tickled my ear. "A mix of lotus, wisteria, and fresh water."

"Good to know. Thanks." A thought crossed my mind. "Could you smell me in the rain or water?"

"No, not really. Your kind smells of watery things to begin with, so the scent of rain dilutes it. One of the many irritating ways of making it hard to find you." He winked and tugged me forward.

"Do I get a question as well?" he asked carefully.

"What could you possibly want to know?" I laughed.

"Where did you get that ring you refuse to take off?" Kyle looked at me from the corner of his eye. My smile melted.

"I found it," I said. Kyle laughed without humor.

"Lucky find," he murmured. "Where?"

"In Texas," I answered gruffly.

Kyle let it go with a simple, "All right. Just curious."

The clearing came into view. Sunlight streamed through wispy clouds, and the scent of honeysuckle clung to the air. I stared out over the long rectangle bordered by fields of heather. Squares of checkered grass stretched across the meadow, looking much like the courtyard of a European castle. The soothing meadow cooled the soles of my feet. I sighed, digging my toes in further.

What looked like wide open-fronted cages on either end of the clearing caught my eye, and I shifted a questioning glance to Kyle.

"I thought you might enjoy watching us play," he said.

"Play?" I repeated, surprised that anyone did anything recreational here. I couldn't even begin to imagine what their idea of play was.

"Soccer," he said as if I'd missed the obvious.

I appraised the odd looking shapes in the clearing with understanding. "Mm-hmm," I said. "But what's with the maximum security nets?"

"We have a little more oomph behind our kicks than most."

"Ah, I see." I smiled, envisioning that.

"We kept whisking balls through the cloth nets like cannonballs. I swear Oren had one smoking one day."

"Well, what if I want to join in?" I asked.

"You?" he questioned with more disbelief in his voice than I appreciated. "You want to play with us?"

"Yeah." I crossed my arms. "You gotta problem with that?"

Kyle bit back a laugh. "Come on, Ash. You can't be serious. Do you even know how to play?"

I balked but stood taller, squaring my shoulders. "Yes!"

Kyle's face stayed in a grin. "No way. You wouldn't even be able to keep up with us."

I couldn't argue the fact. If they played full speed — and why wouldn't they? — it would be impossible. And I didn't think they'd want to devise a new set of rules for playing in water.

My shoulders fell, and I turned to take my place on the sideline.

"Hey. Wait a sec." Kyle grabbed my waist and pulled me back. "Maybe we could improvise. Make it an even game somehow."

I lifted an eyebrow. "What did you have in mind?"

Kyle's gray eyes turned scheming as the rest of the Hawthorne clan emerged from the woods.

"Hey, Ashton! Did you come to watch?" Kyle's oldest sister trotted toward us.

"Hi, Erin. Yeah, I guess so."

"Actually, Ere, Ash was hoping to join us," Kyle said. Everyone froze mid-stretch and stared at me.

Oren, like Kyle, burst out laughing. "You're kidding, right? Does she even know what this thing is?" He held up a checkered soccer ball and twirled it on his fingertip. The colors blurred into a solid orb of red.

"Yes!" I offered him the same response as I had Kyle.

"Well, I had an idea for leveling out the playing field, so to speak." Kyle dashed into the trees quicker than I could blink.

"Long as you have a plan," Oren spoke to the empty space where his brother disappeared.

Several seconds later, Kyle reappeared carrying a length of rope and a pocketknife.

"Good plan there, big brother." Oren offered a sarcastic thumbs-up. "You gonna hogtie us so she can play? Or maybe hamstring me with that knife?"

"Don't tempt me," Kyle said. "I thought we could do it like a three-legged race but let Ashton run by herself."

Kyle unfurled the rope and began cutting sections away.

"You're serious?" Oren scoffed. "That's stupid."

"I think it sounds fun!" Erin chimed, wearing a grin that made her look a lot like Kyle. "We always play by the same old rules. Let's mix it up for a change."

"No way!" Oren opposed. "You're not tying me up."

"What's wrong, Oren? Afraid I'll win?" I quipped. Probably a stupid notion given the fact that Oren lacked a that's-too-far switch in his brain.

Everyone's gaze lighted on me before cutting to Oren. Surprised entertainment washed over their faces.

"In your dreams, hot stuff." Oren grinned. "Or have I already been starring there?"

I wasn't the only one who scoffed and rolled their eyes.

"She's got guts, Kyle." Erin laughed as she jogged over to stand beside me. She gave me a playful nudge in the arm and winked.

Kyle and Oren divvied up the teams. Thankfully, I was on Kyle's, but only because he called the coin toss and chose first.

"So how are we going to do this?" Erin held up her piece of rope.

"Just find someone and tie yourself to them." Kyle fastened his leg to Pearse's.

"You break my leg, and I'm going be to mad," Oren threatened as Erin secured their ankles together. She bit down on her lip, trying not to smile.

"You do know how to play, right?" Kyle leaned down to whisper as everyone hobbled toward the field.

"Sure." I shrugged and pointed. "The little ball goes in those thingies. You're not supposed to use your hands though, right?"

Kyle tried to repress a sigh, but it escaped anyway. "Yeah."

The game started off slow at first. Oren yelled at Erin, telling her to pay attention. She laughed him off and finally let him take the lead. Kyle and Pearse moved without much trouble while Elon and Adare struggled to time their steps. After several minutes, everyone figured out how to move symbiotically.

I followed after Elon, trying to sweep the ball away. In a flat sprint, they flew past me, whizzing the ball toward the goal. I felt sorry for the goalie when he stopped it against his chest. The loud smack of a speeding ball with Dryad flesh sounded like a blue whale doing a belly flop from a mile high.

Erin's mate tossed the ball back out. I swooped in and stole it from Oren, dribbling around him before I kicked it between his legs and zipped down the field. Knowing I couldn't get around the lone goalie, I passed the ball to Kyle and Pearse. Pearse intercepted it and sent it flying over Elon and Adare's heads.

The ball whizzed like a bullet through the air toward the improvised net, rattling the metal as it made contact. Cheers erupted from my team and everyone clapped me on the back for the assist. Even Oren smiled and shook his head.

I flopped down, panting beside Kyle as he and Pearse untied their legs.

"Thanks for this." I gave him a genuine smile.

"You're welcome." Kyle's eyes held mine, warmth coating his expression. "I'm happy to see you smile again."

Erin bounded over to stand at my feet. "Hey, Ash. Are you coming to dinner tonight?"

"I guess so." I looked at my grass stained knees and muddy shirt. "I should clean up first though."

"Don't be ridiculous." Erin grinned. "We'll all be grimy. Don't worry about it."

Everyone else ran ahead while Kyle lingered at my pace. Fun and games aside, my mind reeled with unanswered questions again.

Kyle's eyes raked over me, his brows lowering. "What's on your mind, Monet? You've gone solemn all of the sudden."

I shrugged him off and shook my head.

"Don't do that. What's so bad you won't tell me?" He nudged me. When I didn't return his smile, he stopped. "Ash, what's wrong?"

I bit my lip. Kevin had to be wrong about Kyle's involvement with my mother's death. Still, I had to know, or it would eat at me forever. "I need to ask you something, and I need you to answer me honestly."

Kyle looked at me, concern etched in his face. "What is it?"

I drew a deep breath, my skin cold. "Were you sent to deal with my mother?"

Kyle's expression melted then turned blank. "It was my responsibility," he said then just the hint of his eyebrows pulled up in the middle.

"You didn't answer my question," I said, recognizing the expression.

Kyle grabbed my arm at my elbow and encouraged me forward. When I tried to pull away, he met me with a pleading glance. "This isn't the time or place for this conversation, Ashton. It was my job to fix things, and I did. Please, don't ask me about this any further right now. I know it's hard, but I need you to trust me right now."

His gray eyes burned with sincerity, battling against my emotions. Maybe he had followed instructions, but I couldn't believe Kyle was capable of taking anyone's life, no matter who ordered it. Kyle had proven to be the only true thing in my life.

While I knew there was more to it than he was telling me, I couldn't help but trust him.

"Okay," I whispered. "But I need to know, Kyle. I'm counting on you. You're all I have, and if I thought you had—"

"I know," he interrupted quietly. "I'll tell you everything. I promise. Just not today."

Kevin waited by the door when we filed through the front gate.

"Where have you been?" His lip curled up as he appraised my filthy clothing.

"At the clearing," I said. "We played soccer today."

Kevin stared at me, disbelief or irritation in his eyes. I couldn't tell which.

"She was incredible, man." Kyle stepped forward and draped a friendly arm across my shoulder. "You should've seen her, she totally nutmegged Oren and Erin. Caught them flat-footed and went right between their legs, and that's saying something considering they were tied together. We were in tears." He gave me a mock punch in the shoulder, and I smiled.

"You want to run that by me again?" Kevin said.

Kyle explained his ingenious idea and the day's events to Kevin, who stood wearing an expression that reeked of, Are you kidding me?

"Ashton?" A recognizable voice spoke at the same time the smell of a damp hayfield hit me. I swallowed hard, anger and feelings of betrayal rolling inside. I slowly turned to face the man behind me.

"Come now, don't be like that," Harry said, a derisive smile on his face.

"Why are you here?" Kyle asked, his jaw tight with restraint.

"What? You would have me miss out on seeing my niece and her loving fiancé all this time?" Harry's eyes settled on me. "How are things, Ashton? I see you found your way home after all. Did you have a pleasant trip?"

The flagrancy behind his words rang loud. Heat flooded my body, and my vision ran red. I didn't recognize the mocking face staring back at me. I searched Harry's eyes for some sign of the man I'd always known, but only found disregard. My teeth cut into my tongue and the taste of blood filled my mouth.

"Kev, why don't you get Ash something to drink?" Kyle motioned behind him toward the kitchen. "Ashton, what do you want?"

"He knows what I like," I responded, sounding surprisingly nonchalant.

"I'll be back momentarily." Kevin ran his hand along my arm, gripping my fingers briefly before offering Harry a questioning glance and striding off.

My careful façade wavered. Fury bubbled close to the surface, scorching from my hairline down to my toes. I craved violence for the first time in my life as I stared wordlessly at Harry's smug unrepentant expression.

"What do you think?" He glanced around the palace. "I guess you never expected this." Harry's focus flitted through the hall, and his eyes paused on Kyle who watched us carefully. "He seems to have taken a keen interest in you all of the sudden. What's that about?"

"How. Could. You? How could you do this to me, to my family?" My voice shook.

"It's nothing personal, kid. I just needed a bailout," he stated unsympathetically, as if he were talking about a sports game. "Your mom couldn't finish the job. That just left you. And to be quite honest, this worked out even better. Edlyn's failure turned the tides, so to speak."

Angry tears spilled from my eyes. How could he talk like that, like I was nothing to him? And mentioning my mother? That was beyond crossing the line.

I followed Harry's gaze to see a protective Kyle watching us from across the way.

"What is the issue here?" Harry's voice turned gruff then a slow grin spread across his face. "Ohh, I see. You're good, Ashton. I'll give you that. Well played. A Hawthorne on each arm is quite an accomplishment. Sometimes I wonder just how factual those rumors tend to be about our kind."

"Shut up, Harry. It's not like that," I huffed.

"Isn't it?" Harry challenged, crossing his arms over his chest. "I wonder what your Gabe would say about that? You sure got over him pretty quickly ... Gracie."

"Leave Gabe out of this," I growled, my chest heaving. "He sacrificed everything to help you, and you mock us openly. Is my pain somehow humorous to you?" I felt all eyes on me as I stood toe-to-toe with Harry, shaking with fury.

"I wouldn't say humorous, per say," Harry stated coldly.

"Ashton." Kevin towed me back. "Calm yourself. What's happening?"

Harry gave a sick smile. I saw the assault in his eyes, but cut him off. "H-h-he said that he was sorry he ever helped you, and that you didn't deserve me. He said you'd never be a real leader, and you should stick to your own kind." My voice broke when I caught sight of Kevin's enraged expression.

Kevin pushed me to Kyle, and grabbed Harry by the shirtfront.

"No!" Harry's face glowed red with fury. "It's her, Kevin! She's been with..." His statement was cut short as the back of Kevin's hand struck Harry across the jaw with a loud smack, propelling him to the ground.

"We should've never bargained with you again, bottom-dweller. That was the last time." Kevin snapped his fingers. Six intimidating men charged out of nowhere to stand beside us. "You know where to take him."

"No! Wait!" Harry's voice faded into the darkness, the henchmen making quick work of their removal.

"I do believe he's outlived his usefulness," Kevin said calmly. He wiped Harry's blood from his knuckles then pulled my hand through his arm. There was no flaw in Kyle's reasoning before. Kevin would act first and question later.

I sat dutifully next to Kevin through dinner. The quiet music playing in the background hid the fact that I didn't join the conversation. I stared at my plate, pushing the food around with my fork. How could I fix this? Harry would tell Kevin everything given the chance. Kev would know about Gabe, and who knew the consequences. And what did Harry mean by my mom's failures turning the tides?

"Are you ill, dear?" Ilana asked, her hand sliding over mine.

I glanced up and forced a smile. "Everything's fine. I'm just a little tired."

Ilana held my gaze for a moment longer. Her delicate eyebrows fell, concern etched in her expression. Chairs scraped against the hard wood, startling me. I looked away from Ilana as couples made their way to the adjoining room.

Familiar folk music hummed through the space as the family partnered up and began swaying to the beat. An ache tugged in my chest, taking my breath away. I found a plush armchair in the corner and started to sit when Kevin's hand reached for mine.

"Dance with me," he ordered. Kevin's arm roped around my waist a little too tight. His grip was possessive, like a child who refused to be separated from his favorite toy, and my soul mourned for love.

I warred with the memories of warm cedar, sea-colored eyes, and gentler hands that set me aflame. My mind refused to relent, and for a brief moment, I embraced the indelible mark of Gabe burned into my heart.

The bone deep sadness that followed swept away all emotion, leaving me to the familiar emptiness I'd come to accept. Kyle's knowing eyes met mine with compassion and concern when we passed by. But Kevin twirled me around again, ripping Kyle from me too.

Kevin looked down when I sighed.

I tucked my cheek into his shoulder and tried to hide the nothingness in my eyes. "I just realized. We've never danced together."

"Why would we? There was never a need," he said matter-of-factly.

His phone buzzed, and we slowed to a stop. "I need to take this."

Kevin released me, and he walked away without a second glance, leaving me alone on the dance floor. An infinite weight settled in my chest as I watched the couples surrounding me. Seeing the love in their eyes, knowing I was destined for a marriage of obligation, pinned me in place.

"Mind if I cut in?" Kyle's voice broke through my thoughts.

When I didn't answer, he turned me around in his arms, his hand lightly brushing my back. With every step, we neared the foyer that housed the staircase. Ilana's watchful eye caught mine just as Kyle tugged me through a hall, leading outside.

"You looked like you could use some air." His expression warmed.

"I need a lot of things, Kyle." My lip quivered, and I wrapped my arms around myself.

Kyle's hand brushed across my face, momentarily distracted. "I wish I could give them to you," he whispered then pulled himself together. "I can offer one thing, though. How about a midnight dip?"

I half smiled. "Yeah?"

Kyle nodded and wound his fingers through mine.

"Do you mind if I ask you something?" I kept my hand in his as we walked past the gardens.

He barked a soft laugh. "Does it matter? You'll just ask me anyway."

"True." I shrugged.

"Shoot," he said.

"Why were you so antagonistic when we met in the woods? Why didn't you want me to see you?"

He sighed. "I didn't want any part of this, Ash. I never wanted you to end up here. I knew you'd be devastated — that you'd feel betrayed and lied to, even without everything else that happened. I didn't want a hand in that. I was just so angry about everything, and then I went and blew my cover."

"Why did you do it then?" I stopped to study his face.

My question brought a smile to his mouth. "I couldn't help myself. You and your big plans for escape. You could've ended up in any number of positions with Oren, all of which would've involved someone getting their teeth kicked in."

I smiled, imagining the possibilities. As usual, Kyle was dead on target.

"Sorry about that by the way." I glanced up to find Kyle's expression gentle yet amused as we began moving toward the pond.

"It's all right." Kyle shrugged and eased his toes to the water's edge. "I guess it worked out, all things considered."

I couldn't quite agree.

I skirted the edges of the pond to the place where the willow fronds brushed the water. The petite leaves swayed like ribbons in the wind. I caught a slender branch between my fingers and peeked at Kyle from the corner of my eye.

"So, your mother is an insightful woman," I said. "How she watches us all, taking everything in. She's very ... perceptive."

Kyle laughed once, moving closer to me. "You're sharp, you know that? In all these years, my siblings have never noticed. I imagine it's just commonplace for them."

"Can she read minds?"

Kyle grinned. "No. She sees things."

"Like what? The future? Is she a fortune teller?" I smiled, mostly joking, but the very idea terrified me.

"Not exactly. You've heard the phrase 'green with envy?'" Kyle asked, and I nodded. "My mother can see that. Actually, it's how the term came about."

"You mean, she could tell that I was jealous?" I quirked an eyebrow. "You could tell that, too."

He snorted. "It's not quite that clear-cut. From her perspective, you would look differently. She would almost see you green. She doesn't hear your thoughts, and she can't see the future, but your color — your mood or emotions — they're as clear as if they were written on your forehead. She has to see your eyes though. That whole, 'The eyes are the windows to the soul' thing, is very much in play there."

My skin ran cold as that fact sank in. What had she seen in me at the countless family dinners? Was that the motive behind her sharing her life with me? Did she know all the things I was hiding? The things I worked so hard to forget?

"Are you all right, Ash? You're as white as a sheet." Kyle's hands chafed over mine.

"Why didn't you tell me, Kyle?" I shivered.

"Calm down." He wrapped his arm around my shoulder. "That's not something I would just share with you for no reason. No one knows. I never even considered mentioning it."

"But all this time? What if she knows about Gabe?" I blurted in blind panic. "What if she tells Kevin?"

Kyle's eyes hardened. "Listen. I know my mother. She would never share something unless she felt it was necessary. That's why she's never told the others. Whatever her reasoning, she only did it to benefit you." He drew a deep breath. "If she does know about him, she won't say anything. So don't worry."

Hearing it out loud, I knew Kyle was right. The time I'd spent with Ilana had only strengthened my opinion of her. Maybe I hid my feelings well, or perhaps she genuinely cared about me and was trying to ease me into this new life. Whatever her thought process, Kyle was right about her motives. She harbored nothing negative toward me, and she would never hurt her family.

I stared at the night sky, accepting the fact that nothing had changed, and no one else was at risk. Another full moon shone about a carpet of stars, its beams glistening across the water at my feet. The sound of tree frogs circled the pond, and fireflies glowed throughout the clearing.

I gave Kyle a mischievous smile then very non-gracefully dove in. Seconds later, I resurfaced to find Kyle standing on the bank, water dripping down his front and a playfully putout gleam in his eye. Kyle peeled off his shirt and plunged in after me, sending a tidal wave in my direction.

He resurfaced, wiping the water from his eyes, and swam to meet me. "Can I ask you something?"

"Shoot," I repeated his answer.

"Why did you stay with Kevin?" he asked.

My teeth found my lip, and I stared at the ripples fanning out from our bodies. "Just shallow and superficial, I guess. It was a comfortable lifestyle."

"No." Kyle shook his head.

"No?" I echoed.

"I don't believe that for a second. You already had the money and reputation."

I didn't say anything.

"I know you all too well, Monet," Kyle continued when I didn't respond to his on-target observation. "But this is the one thing we've never talked about. You've always had him at arm's length. I'm not complaining. You were doing the right thing, keeping your distance. But there's more to it. More than you know."

My eyes narrowed. "What's that supposed to mean?"

"Let me take a guess. In the beginning, you were drawn to him, right? Kev was beautiful, charming, endearing — all the things you never thought about but somehow wanted. And even when he wasn't trying to be charming, even when he was being a complete jerk, you couldn't help but need to be with him."

My breathing fell silent.

"But it's different now, isn't it?" Kyle stated confidently. "Even if everything had played out differently, you wouldn't see him the same way because you're not the same. The things that were so enticing about him are missing now. All that charm and charisma, the hypnotic eyes and thousand watt smile, they're just that and nothing more. And I'll bet if you think about it, you won't even be able to remember what you loved so much about him to begin with."

And Kyle was right. The more I tried to understand my attraction, the less it made sense. "How do you know this?" I asked.

"When you began changing," Kyle continued, "the hold Kev had on you began to weaken. That's why he planned that trip for you to Europe. You were actually coming here in case you changed. Kev didn't want to lose his chance with you. A quick marriage, one way or the other."

The wind howled in the treetops, and cold seeped through me despite the warmth of the water. "How is that possible?"

"Before you changed, you were drawn to him because he was a nymph. Humans weren't so far off the mark on that one." Kyle shook his head and climbed ashore.

"Nymphs can compel people?" My eyebrows shot up.

"Mm-hmmm," Kyle nodded. "Well, humans at least. It doesn't work on other nymphs."

"Wouldn't he have tried to compel me sooner?" I plopped down beside Kyle on the shore.

Kyle sighed. "It's hard to say. Maybe he tried and couldn't because you were changing. Or maybe it only worked to a certain degree. Even if he had tried and been successful, if you were more human than nymph, the physical bond wouldn't have formed the same after you ... well, it wouldn't have formed. Kev needed you to be in a position where you couldn't decide to leave later. It was all a matter of which part of your genetics was stronger."

All this time, my nymph side was the catalyst behind everything. My feelings toward Kevin changing, probably his anxiety and push for making a commitment ... maybe even the reason behind his pressing for our physical closeness. In this world, forever was a literal term and one Kevin relied on to keep me from leaving.

"I should probably get you home. Heaven forbid his highness be kept waiting for anything tomorrow." Kyle's eyes hardened as he pulled me to my feet. "But I'll see you tomorrow at the museum for a history lesson, right?"

"If you say so," I murmured, keeping my eyes on my ring.

"If you don't learn your history, you're doomed to repeat the past, you know." Kyle's hand warmed mine as he led me back to the house. We walked in silence, both of us seemingly lost in thought. Kyle opened the gate and ushered me to the porch.

"Night, Monet." He gave a half-hearted smile then turned to leave.

"Hey, Kyle?" I stopped him.

"Yeah?"

"What, um..." I drew a deep breath. "What you said before, when one binds themselves to another, can they find someone else? Someone they truly love?"

Kyle stopped breathing. "Humans are different, but when a nymph commits that fully to another nymph, that bond never ends — it never weakens, never goes away."

Ilana popped back into my mind.

"So what? You're just stuck if your mate is gone?"

"Unless they're killed," he admitted, conflict warring in his expression.

"Killed?" I honed in on his choice of words.

"It's not like we die of natural causes ... mostly." Kyle sighed.

But what of Aiken and Ilana? I thought. "What would happen if a nymph found another partner? Could there ever be two loves and it work?"

"You only have one heart to give, Ash. One time to give it," Kyle repeated Ilana's words. "After that, you have a choice but it's no more than that. You're never whole without your other half."

Then why can't I heal? I didn't ask.

Chapter Twenty-Five
Ancient History

Feathery dogwood petals floated in the air as I walked to museum. I drew a breath and tucked the dreams of last night into my memory vault. Three nights in a row, I'd dreamt of warm cedar and haunting eyes. Each morning I woke to feel of sweat soaked sheets and a tear-stained pillowcase.

The curly-haired shepherd I'd met the day we passed the factory emerged from one of the cabins just off the path.

"Good morning," I greeted and waved.

"Good morning, my lady." He turned toward me and bowed again, a dimpled smile on his face.

"It's a fine day for tending sheep. You have a very important job." I knelt down to meet his eyes.

"Yes, my lady. Thank you. A new lamb was born last night," he said eagerly. "I want to see him and give him a name."

"Eòghan," a deep voice called from the cabin door. "Get along, young man. The sheep won't tend themselves..." The man's sentence trailed away as I stood. His emerald green eyes widened, and he dropped to a knee. "Forgive me, my lady. I meant no disrespect."

"No, please. Stand up. I was just enjoying your son's enthusiasm." I ruffled the boy's curls. "Carry on, Eòghan. Give the new lamb a strong name."

"I will, my lady." He smiled once more and set off toward the western fields.

"You're blessed with a charming family," I said to Eòghan's father.

"Yes, my lady. He's one of four." The man beamed, a broad smile on his bearded face. "Two of my daughters are inside with my wife, not yet old enough to work. My eldest son is living among the humans now."

"Good for you," I praised. "Leaving The Valley requires trust and dedication, I'm told. I'm sure you're very proud. I'd love to meet them sometime."

His eyebrows rose, and he gestured toward his cottage. "Would you like to come inside for tea?"

I began to take him up on his offer when the sound of Kyle whistling broke through the trees. "I would love to, but I'm late as it is. Another day?"

"Certainly, my lady. You're welcome any time." He bowed his head and quickly kissed my hand.

"Very well, enjoy your morning, sir." I took a step back, not wanting to be chastised for speaking with him.

"Morning, Kaede." Kyle rounded the corner, a grin on his face. His eyes locked on me and the grin widened.

"My lord." Kaede backed away and bowed.

"Knock it off. No one here needs to be revered," Kyle joked. "Good morning, Elise."

I followed Kyle's line of sight to the figure in the entrance of the house. A petite woman stepped through the doorway and into the sunlight. A smile crept across the face of the woman, her strikingly blue eyes wrinkled at the corners. Something about her felt odd.

Kaede nodded and retreated toward the cottage. "I'll bid you both farewell then. My lady."

"Kaede," I said, my gaze locked on the woman in the yard.

"Fraternizing with the commoners?" Kyle held a hand to his chest. "What would people say?"

I slapped his shoulder and finally looked away.

"Don't be rude," I hissed. "They'll hear you."

"Please, everyone here knows I'm joking. Kaede and I are good friends. We hunt together all the time."

"Oh," I said, still off kilter.

"You ready to learn?" Kyle pulled my hand through his arm and set off toward the museum.

"Sure," I answered then froze.

Kyle jerked to a stop, his hand up in question when my eyes widened.

"Blue!" I said and slapped my forehead. "She's not a Dryad."

"You noticed that, huh?" Kyle lifted an eyebrow.

I looked at him expectantly.

"She's human," he explained as if there were humans all over The Valley.

My jaw dropped. "How is that possible? I thought humans couldn't know about nymphs or this place."

"She's the first in over two-hundred years," he said as he began walking again. "Save the life of someone important, and you're golden."

"How long has she been here?" I asked. "Kaede said they had an older son who was with the humans. How is that possible?"

"Elise is eighty, I believe," Kyle said on a shrug. "She's been here for about sixty years now."

"She doesn't look a day over twenty," I said. "That's impossible."

"You should know there's no such thing as impossible by now." Kyle grinned and wrapped an arm around my shoulder. "Elise is a prime example of why humans can't know about us."

"Why is that?" I asked.

"She stopped aging. And short of a catastrophe, she'll never die."

I felt the shock on my face. "She's immortal?"

"For as long as she chooses The Valley. It's the grass," Kyle said. "A little tea goes a long way, but if she stopped drinking it or left, she would wither away very quickly."

"Wow." I shook my head then a thought crossed my mind. "What about her children?"

Kyle's expression fell. "They're human. Everyone had high hopes that bringing Elise here, we could figure out how to grow our numbers, but nothing's worked."

My anger rose up. "So what, she's a breeding project? Like a panda in captivity?"

"No, no! Of course not," Kyle said quickly then sighed. "Well, that wasn't the idea in the beginning. She saved my life one day while Kaede and I were hunting. My mother offered her the chance to live here, and Elise, having fallen for Kaede, accepted. When they began having children, we just hoped it might be possible. And her kids are exceptions to the laws here as well. They're given every opportunity and choice she is. They understand the situation."

I sighed, my fingers brushing the mossy oak as we passed through the tunnel. Why couldn't things ever be simple?

"Where's your brother this morning?" I changed the subject. "Off doing something charitable no doubt."

Kyle laughed. "Is that sarcasm I hear? He's working a deal with someone in California. There's a trip planned for next week."

I stopped in place, and Kyle looked at me.

"Do you think he'd take me with him?" I asked hopeful.

"It's hard to say what Kevin will ever do. Let's just focus on educating you for now, all right?"

The smell of sunshine and grass wafted through the air as we neared the museum. An expansive building rose from the trees at the end of the path. I slowed my stride to study the formation of bent limbs and curved trunks.

"Is that the museum?" I questioned in wonder.

Kyle grinned. "Yeah. Pretty neat, huh?"

"To say the least." I walked the path around the building, marveling at the way the many trees grew upward, intertwining at the top to form a roof of heart-shaped leaves and twisted branches. "How did you do that?"

Kyle ran his hand over the white flaky bark, a deep appreciation in his eyes. "We're good at growing things, much like the giant oak tunnel. By manipulating their growth patterns, we don't have to kill the trees to use them."

Marble floors chilled the soles of my bare feet. I followed the naturally formed hallways, peering into a number of rooms that housed everything from a library to a gallery full of paintings and sculptures. The museum felt creepy with only Kyle and me there. While record keeping was important, I figured the Dryads already knew their history having either lived it, or heard the stories. I couldn't imagine the museum got much traffic.

We sat at a long table and Kyle rolled out a logistical sketch of The Valley, explaining a bunch of things I never cared to know.

"Kyle?" I interrupted his lengthy story. "You remember the other day when we talked about nymph influence on humans?"

He suddenly became interested in his map. "Yes."

"I was thinking about that more. And while I was attracted to Kevin, it was never as intense as with..." My voice trailed away when his lips pinched into a thin line. "What I mean is, how was Kevin so sure I wouldn't find someone else? Even when I was drawn to him, I wasn't head over heels stupid."

Kyle's hands stilled and he sighed. "Because he had me follow you. I was ordered to watch your every move. What you did, who you were with, where you lived."

I gasped and watched his profile as he stared down, his eyes fixed on the counter.

"Part of me hated invading your life like that..."

"And the other part?" I asked, the sarcasm back in full force.

He looked at me, his eyes searching. "The other part was grateful I had the opportunity to keep you safe."

I narrowed my eyes and scoffed.

"Look, I didn't invade your privacy like some perverted stalker. I just watched out for you. End of story." Kyle's fingers drummed on the table.

"You're blushing." I tapped his pink cheek.

"No, I'm not." He tried to turn his face away, and I grabbed the bottom of his jaw. His denoting eyebrows pulled up in the middle. The telltale signs of a lie were written all over his guilty expression.

"What aren't you telling me?" I asked.

"It's just, during that time, I had an opportunity to see more of the real you — the one who loves reading and classical music. That's when I fell ... felt like I'd found my best friend. How Kevin could miss all of that, I'll never know." Kyle paused, his eye's probing. "He's missed a lot more than your loving to read though, hasn't he? He doesn't know you at all. Not like I do."

My eyes fell to the map, a frown tugging at my mouth.

"There's so much more to you than the façade you show the world, Monet." He leaned closer, his hand over mine. I cleared my throat. "I've seen more of that girl lately. I've missed her. That is when she isn't trying to hate me and everything about this place."

"I don't hate you, Kyle. Far from it. You're one of the few things here I don't despise."

"Regardless, I miss your smile and carefree ways. Even your walk was different, less edgy. Now, you look like a rubber band that's been wound too tight, ready to snap."

I trapped my lip between my teeth.

"He's never known you," Kyle muttered to himself, bitterness coating every word. "He never will."

I pulled my hand from Kyle's, leaving a cold void where our skin touched, and walked to the window overlooking the stream. "So, you followed me the whole time I knew you?"

Kyle nodded.

"Even leaving the party?"

"Yes," he answered straightforward.

"If you were there, how did you lose me in Arizona? Was it because the bellboy got my car?"

"Yeah," he said. "Oren saw you go out the front and he just assumed."

"Whose idea was it to run me off the road?" My tone turned accusing as I pivoted to meet Kyle's eyes. "And then that stunt in the parking lot?"

He flinched. "The running you off the road thing was an accident. We were trying to fix it when your friend showed up." Kyle's chair scraped the floor as he stood and moved to stand beside me. "Oren was the idiot mastermind behind the parking lot. I could've killed him for being so reckless."

"Figures." I scoffed.

He smiled grimly. "We lost you after that. Your little side trip to Texas threw everything into a tailspin. It all went to pot from there."

I tensed waiting for Kyle to ask. Mercifully, he didn't. Texas was a turning point in my life, and we both knew it. Things would've played out much differently for everyone had Texas not come into the picture. I wasn't sure how I felt about that.

I crossed my arms and followed the length of the room, studying an array of paintings and portraits that lined the walls. Vines wound through the white tree trunks, and disappeared into the ceiling of branches. An iron podium stood at the far end of the room, bathed in sunlight pouring through an ornate stained-glass window.

The walls on either side of the pedestal were lined with books, and the scent of age and musty paper strengthened the closer I moved. My breath caught with a gasp as I stopped, hovering above the open page. I grabbed either side of the podium to steady myself. A yellowed parchment with frayed edges laid, rolled open beneath a Plexiglas box. Blood pulsed through my ears as I took in the shapes of willow trees decorating the top of the page and the wax seals and signatures along the bottom. The pale background emblem held the same seal as the journal I found at the lake house.

"Is ... is this what I think it is?" I asked, my voice trembling at the sight of a familiar ancient language.

Kyle's hand settled at the small of my back. "Please don't do this right now, Monet."

"Answer me, Kyle." I turned my head to meet his eyes.

He drew a deep breath. "It's the treaty, yes."

"I can't imagine you want to read it to me, huh?" I asked, not sure what answer I wanted.

"Not especially." Kyle sighed then added, "But if you ask me to, I will."

I hesitated. "Not now." I shook my head and took a step back, swallowing hard. What would it do for me besides raise more questions? I forced my feelings into the vault and looked at the green vines climbing the wall near the window.

"What's going to happen to Harry?" I asked, twisting the ivy between my fingers.

Kyle scoffed. "Why do you still care after all he's done to you? I would think you have more reason than anyone to hate him."

"I just can't reconcile the two images," I tried to explain, feeling the heartache on my face. "He's my family, Kyle, even when I didn't know it. I have this picture in my head of the man I loved like a father. Then there's the other one — the one that's real, the one of the man who sold me to the enemy. I can't separate the two. I don't know how."

"You feel like you were sold, like a slave?" Sorrow flashed in his eyes. "And my family's the enemy?"

"I've been drugged, stolen, lied to, and manipulated. I don't have a choice in any part of my life or even a say. I can't choose who to love or where to live. Is that not enslavement?" My hand fell. "How would you feel?"

"I would be bitter and full of hate," Kyle confessed with frown. "You have to understand though. Harry was never that man you knew growing up. He's always wanted power, even before you mother was born. Harry's ultimate goal was your grandfather's position. He used someone important as a bargaining chip between our families, pitting us against each other by playing both sides."

Of course. The face of Ilana's curly-haired baby popped into my mind.

"What?" he said. "You're not going to badger me about the identity of this person?"

"No. Why would I?"

Kyle studied my face for a long time. His eyes narrowed. "My mother talked to you, didn't she?"

"Yeah, why?"

Surprise washed over him. "No one knows about that, Ash. You don't understand what a huge ordeal that was for her ... is for her! Not even my siblings know."

Kyle began to pace in front of me.

"She told you," I claimed.

"Did she now?" he challenged, his eyes locked on mine. "What exactly did she say?"

I hesitated, not knowing how to answer him. Ilana had shared her very personal history with me. While Kyle knew some of the story, there was no way to know how much he knew. I wouldn't betray her confidence like that.

"Enough it would seem." I turned away.

Kyle sighed. "Well, getting back to the point, Leith created an elaborate story to tell both sides concerning the child's fate. The Naiads believed that we had the baby and we were trying to use him against them to gain something. Leith told us the same story. But it began to fall apart. And in short, your mother was promised in place of the baby. Well, not the baby so much as the war that brooded over the situation."

"What would happen if the treaty were broken again?" I asked. Kyle lifted a suspicious eyebrow. "Would it mean a war?"

"Our people's numbers are suffering. Kevin wouldn't risk them, but he would find someone to take it out on. You and anyone you ever loved would be at risk until the treaty was met. You're in deeper than your mom ever was."

"But if it was all a lie on Harry's part, why does it matter anymore?" I asked. "Why is he even breathing?"

Kyle's face hardened. I didn't know if he caught the undertone of my question — why was I still subject to the treaty if everyone knew the truth?

"Some of my kind turned stupid," he confessed with disgust. "They uncovered Leith's betrayal and decided to use him for their own wants. They offered him amnesty in a way. He would do what he was told, when he was told to do it, no questions asked." Kyle gritted his teeth. "He was smart though — smarter than those who thought they were controlling him. In classic style, he turned it around to make them believe they had the power when really, he held it. Then my—"

"Ashton? Kyle?" Kevin's voice echoed across the marble floor. Caught up in our disturbing conversation, we both jumped.

"Later," Kyle whispered as he put on a feigned smile, encouraging me to do the same.

Kevin rounded the corner to see us content as we looked over the old drawings.

"Ashton, let's go," he ordered, not bothering with a hello. "We need to talk."

"Fine," I said on a sigh and looked to Kyle. "Thanks for today."

He nodded once and started straightening up.

"Ashton, I'm leaving for California in a few days on business, and I'll be gone for several months," Kevin began as we walked home. "As you know, our family doesn't leave the safety of The Valley, but I maintain the company, and it's necessary I go in person."

"Whatever you need to do," I said, unsure but excited at the thought of not seeing him for months.

"Ordinarily, I wouldn't allow you to leave," he continued. "But having talked to my parents, we've decided to move up the wedding date. I want you with me from now on, and this is the only way I can assure no one will risk staging a rescue while we're away."

My mouth went dry. I tried to take a breath, but it felt like someone had wrapped cellophane over my face. Dots floated across my vision, and I struggled to keep my legs steady.

"M-m-move the wedding up?" I repeated.

"Yes. The ceremony is Saturday evening." A wicked glint shone in his eyes. "Six o'clock and you're mine forever."

"That's tomorrow." I bit back the dread.

"You should rest up now, while you have the chance." His voice grew husky, and my head began to spin.

Kevin opened the gate to the front lawn and ushered me to the door. His hands found my waist, and he pulled me close, his focus trained on my lips. "I've waited a very long time for this."

His mouth moved to mine, his kiss rough and greedy. I shut my eyes, forcing myself not to feel, and waited for him to finish. Finally, he stilled and backed away, wearing a predatory smile.

I clenched my shaking hands behind my back and plastered on false enthusiasm. "I'd better go before I do something to get me in trouble," I hinted, hoping he took it the way it sounded.

"One more day, and you can have all the trouble you want." His finger trailed the length of my jaw. "I'll see you tomorrow."

Kevin traipsed off into the trees, perfectly at ease. I on the other hand, slipped through the doorway and into a panic.

Chapter Twenty-Six
Confessions

Billowing clouds layered the sky, hiding the sun behind a ceiling of gray. Erin and Aurelia danced around me, chattering on about something I didn't hear. Their fingers moved through my hair, twisting and curling pieces here and there. I kept my focus on the floor, avoiding any hint of my reflection in the windows or otherwise. My heart went into overdrive at the thought of today's events. I closed my eyes and drew a steadying breath.

"...and your dress is styled in the traditional form of the Naiads." Aurelia's voice broke through my subconscious. "Mother thought it would be a nice thought for you as well as introduce our people to the new life the treaty will bring."

Erin whisked a garment bag into the bedroom. She unzipped the front and pulled out an intricately designed gown. My body went cold as images of an Arthurian era floated through my mind. The cream-colored satin held a scooped neck bordered with a strip of translucent golden beads. They matched those circling the wide flowing sleeves. An elaborately stitched sash wrapped the midsection of the A-line skirt and swept to the floor.

"Is that it?" I asked, my voice a choked whisper.

"No, this is your reception gown," Erin said. "You'll change into your wedding dress before the ceremony."

Erin pulled me from my seat and untied my robe. She wrapped a corset-type material around my torso and hooked the front together. As soon as she finished, Aurelia began tugging at the laces on the back, squeezing everything up and into place.

"Why am I wearing a reception gown before the ceremony?" I breathed, wincing as Aurelia tied the lace at the small of my back. If the dread didn't kill me, the corset would.

"In our world, the reception comes first then a brief ceremony," Aurelia explained. "This allows the newly matched couple to spend their evening alone without waiting through the party." She winked and my heart sputtered before kicking into overdrive.

Erin dressed me with care, buttoning and lacing the necessary parts of the elaborate gown. Aurelia followed behind, weaving rows of lavender and ivy through the curls tumbling down my back.

"There now." Erin smiled at her sister. "She looks absolutely stunning, wouldn't you say?"

Aurelia nodded and twirled a loose strand of my hair to my shoulder. "And there's still room for the crown."

Erin's smile melted, and she sighed. "I left it at the palace."

"Guess we'd be better hurry back then." Aurelia shrugged. "Ashton, we'll be back with your coronation crown as soon as we dress."

I nodded and swallowed against the knot in my throat.

"Try and relax," Erin offered with a smile as they walked outside. "This will all be over soon, and you can just enjoy being a newlywed."

I shut the door and began pacing frantically, fighting the tears and desperation each heartbeat carried. I couldn't do this! I couldn't be a wife. In all the weeks of worrying about the wedding, it never actually felt like it would happen. Where was my supposed rescuer now? Months had come and gone with no sign of her.

You may as well accept the fact, my brain ordered as I wrung the sash at my waist. The life you chose ran out and left you to hopelessness.

A sharp thud at the door tugged me back into reality. I pulled it open to see Kyle on the stoop. I didn't say anything for fear of losing it. His expression fell as he took in my dress.

"You look absolutely stunning." Kyle's tone was as bleak as the weather. He stepped through the archway, pulling me in behind him, and pressed the door together. Keeping my hand in his, he tugged me through the hall.

Halfway to the kitchen, he turned on his heel to face me. His oversized hands wrapped around the tops of my arms, and he stood squarely in front of me, gazing down to meet my eyes.

"Ash, do you want this?" His hands tightened, and he took a deep breath. "What I mean is, if you could leave, would you? Would you be happy if you weren't here?"

My heart swelled as I considered his question. I took a shaky step back and leaned against the wall.

"Even if you didn't have your first choice of a life? You could be happy, right?" He searched my expression then squared his shoulders. "I can keep you safe. We would have to go somewhere that no one could find us, but I can protect you."

His words sang like a bluebird. And I knew they were true. Kyle would rescue me. He would defy his family. He would rebel against the same laws that brought punishment down on my mother ... the same laws that separated me from Gabe.

"You would betray your family? Abandon your people?" I pressed.

Pain flashed in his face, followed by resolution. "I would for you."

"Why?" I whispered.

Kyle cupped his hands around my cheeks, his thumbs resting on my chin as he refused to let me look away. "Surely by now you know the answer to that, Ash."

"I ... you shouldn't say things like that, Kyle. I'm marrying your brother in a matter of hours. There's no point now."

"Kevin doesn't love you. Your marriage would be hollow and superficial. Just like him." Anger shone in his eyes, his voice low and intense. "You don't know who he is, what he's done. He's capable of a lot more than the bruises he left on you. I can't lose you like that. We're out of time. We have to leave."

His warm breath caressed my skin. I opened my eyes to find his face inches from mine, his resolve waning with every rapid heartbeat.

"Kyle, don't," I spoke softly. "Don't do this to yourself. You know it can't be like that with us. You deserve better than the nightmare you'd live wanting me."

"There's nothing better than you, Monet," Kyle whispered fervently. His lips possessed mine with a need I'd never experienced. Raw passion drove every thought from my head, except one. Gabe.

"Stop, please," I breathed, my body crushed against his. His eyes burned into me, swaying my conscience. "I-I can't do this."

"Ashton, I love you. I know your heart is out there, but he's not here. I am. And I would never hurt you. I would never leave you."

I drew a slow breath and placed my hand on his chest, fighting the selfishness that yelled at me to escape with him. "I know. But I'm not whole anymore, Kyle. All I had to give is gone, and I don't think it'll ever be right again. That's not fair to you. If I can't have..." I hesitated. "If I'm doomed to this life, then let me suffer it alone. Don't make it harder on yourself by betraying your family. There's nothing for me to lose, but you have everything."

"I don't have you," he whispered.

"I'm not worth it." I offered a hopeless shrug.

Kyle's eyes narrowed, his heart picking up pace under my palm. "So that's it? You're just giving up?"

"What should I do, Kyle? Drag you into it for my own benefit?" I shook my head, nothing left in me for arguing. "I won't lie to you. I'm not exactly being noble here. There's just nothing in me to salvage."

"I hate what's he's done to you," Kyle growled, his voice rising with every word. "How can you care about someone who's betrayed you? He's no different than my brother. Gabe's not coming back, and you know it."

My chin quivered as a tear fell down my cheek.

"After everything he's done, you still love him?" Kyle murmured. Pain colored his expression.

I looked away, unwilling to answer him. Kyle yanked the towel from the mirror.

"See what love has done to you. You won't even look at yourself anymore." His voice warmed my ear. "This isn't a result of love, Monet. Love isn't cruel."

My hollow gaze roamed over my expression, taking in the tired eyes with dark circles underneath. The glow had all but vanished; every part of me seemed lifeless.

"You're wasting away. You're a shell of who you used to be. I want you for you, not because of your status, or any dues owed me. I love you. The girl that no one else sees, the one who walks like a kid. I love the girl who reads the same monotonous stories over and over again and sings at the top of her lungs when she drives." He laughed then his expression turned smoldering. "I want that girl."

Desire, longing, and desperation warmed Kyle's eyes as he watched the emotions play across my face. "You don't have to pretend anything with me, Ash. I would know anyway." He swept a strand of hair from my face and tucked it behind my ear.

And it was true. Kyle knew me inside and out, just as I knew him. He understood how I functioned, what I needed. He could take care of me and make me as happy as I could possibly be ... without my insides. But I could never give him the love that he so deserved. How could I steal that opportunity from him?

"It doesn't matter though, does it?" His voice turned cold.

"Kyle," I began.

"Before you turn me away, there's one more thing you have to know." He hesitated. "Do you remember that day in the cave when Oren assured Gabe that the rest of his demands had been met? Did you ever wonder what they were?"

Cold dread washed over me. I slowly shook my head.

"He was exonerated for his own crimes against his people as well as the Dryads. Your Prince Charming has an ugly history. But that's not all." Kyle's tone lowered, his expression torn. "Harry held Gabe's fiancée captive here, but he agreed to let her go in exchange for one thing. You."

"Fiancée?" I wheezed. The room seemed to shift, like it'd been turned on its side, my fractured heart raced on but my labored breathing ceased. It felt like every fiber of my being had been torn to shreds, leaving me exposed and vulnerable. I stumbled back against the wall, panting. My arms pulled around my chest as I doubled over in empty-heartache, struggling to catch my breath.

Kyle's hands moved around my waist, and he pulled me to his chest. Warmth enveloped me as his breath brushed my ear. "I would never do that to you." He kissed my forehead before pulling away just enough to meet my eyes. "I'm not perfect, I won't even pretend to be, but I will not lie to you when I know the truth. And there is nothing in this world or theirs that I would trade for you."

Was it all a lie? Everything Gabe told me, all the emotion, all the turmoil he'd put himself through — was it real? I shook my head, swayed in my beliefs. My whole life had been a lie. What made him any different?

What love? It wasn't enough, if it was ever there at all.

"I trust you," I murmured. Those three simple words warmed his eyes. He smiled, brushing his thumb across my lips, and then leaned in to kiss me once more. Memories of Ilana's words floated through my mind.

"Aiken knew my life, my love, but he still wanted me. And over the years, though I never regained the heart that longs for my Naiad, I love Aiken more than I would have ever dreamed possible. He is more than I deserve, better than I'd ever been allowed to hope."

Maybe it was all I could hope for. Maybe it would be enough for Kyle, for me.

The kiss deepened as Kyle's passion stirred. Hot hands wrapped around my waist, lifting me to his height. I threaded my fingers through his hair, allowing the months of loneliness and grief to fuel my reaction. He moaned softly as he held me tighter, and I reveled in the feel of his love.

The wall slammed against my back and Kyle leaned into me, yet it wasn't close enough. My arms strained against his muscled frame, pulling him tighter still. The overwhelming heat from his body bled through my clothes, combining with the slow simmer inside, warming me from every angle.

Somehow, the logical part of my mind registered that this was wrong — that it opposed my wretched and broken heart violently — but something else silenced it quickly as Kyle's lips burned against mine once more, his warm scent invading my conscience.

My reluctance, my admittance, my love for his enemy, nothing swayed Kyle's love for me. For the first time, he was proving it.

"I love you," Kyle breathed hard, his mouth trailing back to mine.

I didn't say anything as a tear trickled across my cheek.

Kyle backed away, a soft smile on his face. "I have to go. I need to gather a few things before we leave."

The hope in his eyes flooded me with guilt.

"Grab one bag you can carry easily. I'll be back for you in an hour." Kyle's finger traced the bridge of my nose. He leaned in and lightly brushed my lips with his. "I'll see you soon."

With that, Kyle smoothed his hair and stole through the door into the rain.

Why couldn't the man I wanted to be in love with me, love me? I had no desire for Kevin to have feelings for me, shallow or not. I'd rather he lavish his superficial sentiment on someone else.

Kyle's overjoyed expression invaded my thoughts. The throbbing in my chest turned painful. How could I do this to him? He was the only good thing in my life now. All this time, he'd been watching me, watching over me. He'd seen every ugly thing I'd done, yet he wanted to be mine. I was hurting him in so many ways. The one man who loved me.

"What are you doing?" I growled at myself and punched the mirror in the hall. It fractured and splintered from the center, leaving a wet red imprint of my knuckles across the shards. I held my hand up and watched the blood trickle to the floor in fat drops. Within minutes, the cuts faded into dry gashes reminiscent of Gabe's arm.

I wiped the dried blood from my hand and stared out the window at the torrential rain. A low ceiling of encroaching black clouds darkened the sky. I hadn't seen rain like this since … Arizona. Ugh! How many ways did I want to die today?

I had to get out here before I went mad.

Ignoring my dress and perfectly styled hair, I ran for the pond. My feet glided over the smooth grass without a sound, picking up pace as I entered the forest. The rain beat through my clothes, weighing the material down and cooling my skin. I slowed as the giant willow tree came into view then paused at the edge of the water. The sharp rainfall battered the surface as I gazed dissatisfied into the pool that usually comforted me. This wasn't what I wanted. It didn't fix anything, and it didn't help.

Grief, confusion, and heartbreak swirled around me like a cyclone. My world felt like it was closing in on top of me, but I had no escape. I shut my eyes and drew a deep breath through my nose, wincing at the smell of the fresh rain — a scent I hadn't encountered in a while.

I stared through the impenetrable curtain of fog and moisture at the nothingness, depressed by the similarity it showed to my life. My breathing spiked as sobs built in my chest.

Without warning, a cool slick hand wrapped my mouth from behind and squeezed.

Chapter Twenty-Seven
October Rain

"**D**on't speak," the familiar voice whispered. "It's time to go. Do what I tell you, and we might make it out of here."

I nodded. My breathing and heart rate sprinted with a flood of adrenaline. The hand slowly unclamped, fingers extended in a steadying gesture as it pulled away. I wheeled around, and a gasp caught in my throat.

"Allie?" I breathed. My knees went weak as shock, fear, and questions surrounded me from all sides. Allie was the girl? How was it possible? A hint of joy crept in before I could shut it out.

Allie's sapphire eyes crinkled into a grin. She yanked me toward her for a surreal but much needed hug. My arms hung limp, too surprised to offer her much else.

"Hey, Ash. It's great to see you, but don't say anything else. You never know who might be listening." She slipped her hand around my wrist, towing me toward the western wall of The Valley. "I've been waiting and waiting for a rain like this. I didn't think it would ever come. Too bad it isn't the end of spring instead of the end of October

October? Had I been here almost four months?

"I was terrified that you'd spot me before it was time." Allie tossed her blonde curls over her shoulder. "You almost made me the other day at the pond when you decided to chill at the bottom. Any other time of the day and you would have seen me in an instant. Thank goodness for shadows, huh?"

My steps faltered. She had been watching me? For how long? A week, a month, the entire time? Had she seen or heard everything said between Kevin and me? Between Kyle and me? My breath caught in my chest.

"Hey, everything is fine." Allie squeezed my hand. "It's just me. Don't worry about anything that's happened here. I'm amazed you've lasted this long through all the madness. Trust me. I understand," she added, a flush of bitterness in her tone.

Allie suddenly froze.

"Oh, no." Her words were lost in the pounding rain as her fingers flew to her lips, her eyes wide with fear.

My breathing slowed as I waited, unable to hear or see the cause of her alarm. The scent of pine and sandalwood drifted through the clearing. Kevin and Kyle were moving closer, and I had no idea why.

"What do we do?" I asked, my voice high even in a whisper.

Allie froze in thought. "We try not to get caught."

She grabbed my hand and yanked me into the trees, heading to the west. My heart drummed in my ears as gruff voices carried behind us, and the sound of hurried footsteps moved across the ground.

"She's probably gone for a walk. Let's just head to the house," Kyle called from the path, not thirty yards away. Allie backed against an oak, pulling me alongside her.

"A walk in the rain?" Kevin growled.

"She likes the rain," Kyle said. "Besides, where is she possibly going to go?"

A thick silence fell over the woods when the footsteps stopped. I wished I could see them.

"That depends on how much you told her about this place," Kevin said, his tone low and threatening.

"I haven't said anything," Kyle murmured, a hint of remorse in his tone. "Perhaps you should ask Harry."

My blood ran cold. Why would Kyle tell Kevin to talk to Harry?

Allie wrapped her free hand over mine. "It's all right," she mouthed, encouraging my grip to loosen.

"Fine," Kevin said. "But be forewarned, if anyone has aided her in an escape attempt, I will have their head."

"Of course." Kyle cleared his throat.

I held my breath till the rain smothered the sound of retreating footsteps. Allie hesitated by the tree for a moment more. My mind ran circles around my body. What did Kevin mean by asking Kyle what he'd told me? Kyle would tell me if there was a way out ... wouldn't he? And why on earth would he suggest Kevin talk to Harry? We'd done well keeping Kevin away from him.

Allie jerked on my hand, snapping me out of my worry, and led me westward again. Rain continued sheeting down. My dress clung to my skin and weighed down every step. I trained my eyes on the rock-face, trying to make out a shape in the mountainside. The factory swam into focus. How on earth did she plan on getting through this place unseen? Allie paused by the edge of the forest and pulled me to a crevice.

"Absolute silence from here on out," she warned. "I'm going to go ahead and make sure everything is clear. Stay here. I'll be right back for you."

"Wait." I grabbed her hand.

"What's wrong? They're gone." Allie's eyes narrowed against the rain.

"I ... I can't go with you, Al."

"What? Why? How could you even consider staying?" she asked, her tone a mix of confusion and disbelief.

"Kevin won't stop until he's hurt everyone I care about. You included. I can't do that."

"Ash, listen to me." Allie met my gaze, her eyes hard as steel. "Kevin has more than one option when it comes to this treaty thing. You don't have to do this."

My eyebrows fell. "But the treaty..."

"Did you read it?" she asked carefully. I shook my head. "It doesn't have to be you. You were already there, that's all. Now sit tight and let me get us out of here."

My stomach knotted in fear and doubt, but I nodded, forcing my shaking fingers to let go.

"It'll be fine. I promise," she whispered, her eyes fixed on mine before she disappeared into the trees.

I backed further into the crevice and rested against the wall. Trying to calm my nerves, I closed my eyes and took a deep breath then another till my heart slowed. The scent of sandalwood suddenly filled the space, and my eyes snapped open.

"Kyle," I whispered, guilt weighing heavy in my tone.

Fiery gray burned into me with mixed emotion. A muscle worked in his jaw as he fought a feeling I couldn't identify. Kyle took a step forward, his muscled frame filling the tiny space. I searched his expression, trying to find an answer. Finally, his face gave way to sadness, and a wave of betrayal washed over me.

"We don't have much time," Kyle murmured, his voice grim. "Kevin is with Harry."

My hands balled into fists as I silently questioned him.

"I'm sorry," he said and looked away. "I had to get him off your trail. With this rain, I can't tell who's leading you away..." He took a deep breath, moisture building in his eyes. "But you can go."

"What?" I gasped. How did he know?

"Ash, you want to leave. You have to leave." Kyle's tone turned soft yet sad. "And if you were going to wait for me to take you, you'd be back at the house." His expression fell. "Whoever came for you did it without our knowledge. They'll get you out safely. You need to go."

"Kyle, I..." My words failed me. What could I say? He was willing to risk everything for me, and I was just sneaking away. He didn't even care as long as I was safe.

Kyle's fingers brushed my face, his eyes searching mine. "Go and be happy, Monet. You deserve that much." He dipped down to brush a mournful kiss across my lips. Salt water crept into the corner of my mouth as my eyes closed, but I didn't know whose it was.

Kyle's hand fell away, and a bitter cold took its place. I looked up to find him gone, leaving me to the nothing. A fresh hole ached in my chest. What was I doing? Kyle wouldn't be the only one to suffer my vanishing. What would happen to the people here? What would happen to my people? Hot tears streaked down my face.

"Ash?" Allie's quiet voice broke through the sadness. "Are you all right?"

"Yeah." I nodded and wiped my cheeks.

She sniffed at the air, her expression darkening by the second as recognition set in. "It's time to go." Her hand tightened around mine, and we slinked around the corner and through the carved entryway of the factory.

Our bare feet moved silently through the marble foyer. The smell of herbs mingled with the caustic scent of hydraulic fluid. I followed her lead as we pressed our backs into the wall and peered around the corner. Despair seeped through me. Four guards manned the reception area, and workers milled in and out of the doorways, clogging the open space. We'd never get through this place unseen.

"Gentlemen, I need to speak with you outside." Kyle's hard voice rang from an open door across the way. Allie ducked behind the wall, but I watched, knowing what Kyle was about to do. His gaze flickered in my direction before escorting the guards through the entryway.

The men left the desk unattended, and Allie's hand tightened around mine.

"Now or never," she whispered and tugged me past a closed door. We rounded the edge of the hall and crept to a door marked supply closet.

I lifted a brow when she gestured for me to go inside, but followed her direction. Allie clicked the door shut behind us and slid a bolt into place. She looked back to me, and I mouthed, "Now what?"

Allie jutted her thumb toward the ceiling. A small ventilation grate sat in the corner, ten feet over my head. Did she really believe we could fit through that?

My heart raced in my chest and sweat beaded across my forehead. I stared wide-eyed and shook my head in protest. She pointed toward the opening, urgency set in her expression, and laced her fingers together. My vision swam with claustrophobia. The room swayed, and I shut my eyes.

"Search every crevice of this factory," Kevin's irate voice boomed through the walls. "I want her found, and found now!"

My eyes flew open to a panicked Allie. The sound of hurried footsteps sounded near the door. Allie braced her fingers against her knee. I wrapped my long skirt around my waist and fitted my foot inside her grip. Her deceptively petite arms hoisted me toward the ventilation shaft. I removed the grate and tried not to notice the size of the space as I dangled my legs low enough for her to shimmy up.

A wave of hot stagnant air smacked me in the face, filling my lungs with the distinct smell of coolant. My slick palms fumbled over the rock-floor of the passageway, feeling my way through the darkness. The dreary sound of labored breathing and the soft scrape of bare skin against stone echoed through the emptiness. I wasn't so sure I didn't prefer the slow death of misery as opposed to the slow death of suffocation.

Sweat raced down my skin. My hair matted to my face and the moisture caused the sharp pebbles to stick and grind into my exposed flesh. I distracted myself from the pain with thoughts of Allie. I wouldn't be alone after all. No one else would suffer my disappearing...

Guilt punched through my gut. Everyone would suffer my disappearing. Keeping Kyle out of trouble didn't amend what my breaking the treaty could cause. Their race and ours was in jeopardy if Allie was wrong.

The time ticked by slowly, and just when I thought I'd snap, Allie stopped with a relieved sigh. I looked over her head to see a faint glow not too far away. The tunnel widened, and Allie moved to hunker in the taller part of the passage. Relief pulsed through me as I rose to match her, heaving my wet mound of skirt up so I wouldn't trip. We crept to the opening and paused at the mouth to sit down and stretch.

"We're out of The Valley, though nowhere near out of danger just yet," Allie said, directing her gaze outside. I peeked over the ledge and gasped at the masked treetops below. Fog swirled beneath me as the rain continued in torrents. If I thought the claustrophobic tunnel was bad, this was the open equivalent of it. Still, we hadn't come this far just to quit.

I drew a welcomed lungful of air and rallied my courage. "In case I don't make it down in one piece, it was great to see you one last time, and thanks for trying."

"Ash?" Allie frowned. "I didn't rescue you just to go Picasso as soon as we were free. I like my face the way it is."

"Well, how do you propose we get down then?"

"I'm not a mountain goat." She moved some rocks aside at the lip of the cave. "Here, climb into this." Allie handed me some kind of harness, assuming I had a vague idea of what to do with it. I twisted and turned the flimsy thing, trying to find the top.

Allie shook her head. "Like this." She took it from me, turning it right-side up. I managed to slip my legs and waist through the openings, causing my dress to slip up to the top of my thighs. It wasn't exactly designed with mountain climbing in mind.

"I should secure yours to mine," Allie said to herself then pulled out a length of rope. "This isn't the safest way to get down, but I can't just leave a line hanging here for anyone to see, or worse, follow."

Allie looped the cord back through a handle.

"Have you ever been rappelling?" she asked, hopeful. I rolled my eyes and shook my head.

"Oh, well. Too late to fix that now. Hang on tight, and try not to wiggle," she said.

Allie sent me out, supporting my weight with the thin rope. We dangled high above the mist-ridden rocks below, swaying softly as Allie gauged the strength of the rivet that supported us. It creaked and groaned but held.

The air on this side of The Valley was colder. I fought the shivers and kept a death grip on my harness. Allie breathed a tense sigh and began to release the rope through the handle, lowering us at a measured pace as she walked down the stone face.

A sharp crack splintered the silence. Shards of rock rained down from the mountain. Allie's eyes caught mine. We both looked down, but the fog swirled thick below, making it seem as if the ground had been swept away.

"Ash?" Allie said.

"Yeah?"

"Do you trust me?" she asked, not giving me the chance to respond. "Hang on and be quiet!"

With that, she loosened her fingers from around the rope. The wind screamed past my ears and took my breath away. A wall of gray blinded me, heightening my panic as well as my other senses. The sound of our descent caused a compressed echo against the ground we rapidly approached.

It was close ... closer ... immediate.

My body jolted to a sudden stop, and the nylon harness bit into the sensitive skin of my hips. The rope recoiled with a loud snap and dropped us on our backsides. Allie jumped up and yanked me in the same direction as a chunk of the mountain came crashing down, landing on the place where we had been.

"What the heck, Allie?" I wiped water out of my eyes and worked the harness off, babying my new bruises.

"Hey, don't look at me." She loosened her buckles. "It was rigged the best way I could get it. One anchor isn't meant to support two bodies at the same time."

"I'll say." I shook my head and stared around the forest. "But you got us out in one piece. That's what counts."

"We're not in the clear yet. Come on." Allie moved toward the base of the mountain. "We only have a small head start, and we have to reach water."

She gathered up the remainder of the gear and shoved the equipment under some boulders. I noticed her hands shaking and stepped closer.

"Al? What's wrong with your—" I didn't get to finish my question as I flipped Allie's hands over. Her palms and the insides of her fingers looked like someone glued them around a fiery poker then yanked it out. Burnt and mangled skin left way for blisters and exposed tissue.

"Allie!" I gasped.

"They're fine," she said. "They just sting a little."

"Sting a little?" I said with a grimace. "Allie, they're just..."

"Ash, I'm okay." She tried to smile. "They'll be fine in no time. Let's get out of here."

We took off in a sprint, weaving through the forest. The rain persisted chilling my heated skin, though it lightened from a monsoon to a steady fall. My lungs ached but we pressed on.

"Do you smell that?" Allie glanced back as she ran.

I drew a deep breath. The faint scent of a lake somehow stood out from the rain. I smiled and nodded.

"You're learning to tell the difference. That's good. We're close now, it won't be much further." Allie picked up the pace, and The Valley fell further behind with every step.

"Al?" I asked, my breath fogging.

"Yeah?" She slowed to my side.

"How did you know where to find me? How did you know I was in trouble?"

Allie slowed to my side. She looked into my eyes for a moment before turning her gaze down. "I had a run-in with the Dryads a while back," she explained. "Harry was involved."

My stride faltered before I regained my rhythm. "What happened?"

"Harry wanted you. He hoped that I might be of some use in that way, that he could use me as some kind of bargaining chip or ransom if need be. If you didn't do whatever it was they had planned, they'd threaten you by using me. It didn't quite work out like he planned though."

Bargaining chip? Just like Ilana's baby. Harry'd had good success with bargaining chips in the past.

"What happened?" I asked.

"The day we left after the swimming incident, we were expressly forbidden to contact either you or Charlie. And for years we obeyed ... until I disappeared. We were as fooled by Harry as everyone else. Mom just assumed the Dryads were involved. She was afraid they'd taken me to get to you, so she called Harry trying to get in touch with your dad to warn him."

My breaths came too quickly. The shock, the pain, the fear ... the hope, it overwhelmed me.

"My mom said Charlie called you the week before," she continued, her voice low. "He wanted to talk to you about all of this. He was going to tell you everything."

"And I wouldn't come," I muttered, my chest heavy with guilt.

"Don't beat yourself up, Ash. You didn't know. It wouldn't have worked out this way if you had come then," she said. "Trust me; on the one hand, it worked out better."

I couldn't forgive myself so easily.

We jumped over a small ravine riddled with rotten logs, careful not to slip in the dead leaves. The underbrush grew thick, and Allie zigzagged along trying to break as few branches as possible till the dense foliage gave way to a clearing.

"So what happened?" I continued. "How did you escape?"

"Oh, no..." Allie stopped suddenly, her bare feet skidding across the ground with a squeak. I balked behind her, confused when her arm flew up to hold me back.

"Allie, what are you ..." My sentence fell in despair.

A shadow emerged from the trees.

Chapter Twenty-Eight
Resolution

The figured shrouded in mist and darkness inched closer, his cloak billowing in the chilled air. Moisture clung to my eyelashes as my muscles coiled with adrenaline. Blood pounded through my veins like ice. I eyed the imposing shadow moving toward us then scanned the area, a hundred scenarios running through my head. My palm burned against Allie's arm. I yanked her behind my body, more afraid of being separated than anything, and prepared to run.

Allie sighed in exasperation. "Um, stroke! Seriously," she scolded the silhouette. "What are you thinking, creeping out like that? Sheesh!"

"What?" I questioned, taken aback by her reaction. The wind howled at my back, whipping my hair around my face, then witched directions. A hint of warm cedar mingled with the rain. It couldn't be.

I shut my eyes as a wave of mixed emotion overcame me. I couldn't handle this, not now. Not after surrendering to the fact that he was gone and not coming back. That he didn't want me and never would.

"Ash, you okay?" Allie spoke at my side.

I disregarded her question and tried to slow my breathing.

"Ashton?" Another deeper sweeter voice questioned just in front of me.

I shook my head, unwilling to open my eyes. I didn't want to see the face of the man I loved outside of sane boundaries simply staring back at me with cold indifference. I wanted to turn and run the other way, but panic froze me in place.

"What's happened? Is she in shock?" he asked.

"Well, it's not exactly like you left her in the best position, now is it?" Allie quipped. "Maybe she thinks she's hallucinating. Maybe the stress is finally getting to her. I don't know."

Gabe's scent enveloped me. I imagined the look I'd once seen in his eyes — the ocean on fire. My erratic pulse quickened, and the empty space in my chest threatened to drown in warmth. Unwilling to sacrifice what part of me remained, I recoiled and opened my eyes. Gabe wore a half-hearted smile then his gaze moved downward, taking in my once-beautiful dress. His eyes narrowed as comprehension sank in.

"Yeah, I cut it close," Allie said, catching sight of his expression. "But we need to get moving. Now."

A clearing appeared at the forest edge. Allie and Gabe paused at the fringe, their eyes scanning the open area with care. Gabe sniffed at the air then nodded to Allie who grabbed my hand. She lifted her finger to her lips then we set off into the deadly quiet meadow.

Our footsteps glided over the damp ground without a sound, but every sense worked overtime as the peak of the mountain broke through the clouds. Gabe cast repeated glances over his shoulder as we moved, his eyes hard on the place I'd just escaped. Finally, I caught sight of the waning sun glistening off a lake.

Gabe paused as we reached the water's edge and knelt down.

"Stand still," he instructed, his tone as crisp as the evening air. "This is slowing you down."

With a rough yank, he ripped my dress just above the knee then he tore my sleeves away. Goosebumps raised on my exposed flesh. I didn't know if it was the temperature or Gabe's demeanor as he wrapped the torn material around a rock and chucked it into the lake. He followed suit with his cloak then looked to me.

"No one will find see them there. Go ahead," he murmured.

I dove into the lake, relishing in the sensation of the open water enveloping me completely. The water was like a breath of fresh air after being trapped in a cage for months.

An hour into the swim, a small island rising out of the water caught my attention. Skeletons of gnarly evergreens clawed upward as if to pluck the stars from the dimming sky. The land lay eerily quiet, feeling more like a graveyard.

"We'll stop there for the evening," Gabe said to Allie. She lifted an incredulous eyebrow but nodded.

We climbed ashore, and I winced as the sharp rocks scraped against my feet and cold air nipped at my skin. The sun crept behind the mountain, stealing what little warmth remained.

"Why don't you get some firewood, and I'll scrounge up something to eat," Allie said, watching Gabe with a stern expression. He sighed but strode off into the dark trees.

"We'll be right back, Ash," Allie said. "I'm going to catch some fish, and maybe see if I can find anything worth eating on the island."

I plopped down on the soggy ground, but my foot twitched anxiously. I felt edgy, like I didn't really belong here. Perhaps I didn't belong anywhere. Maybe that's why Gabe gave me up to begin with. I only brought heartache to the people around me. Anywhere I went, trouble followed.

Well, you've been rescued, Ash. It's not like you can't handle yourself from now on. Why keep Allie at risk when she doesn't have to be? I thought. Do the right thing and rid everyone of their problems.

I refused to be anyone's responsibility. Determined to make things right, I stood and set off into the forest.

"How could you do this? What were you thinking?" Gabe questioned, his tone quiet yet livid. "Do you have any idea what you've done? What this will mean?"

I froze at the fringes of the forest, and held my breath.

"What was I supposed to do? Leave her there?" Allie retorted. I crept further in as and slipped behind a boulder. "Would you rather she killed herself with misery in that hole? Or were you just going to let one of them do it for her? You saw the dress."

The moon broke through the clouds, and light filtered through the trees overhead. Gabe shook his head, his voice no more than a murmur. I crept forward, peering through the bushes, straining to hear.

"Sorry. You're right. I shouldn't..." Allie's voice trailed off as she put her hands up defensively. Something Gabe said sent her backtracking before making her lash out again. "That's just stupid! It didn't matter," she hissed.

"It's not worth the risk. You should've talked to me first." Gabe's voice dropped as he continued.

"You don't know. Your feelings have nothing to do with my choice," Allie snapped. "I couldn't just leave her to them. I don't care what you say." She turned away from him, her voice became desperate. "You were never stuck there ... you have no idea."

Gabe mumbled something that seemed to reassure her, and she looked at him with a grim smile.

The despair in Allie's voice caught me off guard. I could just make out their profiles through the dimness. Gabe continued speaking too soft for me to hear. It annoyed me to no end. It was like he knew I was listening.

"Best for who?" Her eyes sparkled with unshed tears. "It's so not like that. Sometimes you do what you can. You wouldn't understand."

Gabe snapped his fingers and pointed in the direction where they'd left me on the beach. Allie glowered at him.

I didn't need to hear anymore than this to realize the problem. Me. Allie's rescue meant more trouble for Gabe and his family. It probably negated everything he'd accomplished by trading me to the Dryads in the first place.

I turned back toward the beach. I balled up on some ferns and closed my eyes. Gabe and Allie reemerged from the woods just after me. I watched through slitted eyes as Gabe carried an armload of branches and dried pine needles.

"Is she asleep?" He knelt down to start the fire. The sharp click of his flint rocks making contact carried a connotation of sadness with it. The only other time I'd heard the sound was the night at the mine. A shudder slid through me.

"Get that fire started so we can move her closer," Allie spoke, seeing my tremble.

Someone lifted my body into the air. Warmth wrapped around me as I was laid on something soft and forgiving.

"I know she's beat," Allie said tenderly. A hand brushed my hair away and lingered around my face. The scent confused me; I heard Allie but smelled Gabe. On a reflex, I inhaled. The hand eased away from my hair.

"I've missed her more than you know." Allie sighed. I heard the smile in her voice as she spoke. I wanted to "wake up," to tell her that I'd missed her too, but we could be sisters again. ...I wouldn't do that to Allie though. I wouldn't risk her life just to keep her with me. It was selfish and wrong. I had caused enough damage doing that very thing.

"Eat now and go to sleep. We have a long way to go tomorrow and it's going to be tough enough taking turns at watch." Gabe's voice drifted away.

"Fine." Allie settled near me. "Don't let us get eaten in the middle of the night."

They were taking turns watching. I would be here a little longer. The idea of sticking around set my heart wanting more. The idea of being with Gabe, even if for just a short time, had me itching to stay. And I'd missed Allie more than I realized. We had so much to catch up on.

Maybe a couple of days, just enough time to get me on the right path, I decided before giving into exhaustion.

℣ ℣ ℣

The smell of roasting food stirred my senses. Visions of shadows and distant voices whispered through my head. I struggled through the haze of sleep and opened my eyes. A cloudless blue sky greeted me with a kiss of sunshine and the happy call of a loon. I yawned and stretched, peering around at our discreet campsite.

"Morning, chick. Did you get enough sleep?" Allie sat cross-legged on a piece of bleached out driftwood across from me.

Her smile warmed my heart then set it aching. I didn't want to lose the things I loved again. "Yeah. You?"

She suppressed a yawn. "Yep, I'm good."

Don't get comfortable, Ashton. They're exhausted because of you. Don't keep them in danger. You'll only make things worse.

I looked around and noticed Gabe wasn't in sight. My searching turned panicked when I didn't hear or smell him. Had he gone on without us? Wasn't I even going to get one more day?

"He's fishing," Allie explained, shaking her head at my overreaction.

I made a non-committal sound. Seemed my months of practicing indifference hadn't paid off.

Gabe's head broke the surface of the water, a string of fish in his hand. He slogged on shore and laid the fish out beside Allie.

"Morning, Ashton. Did you rest well?" he asked, offhand. I followed the trail of water streaming down the V at his chest to his face then forced my eyes away.

I cleared my throat. "Yeah. Thanks."

Gabe nodded but didn't say anything as he began preparing our meal.

After eating our fill of breakfast, we cleaned up the evidence of our stay and prepared to leave. Allie dove in first, nodding to Gabe as she darted across the surface of the water before disappearing below.

"You ready?" Gabe asked staring out over the horizon.

"Sure," I murmured and waded out a few feet.

I stared at Gabe's bare chest as he tucked his shirt into his pocket. Muscle rippled over his shoulders as he stretched, but all I could see was his back as he walked away in the cave — the back of someone who didn't even want to rescue me.

He won't have to worry about that much longer, I assured myself, but it didn't help.

We sank beneath the surface, and I peered around. What looked like underwater ferns grew in between fuzzy rocks. Wispy green leaves swayed and danced below me with a ballroom of foliage. The flavor of fresh rain and stirred earth lingered in the water.

I turned, feeling the change in vibrations behind me, and saw Gabe motion for me to surface. My head broke the waterline, but Gabe stayed below. A low drone, barely audible beneath me, carried as I watched him with curiosity.

The sound stopped, and Gabe joined me topside.

"I see you've mastered the swimming technique," he said, his tone guarded.

"I don't know how. It's not like I've been practicing." I frowned at the water.

Gabe stared at a lone goose overhead, and a vague sadness rested on his expression. It set my heart aching again. I only now noticed the bloodshot tint of his eyes and the darkened skin beneath. The scruffy hair on his sallow cheeks hinted at him being in the wilderness for some time. What had happened to him?

"Well, I guess there are a few things I think I should teach you while we're at a safe place to do it," he said. "You should learn this sooner rather than later."

They were planning on ditching me after all, I thought with regret but nodded.

"First thing, we obviously can't speak under water, but we can navigate and communicate as you probably remember."

"Echolocation," I said.

"Essentially. Though there are a couple of differences. We can talk in a way, as well. It's similar to that of a whale song. Though it's more of a learned thing, there are a series of sounds and pitches we use instead of words."

"Were you communicating with Allie just now?"

"Yes, I told her to go on ahead and we would—"

"Catch up in a few miles," I finished his sentence without thought.

Gabe's eyebrows rose. "How did you know that?"

I scrunched my nose. "I don't know. I just did. It sort of felt like humming the tune of a song that I couldn't remember the words to but the melody was still there. The tone conveys its meaning. It's hard to explain but it seems to be ingrained in my memory somehow."

"Hmm." Gabe hovered in thought.

"What else do I need to know?" I suddenly remembered my previous concern. "How do I breathe?"

"You were breathing," he explained like I was missing something. "You don't really need to surface anymore."

"Wish I would've known that sooner." I sighed, feeling relieved but foolish.

A long silence stretched between us as we floated, but I didn't know what to say.

"Ash, I need to know something, and Allie never asked." Gabe's eyes searched mine. "Do you want to go with us?"

"I don't want to be held captive in The Valley, if that's what you're asking," I muttered, trying not to give him the upper hand.

"It didn't sound that way to me," Gabe quipped, his jaw clenching.

"Because you were there? You lived through it all?" I snapped.

Gabe didn't speak for a moment. "Listen. Ashton, I owe you this much. If you ... want Kyle, I can arrange it. You won't have to go back to The Valley." His voice lost all its aggression, but his tone stayed cold.

"No," I huffed. "I don't want Kyle. But don't worry; I'll get out of your hair as soon as we get wherever we're going."

I turned, hoping to hide my heart, and started to swim toward Allie. Slick hands gripped my waist and pulled me back. Gabe's chest warmed me from behind.

"Wait, what do you mean you don't want him?" he asked. "You certainly acted like it."

A sense of betrayal rose up, and I snapped. "Why do you even care? You traded me, remember? What does it matter anymore?" My voice broke as I bit back a sob and slapped at the water. I'd rather die than cry in front of him now.

Gabe turned me around in his arms, his eyes hard on mine. His palm caressed the side of my face when I looked away. "I never left you, Gracie ... never."

"You left me in the cave," I spouted, angry tears streaking over my skin now. I didn't care anymore. "How could you do that to me? I trusted you, and you just bailed like everyone else!"

"Ashton, that night was the most excruciating one of my existence. I can't even begin to tell you how wretched it was!" Gabe paused and took a steadying breath. "I had to force the distance between us. That's why I put up the front for the

Dryads in the cave that day. Whatever you thought, I needed them to believe that I wasn't watching you."

"Yeah, well it worked," I grumbled.

"So I heard," Gabe murmured. "But I was also trying to separate myself from you. I hoped that in what little time we'd spent together, that your attachment wouldn't be fixed on me. Nymphs have such a unique bond with their partners, but you weren't there yet, Naiad wise I mean. I hoped that in time, your feelings would fade. Out of sight, out of mind."

"It doesn't work that way, Gabe." I held my breath remembering all the nights I cried myself to sleep only to watch him leave me a hundred times over in my dreams. Where was he then? "You could've told me. Why would you want me to not love you?"

"Because love will never be enough…" he began, and my heart fell, "to keep you safe. For as long as we live, you'll be the bull's-eye of every target. If you could be happy there, you would at least be safe."

"Happy?" My tone rose. "How could I ever be happy forced to live as a slave?"

"You seemed fairly content your last few moments alone with Kyle," Gabe muttered, his eyes hard.

My heart sank. "You heard that?"

"It was hard to miss," Gabe said, his breathing labored.

"Then you heard everything he said," I argued. "How could you believe I didn't care about you then?"

"I trust you…" Gabe murmured slowly, throwing my words to Kyle back at me. "When you told him that, it was all I needed to hear to know he'd won. His word over mine. And I assumed you'd made your choice."

"My choice?" I said, my voice as frosty as the air. "Nothing has ever been my choice."

Gabe flinched then his expression blanked. "Then make one, Ashton. Right here, right now. Consequences aside, what do you choose?"

I hesitated. The consequences would never be aside. Gabe made a derisive sound when I didn't answer.

"You don't even know what you want yourself," he said, his expression pained but bitter.

"I know exactly what I want." I pulled Gabe close and pressed my lips to his, letting go of all my anger and emptiness. My fingers wound through his damp hair, and I poured every ounce of my heart into his.

Breathless, I backed away. "I want you, Gabe. It will always be you."

Gabe's eyes warmed as his finger swept a tear away. "I never meant to hurt you, Gracie. I will forever be sorry for what I put you through. But if you'll allow me, I will never leave you again."

"I don't want any kind of life that doesn't include you, no matter how temporary," I confessed. Warmth filled my chest, and I smiled, reveling in the fullness.

"What?" Gabe asked, tracing my upturned mouth with his thumb.

"I just missed my heart." I sighed.

"I love you, Gracie," Gabe whispered against my lips.

We continued on toward the shore. Allie was swimming to the equivalent of pacing by the time we reached the opposite bank. She looked over as we closed in, and I practically heard her eyes roll.

"Well, I can understand the connection now." Allie wrung her hair out and tossed it over her shoulder.

"What do you mean?" I asked as Gabe helped me ashore.

"Just look at you two." She waved her hand in our direction. "It's like you're incapable of existing apart from each other."

I blushed. Gabe laughed softly and squeezed my hand.

"Maybe that's a bit of an overstatement. You can exist, just not functionally." She shook her head. I grinned at her sarcasm. Allie had never been in love. Boy was she in for a surprise.

"You know Al, one of these days you're going to find a guy who you're meant to spend eternity with and ... what?" I asked when Allie arched an eyebrow at Gabe.

"Ash?" Allie began in a placating tone, staring at Gabe.

Gabe glared at her, a warning clear on his face. "Don't, he said sternly. "This isn't the time or place."

"Be mad at me if you will, but she deserves to know the truth for once in her life." Allie's gaze shifted to my face. "Ash, you know I love you, right? We're like sisters. Closer than sisters."

"Yeah," I answered slowly.

"Good. And you know that Gabe loves you and only you. He's never wanted anyone else."

"Mm-hmm." I cast him an unsure look.

"Okay then. I think it's best to lay everything out on the table, no secrets, and no omissions." Her gaze flickered to Gabe who stood, arms crossed, irritated by her speech. "That way everyone knows everything and there are never unpleasant surprises. You want the truth right?"

"No," Gabe cut in.

"I wasn't talking to you, your highness," Allie retorted. "You know she has every right to understand."

Gabe let out a tired sigh.

"Here we go. Gabe was supposed to marry me," she said, gesturing flippantly over her shoulder. The horrified sound I made didn't break her rhythm. "We didn't exactly get on very well, so we shot that horse before it ever had a chance to live."

"M-m-marry you?" I choked out.

"I know, right?" She laughed. "It's ridiculous."

Allie was formerly engaged, in a way, to my Gabe? The story about her run in with the Dryads made all too much sense. She was the girl Kyle spoke about. I couldn't even wrap my head around the outcome of that.

Maybe I should've been used to dealing with the unexpected by now but I wasn't. My reaction was probably as bad as Gabe had feared and worse than Allie deemed rational. My mouth hung open, and my eyes were dry from not blinking.

"This is why you should listen to me on occasion," Gabe spoke to Allie. "Ash, this is not as important as it sounds. Things aren't the same for us as they are in your family. It's not an issue."

I fumbled around for a response. Finally, I quit trying and gave him something in the way of a shrug.

"My brave unrivaled Gracie." Without warning, a set of burning lips moved against mine. Liquid fire. Gabe's breath invaded my body, igniting my insides and melting my defenses. Forgetting about the past betrayals and future impossibilities, I simply drowned in the passionate moment of now.

Allie cleared her throat loudly. Gabe sighed and dropped his forehead against mine.

"Do you mind?" Allie rolled her eyes when I looked her way.

"Just wait, Allie." I smiled, anticipating her reaction. "You're going to meet someone who will absolutely sweep you off your feet, and you'll be as dopey and disgusting as me."

She tossed her blonde hair back, wearing a defiant expression. "Doubtful."

"You know they'll chase us to the ends of the earth." Gabe's worried eyes met mine. "Are you sure this is the life you want to choose?"

I smiled warmly. "I made this choice a long time ago. Nothing and no one can ever change that."

"We should get going then." He sighed and laced his fingers through mine.

"Lead the way..." I smiled.

Acknowledgements

There are so many people who made this journey move from dream to reality. I owe each of you more than I can say. Grab a drink and get comfortable, because this may take a while. Much love and thanks to the following:

My amazing publisher, Jeremy Soldevilla and Soul Fire Press, for taking on not only my book but the madness that is my life. Thanks for enduring my ceaseless questions with a smile.

Neil Noah, my cover designer and sanity saver. Your abilities astound me. Thanks for all your hard work and willingness to get things right. I look forward to our future projects.

My parents, Greg and Angie, for always fostering my love of writing and for believing in everything I do. My sister, Erin, for being there to stretch my imagination. So much of our childhood goes into my writing.

My very own Yoda and master editor, Elizabeth Isaacs, AKA Chi. If it weren't for you, this book would've never happened. Your wisdom (and the ability to make me laugh in spite of myself) is worth more than I could ever repay you.

Megan Curd, my cosmic twin, cohort and Twinkie for life. You're a blessing in ways only you could understand. Thanks for filling the gaps in my technology lack of know-how. The check for my I.O.U. tab is in the mail. Have a Peach Nehi on me.

Italia Gandolfo, AKA Rennie. You are my (super)hero in more ways than one. One of these days you'll actually reveal your true identity, right?

Virtual cupcakes to my beta readers, critique partners, and all-around cheerleaders: Alicia Kerr, Erin Walters, Todd Keisling, Trish Wolfe, Mindy Ruiz, Lorna Suzuki, Rachel Harris,

Brandi Kosiner, Layla Messner, Jenn Thompson, Jami Slack, Regan Coomer, Tori Scott, Morgan Lee and all the amazing folks at Chirenjenzie. You are the most supportive and incredible group of people on Earth. Thanks for putting up with me at my worst. I'm honored to call you friends.

Julie Brazeal at *A Tale of Many Reviews*. You have put more work into promoting this novel than anyone, and it means the world to me. I owe you an organ, or at the very least, the biggest, most awkward hug I can drum up.

To the musical stylings of: Luke Asher, Silversun Pickups, Florence + the Machine, The Fray, Bon Iver, Sia, and Stateless. Your creative genius fuels my muse. Thanks for being awesome!

My always sensational daughters, Rylan and Teagan. I'm blessed beyond measure. I love you guys! Thanks for sharing Mommy with her computer. And yes, Rylan, the book is finished now.

Last, but never least: to my husband Matt, who is, and will always be, my supporter, encourager, reader, motivator, promotional guru, best friend, and love of my life. You are the epitome of greatness. Thank you for always believing in me and for pushing me to believe in myself. I love you!

About the Author

Hope Collier was born in Harlan County, Kentucky. Growing up in the Appalachia, she quickly learned that a good imagination, along with the ability to outrun the neighbor's cantankerous dog, was essential to survival. Hope wrote and illustrated her first book at the age of six and never stopped writing. She now lives in central Kentucky with her husband, two daughters, and a menagerie of pets. When not spending time with her imaginary friends, you're likely to find her stalking other writers on Twitter or searching out new ways of fitting square pegs into round holes.

CPSIA information can be obtained at www.ICGtesting.com
Printed in the USA
LVOW111218020412

275770LV00001B/4/P